Hidden Scars

Books by Mark de Castrique

Hidden Scars

A Sam Blackman Mystery

Mark de Castrique

Poisoned Pen Press

First Edition 2017

10 9 8 7 6 5 4 3 2 1

Library of Congress Catalog Card Number: 2017934134

ISBN: 9781464208942   Hardcover
        9781464208966   Trade Paperback

Poisoned Pen Press
4014 N. Goldwater Boulevard, #201
Scottsdale, Arizona 85251
www.poisonedpenpress.com
info@poisonedpenpress.com

Printed in the United States of America

For Linda
and for all who work with
veterans, refugees, and the innocent victims of war

You succeed when you stop failing.

—Richard Buckminster Fuller
upon the failure of his first geodesic dome,
Black Mountain College, 1948

Chapter One

My partner, Nakayla Robertson, had taken a long weekend in Charleston with the women in her book club for the annual retreat they called "Reading Between the Wines." The mid-March rates kept the hotel price down, but the abundance of restaurants and shops guaranteed the money they saved was still spent in the antebellum city.

Left alone in Asheville to run the Blackman and Robertson Detective Agency, I'd goofed off Friday through Monday, not even bothering to come to the office. With Nakayla's return merely hours away, I'd decided I'd better make an appearance, and so I'd worked for almost an hour, sorting through unsolicited catalogues, shuffling a few papers, and forwarding e-mails to prove Sam Blackman was on the job.

Satisfied that all was under control, I made the executive decision to call it a day. I'd grab an early lunch at Lexington Avenue Brewery, swing by Asheville Wine Market for one of their recommended specials, and then wait for Nakayla at her West Asheville bungalow. I hoped her absence, leaving me alone for four and a half days, would lead to a romantic, home-cooked dinner. And I'd stop at my apartment to pick up some clean clothes in hopes that dinner would be followed by the invitation for an overnight reunion. She could even pillow talk the nuances of her book club discussions—a surefire sedative.

As I opened the hallway door, the office phone rang. I was tempted to bolt for the elevator and let voicemail catch whatever charity or robocall wanted money. But, the message would leave a time stamp that could undercut my "slaving-at-the-office" story.

I hurried to my desk and snatched the receiver from the cradle. "Blackman and Robertson, Sam Blackman speaking."

"Sam, is that you?"

The voice cracked and warbled. I recognized it immediately. "Yes, Captain."

"Good. I thought you were one of those damn machines. Sometimes I start talking thinking a real person answered."

"It's me in the flesh."

"Well, I've got a case for you, if you're not too busy."

Other than my plans for lunch and then dinner with Nakayla, the rest of my life was wide open.

"I could probably squeeze in a new case, especially for you."

"Actually, it's for a friend. Violet Baker."

"I don't think I know her."

"One of the new residents. Only eighty. If I were ten years younger, I'd make a move on her."

Captain was just short of ninety-five, and I'm sure if he wanted to make a move on young Violet, his age wouldn't stop him.

"What's her case?"

"I don't know the details. I thought it better if you and Nakayla talk to her in person."

"Nakayla's out of town, but we'd be happy to meet with her."

"Good. I told her we could count on you. Come for a late lunch. You can brief Nakayla when she gets back."

I glanced at my watch. Eleven-fifteen. "You mean like two o'clock?"

"We were thinking twelve-thirty. The crowd will be thinning by then. And today's make-your-own-sundae-on-Tuesday. Half the damn residents are already lined up at the dining room door."

The vision of a burger and pint of porter morphed into a congealed salad and sweet tea.

"Okay, Captain. I'll see you outside the dining room at twelve-thirty."

"Thanks, Sam. I'm sure just talking to you will be a comfort for Violet."

"And you have no idea why she wants to hire a detective?"

A few seconds of silence greeted my question.

Then Captain said, "Didn't I tell you? She thinks her brother's been murdered."

Chapter Two

"Welcome to Golden Oaks Retirement Center. How can I help you?" The woman's voice emanated from a silver speaker on the side of an unmanned guardhouse where a crossbar blocked the road ahead.

"I'm here to see Ron Kline. He's expecting me."

"Very good, sir. Your name, please?"

"Sam Blackman."

"Hi, Sam. It's Joanne. I thought I recognized your voice. I'm covering while Clara's at lunch. Anything exciting going on?"

I'd met Joanne, one of the elderly ladies who was a member of Captain's CIA, Corridor Intelligence Agency, that he'd organized to patrol the halls and keep an eye on the retirement community's well-being. I also remembered Joanne had an eye for Captain, and was one of his harem of admirers. Telling Joanne that I was coming for lunch with him and Violet Baker, the new "young" girl, wouldn't be a smart move.

"He and I are just catching up."

"Well, come on, then."

The bar lifted and I began the twisting, convoluted climb to the retirement community atop a ridge. Ron Kline, aka Captain, was the acknowledged leader of its residents. Our paths had crossed several years earlier when Nakayla and I were drawn together by the murder of her sister. Captain had been involved in several of our cases, and I felt guilty that at least six months had passed since I'd seen him. As Captain was fond of saying,

"At my age, you don't renew your magazine subscriptions and you don't buy green bananas."

Captain had been career Army, and although he'd risen to the rank of Colonel, he preferred to be known as Captain, the commission he'd held in World War Two, when he claimed he and his men performed their finest service to their country and to each other.

As his generation passed into history, some of his band-of-brothers camaraderie had been transferred to me. Captain and I shared a kinship forged by combat, although our wars were separated by more than sixty years. Mutual respect quickly grew into friendship.

He stood outside the open double doors to the dining hall, wearing a red flannel shirt buttoned to the neck and khaki pants with a belt that was hitched higher than his elbows. As I expected, a fawning cluster of elderly ladies encircled him. In a community where the gender ratio of female to male was ten to one, a man could usually enjoy the companionship of the opposite sex if he had one important trait—a pulse. Captain not only had a pulse, but also a charming smile, a quick wit, and the refined manners of a bygone era that could induce a woman to swoon—and possibly break a hip.

Captain caught sight of me when I was about thirty feet away. He stepped clear of the women, squared his shoulders, and snapped a crisp salute. I stopped and returned our ritual greeting.

"Sorry, ladies," he announced. "Duty calls."

His dramatic tone generated a chorus of girlish giggles. One woman with a round plump face and wry smile waggled a finger at me. "I know you. You're Sam Blackman. Don't tie Captain up too long. He's got a pinochle game at three."

"Don't worry, Bernice," Captain said. "Sam just needs a little advice on one of his cases. We'll be through in plenty of time."

"I'm sure you'll solve it for him."

I could have sworn she actually batted her eyes.

Captain grabbed my upper arm and ushered me into the dining hall. I felt him shift a little weight onto me and realized his step wasn't as spry as it had been.

"Where's Violet Baker?" I asked.

"I reserved one of the smaller dining rooms we have for private occasions. She's already there."

Captain steered me through the maze of tables. Everyone either nodded or waved as he passed. We went behind a short partition that formed a narrow hall. Two doors on the opposite wall had brass plaques denoting the Laurel Room and the Rhododendron Room. Captain pushed open the one to the Laurel Room.

In the center was a rectangular table that could have seated ten. Three places were set at the far end with what looked like plates of chicken salad and glasses of iced tea. A woman sitting on the left side rose as we entered.

Her steel-gray hair was cut short in the way favored by many businesswomen who want to look stylish and yet mature. It was not the cut the ladies in Captain's harem would get in the onsite beauty parlor.

Her wardrobe was smart but casual—a cream blouse and navy skirt. Her only jewelry was a small gold cross dangling from a chain around her neck. She was tanned and fit, and I could tell she'd been a beautiful woman in her younger days. Hell, she was still beautiful. Captain might make his move after all.

"Sam," Captain said, "this is Violet Baker. Violet, Sam Blackman."

I offered my hand across the table. Her grip was dry and firm.

"Thank you for seeing me, Mr. Blackman."

"Sam, please."

Captain pulled out the chair at the head of the table. "Why don't we sit down? I took the liberty of ordering salad for all of us. Sam, you want something else, speak up."

"This looks fine."

Captain and I paused while Violet Baker re-took her seat. Then I sat, spread my napkin across my lap, and took a sip of tea before speaking.

"Captain says you're new to Golden Oaks."

She nodded. "I moved in three weeks ago. I've one of the cottages."

Golden Oaks offered both apartment living and stand-alone cottages for those not ready to give up a more traditional home environment. I knew the cottages were more expensive, which meant Violet was a woman of means.

"Did you have a house in Asheville?" I asked.

"No. I sold my home in Albany, New York. But I grew up here. Actually over in Black Mountain."

"So, you still have family in the area," I said, anxious to showcase my deductive reasoning.

"No, it's just me. We left Black Mountain when I was eleven." She shrugged. "Call it being sentimental. An urge to return to the place of my youth." She gave a wistful smile. "Or too many years of too much snow."

"How do you think I can help you?"

"I don't know if you can." She picked up her fork and held it poised over her chicken salad. "Tell me your story first and then I'll tell you mine."

So, while she and the Captain nibbled at lunch, I gave a condensed version of my life. How I'd grown up in Kernersville in the Piedmont section of North Carolina, rebelled against my father's wishes and joined the Army straight out of high school. How I'd risen to the rank of Chief Warrant Officer responsible for criminal investigations and that one of them pitted me against a gang of Army smugglers in Iraq who staged a rocket grenade attack that killed two of my men and cost me my left leg.

I told how I wound up in rehab in the VA hospital in Asheville and became involved in a murder investigation that introduced me to my partner, Nakayla Robertson, as well as Captain. "So, I've adopted Asheville as my home and Captain as my grandpa."

They both laughed.

"Fair enough," Captain said. "I hereby bequeath you all my debts."

"And this murder," Violet Baker said, "Captain told me it happened nearly a hundred years ago."

"I was actually investigating the murder of two people. Nakayla's sister and her great-great grandfather. His happened in 1919."

The woman studied me carefully as if coming to some decision. She set down her fork. "All right. Now you eat and I'll talk."

"Yes, ma'am." I felt like my mom had just told me to finish my vegetables.

"Since the mid-eighteen hundreds, my family had farms in the Asheville area. My father cultivated over a hundred acres in Fairview. My maiden name was Weaver and I had a sister four years older and a brother twelve years older.

"My sister died when I was five. Polio. One of the last outbreaks to hit western North Carolina. I don't remember her that well, but I do remember how devastating her death was to my family. My big brother, Paul, cried like a baby. He was seventeen and I think that shocked me as much as anything.

"As soon as he turned eighteen, he enlisted in the Army. This was in January of 1943. I don't know a whole lot about what he did in the war, Sam. You and Captain have a better understanding of how troop movements are kept secret. We did get the occasional letter saying he was alive and well."

"Do you know if he was in Europe or the Pacific?" I asked.

"Europe. Paul was honorably discharged in 1946. He told my parents he'd been in Patton's Third Army and was a liaison with the 761st Tank Battalion. That was an all-colored unit." She shook her head. "Sorry. I know that's not politically correct. I just grew up in an era when that was the polite way to address black people."

I shot a glance at Captain, wondering if he'd told Violet Baker that Nakayla was African American.

"That was tough duty," Captain said. "The 761st was in combat over six months."

"Paul didn't talk to me about the war. I was only nine when he returned, but I knew he was upset."

"Post traumatic stress?" I asked.

"I don't think so. That wouldn't cause you to fight with other vets, would it?"

"I don't know. I'm not a psychologist."

"Well, he did get in a fight at the American Legion post in Asheville. Then he and my father had a shouting match because Paul said colored soldiers had as much right to be a member of the post as he did. They were arguing so loudly that it woke me up."

"Your brother was right," Captain said. "It was shameful the way we treated our black veterans. That author Stephen Ambrose has a quote I like—'The world's greatest democracy fought the world's greatest racist with a segregated Army.' And the South after the war had no interest in sharing democracy with everyone who fought to defend it."

"Did your brother continue pressing for integration?" I asked.

"If he did, his actions were sheltered from me. Paul moved out of the house and used his G.I. Bill to start college in the fall."

"Where?"

"Black Mountain."

"Montreat?" It was the only college I knew in the little town.

"No. Black Mountain College. It's not there anymore. It closed in the nineteen-fifties. I guess today we'd call it free-form. Artsy."

I'd heard of the school but only as some museum in Asheville. I'd never been in it. "Was your brother in the arts?"

"He wanted to be an architect. Apparently, he thought the college would give him a good foundation. And the teachers were well connected to New York and Chicago. A portal to the top echelons right in his own backyard."

"Did it work out?"

Violet Baker's blue eyes moistened. "Paul never finished. Some men came to the farm one afternoon in the fall of 1948. I'd just come home from school. They walked with my father out to the barn. About twenty minutes later, my father came in and told me I should go do my homework in my room. I'd just started reading when my mother cried out. The men had told my father that Paul had died in a hiking accident. He'd fallen into a ravine."

"You think it wasn't an accident?"

Violet Baker didn't answer. Instead she reached down by her chair and lifted her handbag. It was large enough to carry a week of field rations for a platoon.

She pulled out an old book. The black leather was cracked and the gilded text on the cover was barely legible. Holy Bible. I wondered if she was about to read scripture to us.

"This was my father's," she said. "He died thirty years ago and I put it on my bookshelf. I wasn't a big church-goer and I never opened it. I kept it for sentimental value. But when I was packing to move south, I spent a few minutes flipping through it."

She set the Bible to the left of her plate and opened it about halfway through. A yellowed piece of paper lay folded between the pages. She handed it across the table.

I examined it carefully. The document was a coroner's report to the Buncombe County inquest, dated November 3, 1948. The deceased, Paul Clarence Weaver, age twenty-three, had died on Sunday, October 17, 1948.

I studied the coroner's comments. They weren't the detailed analysis of a medical examiner's report. The coroner called the death accidental, the result of a nearly one-hundred-foot fall from an overlook along the Blue Ridge Parkway. No autopsy was performed but the coroner noted that the funeral director in charge of the burial described bruising across the torso and thighs while the head and arms were relatively undamaged. From the undertaker's point of view, it meant the family could have an open casket without the necessity for extensive cosmetic restoration. He also mentioned a puncture wound, apparently made by a stick that penetrated the trachea. Bark fragments were in the wound, but it was not the cause of death. General trauma from the fall was his conclusion. The corner's findings were accepted by the inquest jury.

"You'd never seen this before?" I asked.

"No. And we left the farm before Christmas. My father sold it to some other family members so they could put in the spring crops."

"Why?"

"My father told me it was for a new job and more money. My mother was crying a lot. She stopped going to church and they kept me out of school from Thanksgiving till we moved."

"Where did you go?"

"Aliquippa, Pennsylvania."

"Where?"

"A town outside Pittsburgh. My father's cousin had a job in the steel mill. He got one for Dad and we moved in with them till we got our own place. None of us ever went back to Black Mountain."

"Until now," I said.

"Yes. I met my husband when we were students at the University of Pittsburgh. He went on to get a law degree and practiced in his hometown of Albany, New York. Then I went for my CPA license. Mort and I never had any children."

"What about the relatives who bought your farm?"

She shrugged. "When letters go unanswered for over seventy years, even when my father wrote that my mother had died, and no one so much as sent a card..." Her voice choked and she looked away.

Captain and I sat quietly.

She took a staggered breath. "Well, then I no longer consider them family." She twisted her tea glass on the table and stared at the melting ice cubes a moment. "Do you believe in fate, Sam?"

"I believe in pivotal events, ones whose consequences can't be seen at the time. But I don't believe things are predetermined. They are the result of choices, sometimes choices I've made, sometimes the choices of others beyond my control."

She nodded. "I believed that too. Up until about six months ago. My husband died and I had no family. More importantly, I had a tremendous sense of unfinished business. As I said, I'd been an accountant and worked my whole life making sure that books balanced. Well, there was a gap in my ledger."

"Knowing what happened to your brother," I said.

"Exactly. Once I felt that pull, I realized I had to act upon it. And then I found that coroner's report when I easily could have packed the Bible without opening it. I came here and rented a cottage. I met Captain, and I learned about you from his harem." A smile broke through the serious cast of her face.

I glanced at Captain. The tough old veteran was blushing.

"So, here I cross paths with a man who has worked with a private detective. I ask him about you and then did my own research on your successes. Very impressive."

I didn't say anything, but I suspected Captain was not the only one blushing.

She took back the coroner's report. "I thought since this existed there might be other documents regarding my brother's death. I'd thought about hiring a local lawyer, but I'm not sure I want to be quite so official, at least not at first."

"Why do you think your brother's death wasn't an accident?"

"He was raised in these hills. He could have hiked those trails in the dark or even blindfolded."

"And the men who came to tell your father. Do you remember if they were police or sheriff's deputies?"

"I don't know who they were, Sam. They came in a black car and wore black suits. They looked like the Bible salesmen who sometimes went door-to-door back then."

They could have been plainclothes detectives, I thought. But the sudden upheaval of Violet Baker's family suggested something else was at play.

"I know it's not a pleasant alternative, Violet, but do you think your brother could have taken his own life?"

She took a deep breath. "I've thought about that a lot. I don't think so. He loved the college. He took me there one day when we had a school holiday. Why would he throw himself and his dreams off a bluff? It makes no sense."

I didn't have an answer. Suicide is rarely a rational decision.

"If it had something to do with the college, do you know if any of his classmates are still in the area?"

"Probably not. Most of them were from out-of-state, and many have probably died." She reached into her handbag again. "But I believe fate is driving me forward." She pulled out a section of the *Asheville Citizen-Times* and slid it across the table. "This is what spurred me to have Captain call you this morning."

The headline of the newspaper article read, *Black Mountain College to "Re-Open."* I noted the quotation marks around Re-Open and skimmed enough of the story to learn a movie was shooting, using the location of the former college as its setting. The producers were working with the Black Mountain College Museum and also welcomed information any local residents could provide regarding life at the school.

"They're recreating the college, Sam," Violet said. "They're going back sixty or seventy years, and maybe, just maybe, in their quest for historical accuracy, the truth about my brother lies waiting to be discovered. But I need your help."

Captain had sat listening to our exchange without comment. His fork clanged as he dropped it on his plate. "So, what's to think about, Sam? Take the lady's case."

I had to laugh. "Violet, I guess I've been given my marching orders."

Chapter Three

"I thought I was through with the damn book." Nakayla slid the newspaper article across the table to me. "Maybe Violet Baker's right. It is fate."

We sat at Nakayla's dining room table. She'd returned from Charleston an hour earlier and we'd opened my bottle of Pinot Noir to celebrate our new client. I'd given a detailed report on my lunch meeting with Captain and Violet Baker. Violet had made a photocopy of the coroner's report and I showed it to Nakayla. Her ears perked up when I said we'd need to visit a movie location, but something in the newspaper story set her off.

"What book?" I asked.

"*Love Among the Ridges*—one of the book club novels we discussed this weekend. The author thinks he's Asheville's version of Nicholas Sparks."

"And it's about Black Mountain College?"

"It's set there. That was the most interesting part. The school's a legend. Albert Einstein was on the board of advisors. Buckminster Fuller taught there. I understand why Violet's brother would have chosen it. The faculty had immigrants from the Bauhaus."

"The what house?"

Nakayla frowned. "You've never heard of the Bauhaus?"

"Maybe I have, but maybe I forgot that I have. I've heard so many things."

"Yeah. Sure. In one ear, out the other. Well, since it's now an integral part of our investigation, try to hold on to what I tell you, Sherlock. The Bauhaus was an art school in Germany that combined crafts with fine arts. They designed furniture, textiles, buildings, working in an entire spectrum of disciplines that kept the arts at their core—a concentration of very progressive thinkers whose impact was one of the milestones of design in the twentieth century."

Nakayla paused her mini-lecture for a sip of wine. "This is very good."

"See. I know some things." I topped off her glass.

"Of course, such creative forces soon ran afoul of Hitler and his henchmen. The Nazis declared the school a center of Communist intellectualism and, in 1933, its leadership closed it before Hitler's regime exerted more aggressive action."

"And these intellectuals came to little ol' Black Mountain?"

"Some of them. Most notably Josef Albers and his wife, Anni. The founder of Black Mountain College had been fired from a school in Florida, and he, some colleagues, and a handful of like-minded students were determined to put their own revolutionary theories of education into practice. They started in an existing camp assembly that was dormant outside of summer and lured Josef and Anni Albers and other progressives to become faculty for not much more than room and board. It was a great experiment."

"A commune with classes," I said.

"Not a bad way to put it," Nakayla agreed.

"So, *Love Among the Ridges* was long on romance and short on substance."

Nakayla arched an eyebrow. "You're saying romance is without substance?"

I backpedaled as quickly as I could. "Certainly not *our* romance. I'm just agreeing with you about the book."

"The book you haven't read."

"But you have. And I trust your literary judgment. I'll stay clear of this purveyor of vacuous romance. Why waste time with cheesy fiction when I'm living the real thing?"

She laughed. "You're as full of it as L.T. Hart."

"Who?"

"The author. At least that's the pen name. L.T. He says it stands for 'Loving Tender.'"

"Oh, God," I groaned.

"Yeah."

"Well, maybe you'll get to meet him and have him sign your book. L.T. Hart. I bet he writes a little heart symbol in place of the 'a' in his name."

Nakayla raised her glass to me. "Smart boy. Sally in our book club bought an autographed copy at Malaprop's. He wrote Hart with a heart for the 'a.'"

I shrugged. "What can I say? I'm the world's greatest romantic detective. If the movie director meets me, he'll probably recast the leading role."

"Sam, it's not a comedy."

• • ● • •

The next morning Nakayla and I left her bungalow and I drove us to Black Mountain in a drizzling rain. We didn't know where the film would be shooting, if at all, but since the newspaper had reported the production was based at the former site of the college, we figured that was as good a place to start as any. Nakayla also did a quick online search for information at the North Carolina Film Office. We learned the executive producer was a local real estate developer named Arnold Osteen. I was unfamiliar with him, but Nakayla had dealt with his company on some insurance claims before we started our agency.

"Would Osteen remember you?" I asked. We were about five miles out of Asheville and headed for Lake Eden, the only GPS target we had. The college had moved to its shore in the early nineteen-forties.

"No. I only dealt with his legal team. They had some theft issues at one of their sites. We were investigating the accuracy of their reported losses and if proper security had been in place."

"And?"

"The insurance company paid. Someone had cut through a chain-link fence at the far end of the site and hot-wired some of the construction vehicles. Drove them away out of earshot of the guardhouse. We figured the trucks went straight to a paint shop and probably wound up in Mexico, or machine guns were mounted in their beds by terrorist groups in Africa or the Middle East."

The terrorist possibility wasn't as far-fetched as it sounded. I'd read the story of a man in Texas seeing his company's logo on a pickup truck in Syria commandeered by ISIS.

"Well, I'm sure security's tight on a movie set," I said. "We'll have to talk our way in."

"With my brains and your looks, how can we fail?"

"Let's just say your chances are a hell of a lot better than mine."

The GPS led us over a few miles of rolling farmland that suffered pockets of new housing developments bearing witness to the growth of neighboring Asheville.

A lake appeared on our left and the road narrowed. Pine trees lined the shoulders, signaling we were entering an area that had been landscaped long ago. A series of handmade posters on stakes read "L-A-R" and arrows indicated we were to proceed straight ahead.

"L-A-R," Nakayla said. "Love Among the Ridges."

"At least the 'A' isn't a heart."

We were visually instructed to turn left at the far end of the lake and then signs proclaimed two choices for parking: one for deliveries/guests/extras and the other for crew. The deliveries/guests/extras route passed by a security guard seated in a metal folding chair and wearing a yellow rain slicker. The crew route went to a field that looked like an Army encampment. Eighteen-wheelers with CineVision Rentals logos on their sides were circled like covered wagons. I figured they held lighting, rigging, and camera equipment. Six or seven RVs sat near a large catering truck. I assumed these were those famous trailers where the movie stars retired to relax or pout, depending upon how their scene had gone.

"What do you think?" Nakayla asked.

"It's clear the guard will stop us. Crew parking looks to be more open." I saw people scurrying around the multitude of vehicles but no one seemed to be checking credentials. "I'm tempted to skip a formal approach where we'll be told no and try coming through the back door with the crew."

"And if someone asks you what your job is?" Nakayla asked.

"You watch movie credits. I'll say I'm a grip or a best boy."

Nakayla cocked her head. "Best boy? Do you even know what that means?"

"Sure. Someone who's better than a good boy."

"Stick to what you know," she admonished. "We go to the guard, flash our creds, and tell him we have some questions for Mr. Osteen. And the guard might be one of Nathan's."

Nathan Armitage was a friend who owned Asheville's largest security firm. The guard would probably recognize our names and at least treat us with a degree of courtesy.

"Good point," I said. "Act like we know what we're doing."

"It's a movie set, Sam. Everybody's acting."

I drove forward. The guard got up from his chair, signaled me to stop and walked to my window. He was a stocky man, at least six-two and two hundred-fifty pounds. Some of that weight had gone from muscle to flab, but I could tell from the swagger in his stride that in his mind he was twenty years younger.

The rain slicker parted enough for me to see his badge. It simply read "Officer." The words "ACME SECURITY" were embroidered above it. He held a clipboard in his left hand and stared past me to study Nakayla in the passenger's seat.

"Are you two extras?"

I wanted to say we were extra special but decided the man probably wasn't into sophisticated humor. Instead, I flipped open my P.I. license. "Sam Blackman and Nakayla Robertson to see Arnold Osteen."

The guard scowled. "They called you already?"

I looked at Nakayla. She gave a nod to play it forward.

"Why wouldn't they?" I asked.

"The police left no more than thirty minutes ago. You'd think these Hollywood people would give them a chance to do their job."

I had no idea where this script was going so I fell back on my safest response. I agreed with him.

"I know. What can I say?"

"Well, a word of advice, pal. You could have been called without Mr. Osteen's approval. He might just want the police to handle it. So, don't be surprised if he says, 'Thanks, but no thanks.'"

"Got it." I winked at the guy like we now shared a closely guarded secret. "Where will I find him?"

He turned and pointed up the road to a rectangular building near the lakeshore. "The movie people have taken over the camp's administration offices. You can bet Mr. Osteen will be close to anyone writing checks."

We followed the looping blacktop as it curved left and ended at a grassy patch where about ten vehicles were parked. Most looked like rental vans and SUVs. A silver Mercedes angled closest to the building's entrance. I parked behind it.

"What do you think that was all about?" Nakayla asked.

"Something must have happened earlier this morning. Something involving the police."

"I got that part. I meant about Mr. Osteen's approval. The guard assumes we're not going to be welcomed."

"Maybe it's something minor and he thinks Osteen doesn't want to shell out any money. Anyway, we're here and we'll play it straight, like you suggest."

I flipped the hood up on my rain jacket and got out of the CR-V. The precipitation had subsided to a fine mist that I thought must be playing havoc with the film gear.

The building was made of wood and corrugated metal—clearly functional and economical construction. If the building had been made of Legos, there would have been one missing on the ground level because the first floor was only a part of the overall footprint. Beneath the second story, a concrete pad without sides created a versatile patio with overhead shelter. Nakayla and I crossed the patio and walked to the door with a temporary sign, "Production Office," taped to its window.

I put my hand on the knob and then hesitated. "Now, we're not signing anything before checking with our agent."

"I wouldn't worry about it," Nakayla said. "The only agent we're likely to have will be selling us insurance."

We stepped into a large room populated with gray metal desks that looked like they'd been commandeered from a used furniture store. Eight were arranged in the center in two rows of four. Another five were pushed facing the walls. The person at each was armed with a computer and cell phone, and most were using them simultaneously.

A young woman at the nearest desk looked up from her laptop and frowned. "Didn't your agent tell you? Extras have been canceled for the day. We'll let you know when the build scene's rescheduled."

"We're here to see Mr. Osteen," Nakayla said.

The woman's frown deepened. "He's in a meeting. I don't know how long he'll be."

I stepped closer to her desk. "Would you get word to him that Nakayla Robertson and Sam Blackman from the Blackman and Robertson Detective Agency are here?"

The woman stood. I noticed she wore no makeup and sported bags packed for an ocean voyage under her eyes. She couldn't have been more than twenty-five.

"Look," she said, "I don't care if you're from the office of the President of the United States, Mr. Osteen is in a meeting with the director and line producer and is not to be disturbed."

"It's about the incident this morning." I tried to sound like I knew what the hell incident I was talking about.

"Then I'm sure he'll want to see to you. BUT..." she barked the word... "it will be after they're finished. We have no spare chairs, so if you can wait in your car, I'll signal you from the door when he's free."

I looked at Nakayla. She shrugged. Neither her brains nor my good looks were getting us beyond this dragon lady.

"All right," I said, "but he'll be upset if he doesn't know we're here."

"Don't worry. There's no way he'll be more upset than he is already."

She glanced over her shoulder just as a door swung open on the back wall. A man came charging out, his face as red as his scarlet golf shirt. He stopped and swept his gaze across the bullpen.

"If I find it was someone on this crew, I'll kill the son of a bitch. I swear I will."

The woman turned back to us and smiled for the first time. "Mr. Osteen will see you now."

Chapter Four

"Come on." I moved quickly around the pod of desks in an attempt to intercept Osteen.

Instead of following me, Nakayla circled to the other side so that unless Osteen ducked back through the open door, he would have to encounter one of us.

Arnold Osteen was a tall, lanky man whom I pegged for early sixties. He had a country club air and a golf tan. He glanced over his shoulder at a woman and two men trailing behind him.

"I mean it," he said. "Goddamn it, the lapse was inexcusable."

The woman looked to be in her late thirties, small and thin, but carrying lightning in her eyes that flashed at the bigger man with an intensity that told me she wasn't intimidated by Osteen's rant. "And if you'd hired the firm I recommended, this never would have happened."

Osteen wheeled around to face her. "You don't know that."

"Neither do you," she shot back.

The two were unconcerned that their shouting match took place in public view.

Osteen stepped closer to her. "It's my money paying for all this." He swept his right arm in an arc across the room.

"Well, with Acme Security, you certainly got what you paid for, didn't you?" She pivoted, pushed her way between the two other men, and disappeared back down the hall.

"Mr. Osteen, may we have a word?" I interjected the question before he had a chance to shout at anyone else.

He turned, ready to bark at whomever had interrupted him. When he saw I wasn't one of the staff, he checked his anger. He also looked beyond me, searching for why I'd said "we."

Nakayla joined me. "We're from the Blackman and Robertson Detective Agency," she said. "We just need a few minutes of your time."

Our names sparked recognition in his eyes. "Who called you? The police are handling everything." Osteen turned to the two men still standing in the doorway. "Marty, tell Nancy to order the replacement materials. Tell her to make sure Raymond gets both sets of receipts—originals and replacements. I'll find the money somewhere."

Marty ignored him. He studied Nakayla like he was examining a piece of sculpture and was pleased with the appraisal. The man was about my height, five-nine or five-ten. I estimated his age to be around forty. He had bushy blond hair and one of those beards that looked more like he'd forgotten to shave.

His eyes were sky blue, and for all I knew the striking color could have come from special contact lenses. There was an air of urgent energy about him, the kind I'd seen in men in the service who were never at ease.

"Are you a dancer?" he asked Nakayla.

She laughed. "Not since I was twelve."

"I've got this, Marty," Osteen said. He focused on me. "Thank you for your interest, but I'm satisfied that the police will do all that's possible."

I decided I needed to get the man's attention. "We're here about a suspicious death, Mr. Osteen. Surely that merits a few minutes of your time."

Marty and the other man, who had yet to be introduced, froze. Osteen made a small O with his lips and shifted his gaze between Nakayla and me.

"In that case, let's go someplace where we can talk."

"Who is it?" the second man asked. He appeared to be in his late twenties —pudgy with thinning black hair. He wore a tweed sport coat although the temperature had to be at least seventy. He clutched an iPad in both hands.

Osteen cleared his throat with a guttural growl. "They want to talk to me, Roland. You and Marty concentrate on salvaging today's shoot. I don't want the crew sitting on their asses all day. And no overtime."

Osteen motioned for Roland and Marty to step aside. "This way," he told us and walked back into the hallway.

We followed him through several rooms until we reached a stairwell. We climbed to the next level and then walked down a long narrow corridor with windows on the right and closed doors on the left. It was like walking down the hall of a nineteen-fifties motel.

About halfway down the length of the building, a door opened on the right and Osteen led us out onto a second-floor covered balcony. Although the mist still hung low, I could see the lake only fifty yards away at the far edge of the lawn.

Osteen motioned to the patio furniture clustered near the balcony's railing. "If this is too damp for you, we can move inside. Myself, I like fresh air and a little privacy."

"This is fine." Nakayla sat on a cushioned chair.

Osteen and I took seats facing her. The real estate developer-turned-movie mogul leaned forward, elbows resting on his knees. "So, what's this about a suspicious death? We've had no accidents."

"It happened in 1948," I said.

Osteen leaned back and laughed. "Well, I've got the perfect alibi. I wasn't born until 1950."

"We're not here looking for suspects," Nakayla said. "A young man fell to his death in what appeared to be a hiking accident. He was a student at the college. His sister has reason to believe his death might not have been accidental."

Osteen threw up his hands. "Look, I'm sorry that whatever happened happened. But that was nearly seventy years ago. I don't see how I can help you."

"This film you're producing is set at the college," I said. "What time period?"

"Late nineteen-forties and early fifties. I understand they're collapsing some events into a tighter timeframe. Story structure, they call it."

"So, our young man's death falls within the period of your film," Nakayla said.

"Yes. And, frankly, it sounds more exciting than the script we're shooting." He spread his hands in a gesture of cooperation. "Look, maybe Roland knows something about your case. He did a lot of research."

"The guy downstairs with Marty?" I asked.

"Yeah. Roland Cassidy. He wrote the book."

I shot a glance at Nakayla.

"L.T. Hart's his pen name," she explained. "You bought the rights?" she asked Osteen.

"I got the family discount. Roland's my nephew. My sister's boy." He shook his head. "This whole thing could become a goddamned nightmare. At least in real estate, if a deal goes bad, you still own some dirt. Make a bad movie and you can't pay people to watch it."

"Didn't the book sell well?" Nakayla asked.

"Well enough, I guess. But plenty of books have been screwed up for the big screen."

"Is Roland writing the script?" she persisted.

"Good God, no. That's why I brought in Marty and Nancy. They've got Hollywood creds. I told Roland if I'm going to crawl out on a limb with investors, we're not making this some glorified home movie. That means hiring people who know what the hell they're doing. Of course, that pissed off Roland. He not only wanted to write the script, he wanted to direct." Osteen gave a humorless laugh. "He's my flesh and blood, but he couldn't direct a one-car funeral."

"Who are Marty and Nancy?" I asked.

"Marty Kolsrud is a director/writer. He did that TV series *Into the Depths* about the fictional West Virginia family where one son went from coal mining to meth production while his brother went from coal mining to law enforcement. Got good ratings and I'm told working on a TV budget is good training for an independent film. And Marty's hungry. I got him at a good price. Nancy Pellegatti is the line producer. She's supposed to be able to squeeze blood out of a nickel. My kind of woman."

I thought about the confrontation between them we'd witnessed downstairs. "You seemed to believe we were here for some other reason. Is there some way we can help?"

Osteen stood. Nakayla and I remained seated, not accepting his signal that our conversation was over.

He leaned against the balcony's railing and did his best to appear nonchalant. "We had some construction materials stolen last night. Lumber, steel, nails, that sort of thing. The students at Black Mountain College actually built this building and several cottages. We're recreating those events in some of the key scenes. We were supposed to start today, but the weather nixed those shots. Just as well, since we have nothing to build with."

"And your security?"

"You mean lack thereof?" He pushed himself away from the railing and started pacing. "They say it was a schedule screw-up. The night guard claims he was told he wouldn't be needed. The man on the previous shift said he got a call that we were cutting back overnight coverage and when his eight hours were up, he could leave."

"Who made these calls?" I asked.

"Someone identifying himself as Curt Altman, an assistant producer speaking for Nancy Pellegatti. We have no Curt Altman on the film."

Nakayla shook her head. "And the guard just walked off without confirming with anyone? Where'd you find this security team?"

Osteen reddened. "I screwed up. I got a temp company to supply some guys. It wasn't like they were carrying guns or anything. Just be onsite and check people in and out. They were cheaper."

"And the name Acme?" I asked.

"It was the name on the costumes we rented."

"Well, it sounds like an inside job," I said. "Someone knew the materials had been delivered and made the calls. If the guards didn't comply, then the theft wouldn't have happened. When the ruse worked, some trucks rolled in and were loaded and gone in a few hours."

"Yeah. That's what the police said. Guess I'm going to have to eat the loss because we have to have the materials."

Nakayla gave a slight nod of her head signaling she had no more questions. We both stood.

"Thank you for your time," Nakayla said. "And it sounds like Roland Cassidy is the person we should speak to."

"Yes. Let's go to his office and see if he's free."

We followed Osteen farther down the narrow hall to the last door on the left. He gave a sharp rap and opened the door without waiting for a response.

Cassidy sat hunched over a scarred wooden desk, his face buried in pink pages spread across its top. He jerked up as Osteen entered. "What now?" he snapped.

Osteen stepped aside to reveal Nakayla and me. Cassidy reddened slightly, then tugged at the lapels of his tweed jacket in case we didn't notice his writer's trappings.

"I believe you can help, Roland. I would appreciate if you took a few minutes out of your busy schedule to talk with them." The sarcasm in his voice embarrassed everyone but Osteen.

I looked at the desk. Stacks of paper in a rainbow of colors gave the impression the man was hard at work on something.

Nakayla stepped closer. "We'll only take a few minutes and then we'll be out of your hair." Her soothing tone eased the tension.

Cassidy nodded. "Of course. Anything I can do."

"Good. Then I'll leave you to it." Osteen headed out the door, and then pivoted. "And if I don't think the police are doing their job, I'll be in touch."

As his footsteps echoed down the hall, I closed the door to Cassidy's office and leaned against it. Cassidy frowned at the prospect of being a prisoner.

"I'll stand," I said. "Nakayla can have the chair." I gestured to the single guest chair in the corner of the small room.

Nakayla sat and leaned forward. "It's an honor to meet you, Mr. Cassidy. I'm a big fan. In fact, my book club was discussing *Love Among the Ridges* this past weekend."

Cassidy puffed out his chest and smiled. "Really? Well, you should have contacted me. Perhaps I could have been there."

"That would have been marvelous. Perhaps with your next book? I do hope you're writing one." Nakayla fawned over the man like she was a member of Captain's harem. If she fluttered her eyelashes, I was leaving.

"Well, I am," Cassidy said. "But it's hard to make much progress when this script is so all-consuming."

"I thought Marty Kolsrud was writing the script," I said.

Cassidy gave a dismissive wave. "He's making some minor tweaks—for camera blocking."

I looked at the stacks of pages on his desk and the rainbow of colors. "Minor tweaks?"

"Yes," he insisted. "Even minor tweaks generate a reprint of the scene. Everything is color-coded so we know we're all working from the same version."

I looked at the pages he'd been reading when we entered. "And today is pink?"

"Yes. The weather forced us to shoot a simpler scene in one of the cabins. I'm revising the dialogue for authenticity." He turned to Nakayla. "It's rather my specialty."

"I loved the dialogue in the book. So real. It was like my mom was talking to me."

"Your people had a mountain dialect?" Cassidy blurted the question without thinking how patronizing it sounded.

"Yes, we've been out of Africa, oh, almost three hundred years. And we're very quick learners."

Cassidy blushed. "I'm sorry. It's just that you don't have any accent at all."

"I've been giving her elocution lessons," I said. "Tell the man about the rain in Spain staying mainly on the plain."

Nakayla shot me a glance that would have killed a lesser man. "Don't mind Sam," she told Cassidy. "He's always wanted to use the word elocution."

Cassidy looked at me warily. "Whatever."

Nakayla slid her chair closer to his desk. "As we said downstairs, we're investigating a suspicious death. He was a Black Mountain College student in 1948."

"In 1948?"

"Yes. We know that falls within the time period of your research," Nakayla said. "He fell from a bluff while hiking."

Cassidy shook his head. "It doesn't sound familiar. What was his name?"

"Paul Weaver. He was a World War II vet, here on the G.I. Bill."

"There are lots of Weavers in these hills, but I don't remember one at the school. Of course, I mainly focused on the famous people—Buckminster Fuller, Arthur Penn, Merce Cunningham—you know, the people who went on to do great things."

"But your main characters weren't famous," Nakayla said.

"Because I made them up. Yes, some were composites of people's stories, but none of them fell off a cliff."

"Where did you get these stories?" I asked.

"Talking to the old-timers. There are still a few alive who remember the college." His face brightened. "You should talk to Harlan Beale. He's working as an advisor on the picture."

"Was he a student?"

"No. He worked as a handyman—part time, since the college was always hurting for money and couldn't pay full-time wages. He was like sixteen when he started. That was back in 1948. If anybody knew this Paul Weaver, it would be Harlan."

"Where can I find him?"

"There's a makeshift carpentry shop up on the knoll by the entry road. It's a big white tent." Cassidy paused. "But he might not be there now. I think Nancy sent the carpenters home."

"Because of the theft?"

"Yeah. We probably won't get a replacement delivery for a day or two."

"Do you have his home address or phone number?" Nakayla asked.

"Sure. He lives up near Ridgecrest." Cassidy pulled a cell phone from his jacket pocket and swiped through his contacts. He picked up one of the pink pages of script and wrote Harlan's information on the back. He passed the paper to Nakayla. "A little souvenir of the movie."

"Would you sign it?" she asked.

"With pleasure." Roland Cassidy, aka L.T. Hart, scribbled his name with a flourish.

Nakayla risked giving me a wink. The woman was shameless.

Chapter Five

We left Cassidy all smiles and headed downstairs.

"Do you want to call Harlan?"

"What's his address?"

She examined the script page where Cassidy had written the information. "1426 White Pine Road. It can't be too far, if he's this side of Ridgecrest."

"Then let's drive. It'll be harder for him to turn us down if we're face-to-face."

"My brains and your looks again?"

"Maybe we should reverse that."

She laughed. "I didn't see the director and producer fawning over either one of us."

"Then you didn't see the gleam in Marty Kolsrud's eye. I'm not letting that guy near you."

"Don't worry. The only way either one of us will get into the movies is to buy a ticket."

We returned to the large room filled with desks and scurrying assistants. As I pushed open the outside door, a voice yelled, "Sam Blackman. Wait!"

I turned to see the young woman we'd first met jump from her chair.

"Yes?" I said.

She hurried to us. "Marty would like to speak with you."

"About what?"

"I don't know. He phoned down from the location and asked if both of you could see him for a few minutes."

"Maybe we won't have to buy a ticket, after all." Nakayla smiled.

"Ticket to what?" the woman asked.

"To this movie," I said. "We wouldn't turn down a free pass."

The woman lowered her voice. "If it doesn't go straight to video." She rolled her eyes at the ceiling. "The fastest way to improve this film would be to have Ernest Hemingway up there fall off the planet."

"Problems?" Nakayla asked.

"Nancy says the best authors for movie adaptations are dead authors. They don't argue about artistic integrity."

"I think you'd have to have it to argue about it." Nakayla's comment came so unfiltered that she winced.

The woman pumped her fist in the air. "I like you, girlfriend." She opened the fist into a palm and gave Nakayla a high five. "I'm Camille. Camille Brooks. I'm an A.D. running the production assistants."

I assumed A.D. meant assistant director, but decided not to ask and confirm that I didn't know a best boy from a best man.

"I guess Osteen told you about the theft," she continued. "Between that and the weather, it's a real zoo this morning."

"Where do we find Marty?" I asked.

Camille Brooks walked around her desk. "I'll take you to him."

We followed her out the door and into the open space underneath the second story. A two-seater golf cart was parked near one of the support poles.

Camille looked at me. "You game to be a bag of clubs?"

"I think I can hang on." I sat facing backwards with one hand gripping a pole supporting the cart's canopy.

Camille slid behind the wheel, but Nakayla hesitated. "You're sure you're okay? I can switch with you."

Her doubt fueled my determination not to look like a wimp.

"I could ride for days like this."

"Where'd you find Mr. Macho?" Camille asked.

"Yard sale. It was either him or an old blender. Sam mixes a better drink."

I shifted to put more weight on my good leg. "Yuck it up, ladies. I'll hop off and encourage Roland Cassidy to make new script changes."

"Good God, no." Camille sent the golf cart leaping forward.

We cruised along the side of the building and then picked up a single-lane road that climbed a wooded hillside. As the angle steepened, my butt slipped and I clutched the pole tighter.

We passed a few cottages nestled in the pines. They were small and unassuming, the kind of construction that looked like they could have been a student project.

The road leveled and we maneuvered around some smaller trucks parked in spaces that were too tight for the longer eighteen-wheelers I'd seen at the main equipment site.

As I bumped along, a thought struck me. If the location had been left unattended last night, why weren't the more valuable items stolen? Cameras, lenses, and other movie equipment had to be worth more than some building supplies.

An aura of sunlight broke through the forest. It wasn't coming from the overcast sky above but as if a second sun hung just below the tree line.

Camille braked to a stop. "We'll walk the rest of the way, in case they're filming."

Although there was a gravel driveway, Camille stepped along adjacent pine needles. I heard a low hum behind us.

"What's that noise?"

Camille looked back over her shoulder. "The generator. It's blimped and won't be audible at the set. Although the scene is an interior, Marty wants sunlight streaming through the windows so we have the big HMIs to make our own."

I assumed that was some kind of lighting device and nodded like I carried a couple in my trunk.

Short bursts of a ringing bell sounded from in front of us.

Camille stepped onto the gravel drive. "Good. They've cut. Marty will have a few minutes while they reset." She picked up her pace and we followed. The driveway curved and we saw the lights first. Two large blazing instruments atop fifteen-foot stands. They were aimed at the windows on the left of the cottage—a cottage constructed out of the same corrugated steel and wood as the production headquarters.

A table with two monitors sat just to the side of the front door. I gathered the screens displayed whatever was being captured by the cameras.

The door was open and bodies crisscrossed back and forth as the crew inside prepared for whatever came next.

"Wait here," Camille said. "I'll get Marty."

She disappeared into the cottage.

A man with a gray beard and blue-checked bandanna knotted on his head came out. He must have been around forty. He peeled off leather work gloves and extended his hand. "Sam Blackman? I'm Mick Ritchie."

I shook the calloused hand, trying to place where I'd met him.

"Mick Ritchie," he repeated to Nakayla. She also shook the offered hand and studied his lined face.

"Electrician," she said. "At our office a few years ago."

I remembered. Nakayla and I had added some power outlets for our computers, copier, and printers. Mick Ritchie had done the wiring.

"I didn't know you were the electrician to the stars," I said.

He laughed. "Actually, I started in film electric work. Back when this state was hopping. We had competitive incentives and a great crew base." He cocked his head. "Don't know about your politics, but the damn Republicans blew that industry sky high. Made the incentives so restrictive and damned complicated that Hollywood said, 'To hell with North Carolina.' Then our so-called leaders hammered the nails in the coffin when they passed anti-gay legislation and dictated who can pee where."

Ritchie was so riled a vein rose on his forehead. "They ran everybody off to Georgia, who rolled out the welcome mat. I could get all the work I want in Atlanta. But Atlanta ain't Asheville, that's for damn sure. Anyway, I'm grateful Osteen was able to get the funding to make his movie here. Nice to work on a film and sleep in your own bed."

A man on a ladder by one of the big lights shouted, "Hey, Mick! We need extensions on these stingers."

"Coming right up." Ritchie turned to us. "I heard you two were here. I told the director all about you."

He hustled off.

"What's to tell?" Nakayla whispered.

"Well, we are a cute couple."

"Couple of what?"

Before I could think of a witty response, Camille and Marty stepped outside.

The director raised his hand in greeting like he was an alien emerging from his spaceship. "Thank you for seeing me. Mick told me all about you." His eyes moved from Nakayla to me. Instead of looking at my face, he gazed intently at my legs. Mick Ritchie had told him about my war injury.

He turned to Camille. "Ask Grayson and Nicole to join us for a moment."

His A.D. returned to the cottage.

"I want you to meet our stars," Marty said. "They're terrific. Each has a picture in post-production that will escalate their box office stature. We were lucky to get them while they're still affordable."

I tried to look excited.

"Where's your crew staying?" Nakayla asked.

"A block of rooms at the Holiday Inn between here and Asheville. Osteen made Nancy hire as many locals as she could." He lowered his voice. "Not as many experienced crew are available as when I shot here before."

"Gone to Georgia," I said.

Marty nodded. "So, you're familiar with our business. If Black Mountain College wasn't our core setting, I guarantee we'd be shooting this film in Georgia."

"Are your stars staying at the Holiday Inn?"

"Oh, God, no. Osteen worked out several rental houses in the Montford neighborhood in Asheville. When we can, we take advantage of the Asheville scene."

Montford was a rejuvenated section of Victorian homes and Arts and Crafts bungalows within walking distance of the downtown, a mecca for brew pubs, mountain and bluegrass music, Friday night drum circles, and probably the highest number of excellent restaurants per capita in the state. I could understand the Hollywood crowd wanting to be in those surroundings.

"You wanted to see us?" A young man with slicked-back brown hair asked the question as he stepped from the cottage. He wore loose-fitting jeans with the cuffs turned up and a white T-shirt whose short sleeves were rolled to the shoulder. I knew the outfit was pre-designer name brands and before every T-shirt was an advertisement for a shoe company or a brewery.

Behind him came a young woman in blue cotton shorts and a sleeveless yellow blouse. She stepped gingerly onto the gravel with her bare feet. Her jet black hair was cut short and the bangs were pulled off her forehead with a red plastic band. Her smooth olive skin and high cheekbones projected an exotic Mediterranean air. She couldn't have been more than twenty-five.

"Nicole Madison and Grayson Beckner, meet Nakayla Robertson and Sam Blackman." Marty stepped back like he expected the four of us to have a group hug. Instead, we exchanged formal handshakes and responses that ranged from "Nice to meet you" to "A pleasure."

We all looked back to Marty who stood with his arms folded and his eyes rapidly moving between Grayson and me.

"Nakayla and Sam are private detectives," he said.

"How terribly interesting," Nicole said.

This time I heard what could have been an accent from Australia or New Zealand. She didn't look like a native of those countries, but I really had no clue what those people should look like.

"Are you working a case?" Grayson asked.

His accent came straight from Brooklyn. The two actors sounded worlds apart from western North Carolina and from each other.

"Just getting some information on something that happened a long time ago," I said. "Nothing to do with the movie."

Grayson winked. "I understand. The 'private' in private eye."

"Something like that."

"Marty, we're ready." A young man in cargo pants layered with pockets stood in the doorway.

The director clapped his hands. "Excellent. Sam and Nakayla, would you like to see the set and then watch the video assist?"

Nakayla looked at me and then the two actors. "If we're not in the way."

"Nonsense," Grayson said. "We block out everything around us."

Nicole laughed. "Including Marty's direction."

The front room was stripped bare except for a handcrafted round wooden table and two straight-back chairs. The walls held a few woven tapestries and a shelf of pottery—a pitcher, some goblets, a few mugs.

Two cameras near the table were positioned ninety degrees from each other, and I could see the wall objects were mounted at odd places to be within camera range.

"Sit at the table," Marty said. "Grayson and Nicole need their makeup freshened. Now when you see this scene on the big screen you can say you were there."

"Your big chance." Nakayla pointed to a deck of cards on the table. "I'm pretty sure this is the strip poker scene. Robbie loses."

"Who?"

"Grayson's role. Robbie Oakley, the main male character."

"With a looker like Nicole, the movie has the guy lose?"

"Sexist." Nakayla glanced to the other side of the room where a woman fussed over Grayson's hair. "He looks hot to me. I'd buy a ticket."

"Sam, you and Nakayla look at each other." Marty stood beside a camera operator whose lens was focused on me. "You're a good stand-in for Grayson while we tweak the shot."

Sam Blackman. Stand-in for a younger actor with a hot body. I could live with that.

Nakayla read my mind. "Must be a real wide shot so don't get your hopes up." She patted the deck. "And I was kidding about the strip poker. Robbie and Sacha are building a house of cards while sharing their background stories. Another one of L.T. Hart's not-so-subtle metaphors."

"What are the background stories?"

"Robbie's a World War II veteran who wants to be a painter. He's local but he saw a lot of action in Europe. Sacha Molter is a camp survivor. Her father was German and owned a biergarten. Her mother was Jewish. Her father was killed trying to protect them and the mother died in Ravensbrück, a women's concentration camp north of Berlin. Sacha was liberated and came to Manhattan to live where her aunt had immigrated a few years before the war. Sacha wants to be a dancer. Both are broken, trying to expunge their inner demons through their art."

I thought I saw where a chick lit story was headed. "One of them dies, right?"

"Sorry, you'll have to read the book."

Marty's shadow fell across the table as he stepped in front of the window and leaned over us. "If the film weren't already cast, you could be my leading roles. Come outside and watch the scene with me."

He led us to the area with the monitors. Extra director chairs were set up and a technician handed Nakayla and me wireless headsets. We watched Grayson and Nicole take their places. Instead of the clapstick slate depicted in the movies, a slate with flashing red sequential numerals was inserted into the camera shots. I read "Love Among the Ridges, scene 46, A&B reversals, Take 1." A voice read the information aloud, then said, "Mark it," and a beep sounded as the slate flashed white for a split-second.

The slate withdrew, the cameras reframed on the actors, and Marty spoke into a microphone. "Action!"

Grayson picked up the deck of cards and began building a tower. "How did you come to be here?" The Brooklyn accent had been replaced by a pitch-perfect mountain twang that could have come out of a moonshiner's mouth.

"My aunt. She arranged for me to study with Merce Cunningham. I think she just wanted to get me out of New York." Nicole added a layer to the card tower. Her accent had transformed into a German-tinged English.

"Are your parents away?" Grayson stacked another section of the card house, not really looking at Nicole. A little time passed before he realized she hadn't answered him.

Nicole had tears flowing down her cheeks.

Grayson sat up straight. "Sacha?"

"Merce says a dancer must have joy in her soul. But I look in my soul and I find..." Nicole pressed her hand against one of the bottom cards and the whole structure toppled. "Destruction. Around me. Within me." She jumped up from her chair and out of frame.

"Cut!" Marty pounded me on the back. "Brilliant. Brilliant." He pulled off his headset. "See what I mean? These two will make something out of this pile-of-shit script." He practically ran into the cottage to congratulate his actors.

"What do you think we're supposed to do now?"

Nakayla started walking down the driveway. "Last I heard we were working a case. It's time to see Harlan Beale."

I caught up to her. "But don't you think that was odd?"

"Odd? They were good performers."

"Odd that Marty wanted to speak to us, but what did he say?"

Nakayla stopped and looked back at the cottage. The tech crew was already striking the lights. "I guess he was trying to impress us."

"Yes. Which leaves us with one big question. Why?"

·

Chapter Six

The rusty mailbox bearing Harlan Beale's address looked like it had been there since first-class stamps were three cents. No house was visible. We turned onto a single lane driveway strewn with pine needles and rode about fifty yards until the road took a sharp left. The woods parted to reveal a one-story cottage centered in what appeared to be more pasture than lawn.

A vintage 1970s Ford F-150 light blue pickup was parked near cinder block steps to a warped wooden porch. Set back on either side of the main cottage were two outbuildings. One sheltered an old tractor and the other anchored a fenced area containing chickens and guinea hens. They perched tucked together as feathered balls against the light drizzle.

The three structures looked like they'd been salvaged from the materials used at Black Mountain College and never been renovated since.

I parked in the scruffy grass about ten yards behind the truck. A bluetick coonhound rounded the corner of the porch, sat on his haunches and let loose a mournful howl.

"Better than a doorbell," I said.

Nakayla unbuckled her seat belt. "Let's get out and stand by the car where Harlan can see us."

"In the rain?"

"Yes. He'll see we're harmless."

"Or stupid."

"Speak for yourself." She opened the door.

I followed but stood behind my door, a ready shield in case Harlan was one of those mountaineers who greeted unwanted visitors with a load of birdshot.

The dog stopped howling and scratched one of his long floppy ears with a hind paw. He seemed to have discarded us as a threat.

The door to the house swung open and an elderly man stepped out. His long white hair was pulled back in a ponytail that hung below the nape of his neck. White whiskers draped to the chest of his bib overalls. If he'd had a guitar, he could have been an ancient member of ZZ Top.

He cocked his head and studied us a few seconds. "Can I he'p you folks?"

"We're here to see Harlan Beale," I said. "The movie people gave us this address."

"Well, y'all are seein' him. So, you can get back in your car or come in out of the rain and tell me what else y'all want."

We hustled onto the porch with the coonhound trailing behind. Beale held the door open and ushered us in. The front room was sparsely furnished with a worn sofa with sagging cushions, mismatched armchairs, and a bentwood rocker. The dog went to a throw rug in front of a stone fireplace, shook the water off his back, and collapsed on his side.

"Don't mind ol' Blue. He just listens, he won't interrupt." Beale took the rocker and motioned us to the sofa. "Well, who are ya and why'd the movie people send ya?"

I nodded to Nakayla to take the lead. The house clearly lacked a woman's touch and I thought Beale might be receptive to a little feminine conversation.

"Mr. Beale, the movie people didn't send us. I'm Nakayla Robertson and this is Sam Blackman. We're from the Blackman and Robertson Detective Agency in Asheville. We've been hired to learn what we can about a death that occurred in 1948."

Beale folded his hands across his lap and started slowly rocking. "1948? Ain't y'all a little late?"

Nakayla smiled. "The sister of the deceased has some

questions, and, well, she's at the age where she'd like a little more certainty about what happened, if you know what I mean."

"Yep. She's got to be close to my age and about to finish up. I reckon I can see that. Who is she, if you don't mind me askin'?"

"Her name's Violet Baker."

Beale shook his head.

"Her maiden name was Weaver."

He stopped rocking. "Weaver, ya say? My wife was kin to some Weavers over in Fairview. Of course, there's Weavers all over these hills. Weaverville is loaded with them."

I laughed but then realized Harlan Beale hadn't said it as a joke. Ol' Blue lifted his head off the rug and stared at me.

"That makes sense," I said. "But Violet Baker was from Fairview."

Beale resumed his slow rock. "It's a pity my Loretta's passed over. She probably knew this Violet girl. How old was she in 1948?"

"Eleven," Nakayla said. "Her brother was Paul Weaver and he was twenty-three. He was a student at Black Mountain College. That's how we came to see you. Roland Cassidy said you were his unofficial historian."

Beale expelled a puff of air that lifted the whiskers around his mouth. "Hell, I ain't no historian. I just lived through it all. In 1948, I was sixteen and I worked part-time at the college. I'd just started that summer so I didn't know a lot of people."

"What did you do?" Nakayla asked.

"I reckon you could call me a handyman. There was always stuff to repair and some of them folks had wild ideas, building new things. One guy tried to make this dome thing out of triangles. Everyone was real excited but it fell apart. Next year he came back and it worked."

"Buckminster Fuller," Nakayla said. "It was called a geodesic dome."

"Yeah, The movie people were interested in that. As for me, give me a stack of two-by-fours and a keg a' nails."

"Did you build this house?" I asked.

"Yep. And I'll confess I did learn some tricks from the school. But I don't remember anyone dying there."

"Paul didn't die at the school," Nakayla clarified. "He fell from an overlook on the Blue Ridge Parkway. Coroner's report said he'd been hiking."

A glimmer of recognition flashed in his eyes. "Yeah, I do recollect something about that. And ya say he was local? Most of the students were from up North."

"As local as you," Nakayla emphasized. "And his sister says he knew his way around these trails in the dark. That's why she thinks the whole story might not have come out."

"Where's this Violet Baker been all these years?"

"Albany, New York. The family moved to Pennsylvania after her brother's death. She married a man from Albany and he recently died."

"And she came back here to finish up," Beale said.

Succinct and true, I thought.

"Do you remember if there were any troubles at the school?" Nakayla asked.

"Troubles?"

"Tensions. Conflicts between the students or the faculty."

"There was always tension about money. The place ran on a shoestring. Sometimes I'd go a month or longer without getting paid. Or they'd pay me with leftover construction materials." He looked around the room. "Half my house came from the school."

I thought about the pilfered supplies that morning but decided bringing it up could sound accusatory.

"And then there was tension with some of the town people," Beale said.

"About what?" Nakayla asked.

Beale focused on me as if I would more likely understand his answer. "Mostly about the coloreds." He lowered his head and looked at Nakayla through bushy eyebrows. "Sorry, Missy. That's just the way it was back then." He turned to me. "Our world was segregated. The college didn't hold with that. Everybody mingled. Blacks and whites, with lots of Jews thrown in. Some of the town's people didn't cotton with that."

"So, who was threatened?"

"Well, nobody threatened nobody specifically. You asked me about tension."

The old guy was correct. Tension didn't mean Paul Weaver had been targeted.

"So, there was no violence?" I asked.

"Nope. Just grumblin'. People who felt that way kept their distance."

"What if Paul Weaver was particularly friendly to a black student?"

Beale thought a moment. "If it stayed at the college, no one would have interfered. People looked at it as another world—like goin' to a foreign country. But elsewhere," he shook his head, "it might not have gone over so well. Particularly if they were boy and girl. You know what I mean?" Again, he turned to Nakayla and repeated, "That's just the way it was back then."

"I know," she said. "My family's been here since the eighteen hundreds."

Beale threw up his hands and rocked forward. "Well, there ya go. I ain't sayin' nothin' you don't already know."

I thought about Violet Baker's story of her brother getting into a fight at the American Legion post over not admitting black veterans. Had he dated a black girl in public to make a defiant, in-your-face statement? "Would there be any photographs from that era?" I asked. "You know—of dances or activities where Paul Weaver might show up?"

"Maybe. They'd be at the museum in Asheville. But if it was a suspicious death, wouldn't there have been some kind of police report? Not the Asheville police, but the county sheriff?"

"Yes. If they keep records that far back. That's on our list of things to check."

"I'll ponder it myself. See what I can find. And I'll check some of my kinfolk. Got a cousin still livin' who's in her nineties. She might have some recollection."

"We'd appreciate it, Mr. Beale." Nakayla handed him her business card. "If you think of anything else, please give a call. And do you have a phone where we could reach you?"

Beale unsnapped a chest pocket of his overalls. "Sure. Roland Cassidy got me a cell phone so he could get in touch." He shook his head. "Didn't know it would be all hours of the day and night. That man's what I call a troublin' mind. Everything's high drama." He handed Nakayla the phone. "Don't never call myself. Find the number and write it down."

"Nice iPhone," Nakayla said.

"They tell me I can even use it to deposit checks in the bank. Don't know about that. What if I dial a wrong number?"

"I'm with you, Mr. Beale," I said. "I like to hand my money to a person."

"Got that right. I did learn to take pictures. Comes in handy at the movie when we finish a set and want a record of how it looks. In case somethin' happens to it."

"Any idea what happened to those building supplies that went missing this morning?" I asked.

"Somebody stoled them. They're probably down on the flatlands by now. Them security guards are about as useful as tits on a bull." A tinge of red showed beneath his white beard as he thought about what he'd said in front of Nakayla, but he didn't apologize. He'd pretty well summed up what we thought of the Acme Security men in their movie costumes.

Nakayla scribbled a number on the back of one of her own cards and handed the phone to Beale. "Thank you. I promise not to call you day and night."

The old mountaineer took the phone. "For you, dear, you call whenever you want."

Ol' Blue got up and shook himself from head to tail. He'd heard enough.

Chapter Seven

"What do you want to do now?" Nakayla asked the question as we pulled out of Beale's driveway.

"I'd like to see where Paul Weaver's body was discovered, but there was no exact location for the fall mentioned in Violet Baker's copy of the coroner's report. Just a trail or overlook along the Blue Ridge Parkway."

"There should be a police report or newspaper story," Nakayla said.

"Then let's go back to Asheville and split up. I'll check the police department and you cover the archives at the *Asheville Citizen-Times.*"

"They were two papers back then," Nakayla said. "A morning and an afternoon."

"That's probably good because it means there's twice the chance it was reported."

The drizzle became a heavy downpour and I flipped the wipers to high speed. "Good day for inside work. Let's grab lunch someplace with close and easy parking."

"And what barbecue place would that be?"

"Well, if you insist, I think Luella's will be perfect."

After Nakayla sensibly ate a barbecue chicken salad and I downed a platter of chopped pork and hush puppies that not only filled me but primed a rainy day afternoon nap, I had Nakayla drop me at police headquarters while she went searching for microfiche of the Asheville newspapers.

I recognized the duty officer seated behind a glass partition in the small lobby. Jake Barber smiled and waved me over as soon as I entered. Police and private investigators often clashed, but I enjoyed an exceptional relationship with the Asheville department. Several years earlier, I'd discovered the man who'd murdered one of their detectives, and I was as close to being a member of the force as I could be without carrying a badge. Plus, the partner of the murdered detective had become one of my closest friends.

"What can we do you out of, Sam? Or are you here to turn yourself in?"

"Wondered if Newly showed up for work."

"You his parole officer?"

"Talk about cruel and unusual punishment. I wouldn't wish that on anyone."

Jake laughed. "He's in the pen. I'll buzz you through."

The "pen" wasn't the penitentiary but the bullpen, the open space where the detectives worked as paired partners. Curt Newland, known to everyone as "Newly," was the senior detective on the force. He could have retired a decade ago, but he once told me his wife didn't want him underfoot. She'd hound him to get a job at Walmart, if it got him out of the house.

I spotted him at his desk doing what consumes the time of most law enforcement officers—filling out some report on his computer.

"Doing some creative writing?" I slid into an empty chair at the desk across from him.

He looked up from his keyboard. "Oh, hell, just when I thought the day couldn't get any worse."

"Good to see you too."

Newly ran his fingers through his thinning, graying hair. "Better to be seen than viewed, my friend. This a social call?"

"Always. But now that I'm here, I need—"

"A favor," he said in unison. "What are you fishing for?"

"I'm looking into a suspicious death."

Newly's eyebrows arched. "Did we miss something?"

"Maybe. Where were you in October of 1948?"

"Good question. It depends on if there's life before birth. You want to fill me in?"

I shared my conversation with Violet Baker, showed him a copy of the recently discovered coroner's report, and summarized that morning's interview with Harlan Beale. Newly listened without interrupting.

When I finished, he tapped the coroner's report lying on the table. "If there's no evidence that Weaver's death occurred within the city limits of Asheville, then I doubt I'll find anything in our archives. Your best bet would be the Buncombe County Sheriff's Office."

"But they don't love me like they love you."

"You're right. I bet every morning the sheriff scans the newspaper for my obit and is disappointed. We've had jurisdictional fights that Don King could have promoted." He pulled a notepad from his desk drawer and scribbled a name. "Here's the administrative assistant in charge of their records. Gladys Daily."

"Why will she help me?"

"Her best friend is Roy Peters' widow. Say nothing more than your name and that you need help."

Roy Peters had been Newly's partner until he was assassinated in cold blood in Asheville's Riverside Cemetery. I'd not only tracked down his murderer, but Nakayla and I had made sure Peters' family had been financially taken care of. Our involvement was supposed to be confidential, but maybe it hadn't been kept as quiet as we'd wished.

"And I'll see what I can dig up," Newly said. "But I'd like a favor in return."

"Like what?"

"Like you discover anything that could blowback on our department, you give me a heads up."

"Newly, it was almost seventy years ago."

He shook his head. "When it comes to embarrassing the police, there's no such thing as a statute of limitations."

The rain had stopped so I decided to walk to the Sheriff's Department in the county office building on the other end of Pack Square. I could not only drop in on Gladys Daily but also visit the archived records department next door and see Paul Weaver's death certificate.

Getting into the courthouse was like going through a TSA pat-down at the airport. Once cleared, I rode an elevator to the fourth floor and stepped into a well-appointed lobby. When I asked for Gladys, a deputy told me she was in a meeting and should be out in thirty minutes. I told him I'd be back but didn't leave my name. No sense tipping my hand that the famous Sam Blackman was on the prowl.

In the meantime, I left the courthouse and walked half a block down College to the Register of Deeds office, where I hoped their vital records would include Paul Weaver's death certificate. Although there was only a slim chance that the cause of death would be more detailed than the coroner's report, I needed to pursue all possibilities.

The woman at the desk looked like she could have attended the building's official ribbon-cutting in 1928. She frowned when I gave her the date. "The funeral home might have easier access," she said.

"I don't know the funeral home or even if it's still in business."

She peered at me over reading glasses thick enough to be bullet-proof. "Have you tried, sir?"

I fought back my rising temper. "The police department told me your records are impeccable. This is a pending police investigation." Technically, I'd talked to Newly so I wasn't lying.

She was torn between being officious and demonstrating the superiority of her records.

"What's the name, sir?"

"Paul Clarence Weaver. His date of death was October 17, 1948."

"Excuse me. I'll need to go to our central archives." She turned away and I found an unoccupied bench along a wall.

I sat there for twenty minutes, wondering whether the woman was actually looking for my document or just being a pill by making me wait while she drank a cup of coffee.

"Mr. Blackman?" The woman frowned at me from behind the counter.

I walked over to her.

"Are you sure about the date of the death? October 17, 1948?"

"Yes." I unfolded the photocopy of the coroner's report. "Here's the record of the inquest."

She studied it. "Where did you get this?"

"The deceased's sister. Her father was given a copy."

"So, you have proof that Mr. Weaver died."

"That was never in doubt. But the police are reviewing the cause of death and I'm representing the family. The documents are available to the public."

She bit her lower lip, clearly frustrated that I wasn't going away. "Well, since this document exists," she tapped the coroner's report with a crooked finger, "maybe the death certificate was misfiled with it."

"You're looking at paper copies?"

"No. But the paper documents might have been digitized and catalogued incorrectly." She picked up the photocopy. "Mind if I borrow this?"

"Be my guest. I'll use the time to check with Gladys Dailey in the Sheriff's Office."

She smiled for the first time. "You know Gladys?"

"She's a peach, isn't she?"

The woman lowered her voice. "Let me make an extra copy for Gladys. Tell her Lois says hello."

I left my new friend and went back through courthouse security in search of Gladys.

The same sheriff's deputy greeted me. "Gladys is back," he said. "Give me your name and I'll page her."

"Blackman. Sam Blackman. Tell her Lois sent me."

The deputy reached across his desk and offered his hand. "Sorry, Mr. Blackman. I didn't recognize you. I'm Mike Simmons."

"Have we met?"

"No, but I've seen your picture in the paper. You broke some pretty big cases."

"You know how it is. Sometimes you're in the right place at the right time."

He picked up the phone. "Gladys. Your guest is back. Mr. Sam Blackman." He winked at me. "That will get her out here. She told me what you did for Roy Peters' wife and kids. We butt heads with the Asheville police once in a while, but when an officer falls in the line of duty, it's an assault on all of us. Know what I mean?"

"Yes. I do." Those same feelings existed in the military. Especially among those of us who'd seen our buddies fall around us. We might have been serving our country, but we were fighting to save each other.

"Mr. Blackman?" A middle-age woman with gray-streaked brown hair stepped through a door behind Simmons. Her broad smile was a sharp contrast to the bureaucratic countenance that had greeted me in county records.

"Yes, Ms. Dailey. Have you got a few minutes?"

She waved me forward. "Definitely. Come on back."

I followed her to a small conference room that looked like it was doubling as someone's office. Manila folders stacked in various heights covered the back half of a rectangular table. Two cups, half-filled with cold coffee, sat abandoned near the front edge.

Gladys pushed them away. "Sorry for the mess. Have you ever been in a law enforcement office that had enough room?"

I slid into a chair across from her. "I'd be suspicious of one that wasn't busting at the seams."

"What can I do for you?" She swept her hand toward the folders. "That doesn't involve paperwork."

"No such luck." I explained I was looking into the death of Paul Weaver and showed her the copy of the coroner's report. "Lois in county records is searching for a death certificate and any information from the inquest. I'm hoping you might have a report if the Sheriff's Department was involved."

"Do you know where the death occurred?" Gladys asked.

"Mr. Weaver's sister was told a trail along the Blue Ridge Parkway near Black Mountain."

"That's in our jurisdiction." She rose from the table and picked up the cups. "Can you wait a few minutes?"

"No problem." I pulled out my cell phone. "Always work to do."

Gladys smiled and left. I texted Nakayla:

> At sheriff's waiting on copy of report.

That was the work I had to do. I looked at the stacks of manila folders, tempted to read one of the files. The barbecue rested heavy on my stomach and I feared Gladys would return to find me asleep.

The door opened. Deputy Mike Simmons entered. "Thought you might like a cup of coffee. I know you hang out with Newly and the city boys. Their brew would peel the paint off a patrol car." He handed me the mug, clearly not a refill of one of the dirty cups. "It's black. I figured as ex-Army you weren't the cream-and-sugar type."

I took a sip. "Pretty good. You need to give Newly some pointers."

Simmons laughed. "You tell him. He wouldn't ask for my help if he was on fire."

The deputy left. My phone vibrated and I saw a text from Nakayla:

> Both Citizen and Times have brief stories. No obits.

> Going to library. Meet at office.

At least one of us was making progress.

I stretched the coffee over the next fifteen minutes and was thinking about finding a refill when Gladys returned.

Her smile was gone. "I'm afraid I've got bad news and more bad news."

"No records?"

"No. And there should be something there. We would have been called to the scene."

"What's the other bad news?"

"Lois phoned me. She has no trace of either the coroner's inquest or a death certificate. From our standpoint, your Mr. Weaver never died."

• • ● • •

"So, all the official paperwork is missing?" Nakayla had slipped off her shoes and sat in the corner of our office sofa with her feet tucked under her.

I sat in the chair opposite, nursing another cup of coffee, the best brew of the day. "Yes. The Sheriff's Department even contacted the Office of the Chief Medical Examiner in Raleigh, where all original autopsy and M.E. reports are archived. Nothing. It has to be more than a coincidence or sloppy record-keeping. And I called all the area funeral homes. None of their files go back that far."

"The newspaper articles simply refer to a Black Mountain College student falling from a trail along the Blue Ridge Parkway," Nakayla said. "They gave his name and a quote from a deputy sheriff named Thigpen, who has to be long dead."

"The papers didn't pick up that Weaver was local?"

"No. He was identified as a resident of the college who ventured too close to the edge of an overlook."

Nakayla hopped up, went to her office, and returned with two books. "I got these from the library. They're about the college and have pictures. I thought the captions might identify the people in the photographs."

She handed me one of the volumes, a thin soft-cover book titled *Images of America—Black Mountain College*. I flipped through the roughly one hundred pages containing three to four pictures to a page. Short paragraphs of interspersed text explained the photos and identified some, but not all, of the people.

I glanced at my watch. "It's a little after five. I'll call Violet Baker. She should be the one to review these pictures. They all eat so early at Golden Oaks, we could probably see her at six."

I dialed Violet's number.

"Violet Baker speaking." Her cheery answer belied her age.

"It's Sam Blackman. I hope I'm not interrupting your dinner."

"My Lord, no. I can't swallow a morsel before six-thirty. These early-bird diners think I'm crazy." Her voice turned serious. "Did you and your partner find out anything?"

"We've made some progress, but the records are very limited. Nakayla has some books with pictures of Black Mountain College, and we thought you might be able to identify your brother. If he's in group shots, they might tell us who he hung out with."

"Can we do that now?"

I looked at Nakayla and silently mouthed, "She wants to meet now."

"Tell her we can be there in thirty minutes," Nakayla whispered.

"What if we meet somewhere at Golden Oaks in half an hour?" I asked.

"Don't you have an office in Asheville?"

"Yes. On Pack Square."

"Then I'm coming to you. I can only stay on this mountain so long. We'll look at pictures and then I'm taking you both to dinner. A girl's gotta have some fun."

Violet knocked on our office door in less than thirty minutes. I ushered her to one of the armchairs and joined Nakayla on the sofa.

My partner handed Violet one of the two books she brought from the library. "I thought you might be able to find your brother in one of the photographs. If he's with some other students who are identified, that might give us a chance to find someone still alive who knew him."

Violet glanced at the thin volume, *Images of America—Black Mountain College*. "I've seen this book. My brother's not in it."

Nakayla passed her the thicker volume. "How about this one? It was published in Germany but the text is in English."

"Must have been tied to the Bauhaus," I said, pleased that I could show off my new knowledge.

"No, I've not seen this one," Violet said. "Do you want me to take it home and go through it?"

"No," Nakayla said. "We have time now, if you do. I'll put on a pot of coffee."

Violet nodded and opened the book to the beginning.

I didn't want to just sit there staring at her flipping pages. "Excuse me. I've got some paperwork to tend to."

I retreated to my office but left the door open. My paperwork was a half-finished detective novel I'd picked up at Asheville's used bookstore, The Battery Park Book Exchange. Books, wine, and appetizers were their specialty, not to mention every other person brought a dog into the shop. I fished the paperback out of my desk drawer, an underrated hard-boiled, fists and guns adventure by Ralph Dennis, whose detective, Jim Hardman, worked tough cases in Atlanta in the nineteen-seventies. If I used Hardman's tactics in Asheville, I'd be in jail faster than my suspects.

I flipped back several pages to refresh my memory of the plot, but had read only a few paragraphs when Violet called out with unrestrained excitement. "It's Paul. I found a picture of Paul."

Nakayla beat me into the room and stood beside Violet. Our client was pointing to something on one of the pages.

"He's the tall boy with blond hair sitting between the two young women," Violet said.

I circled behind them and peered over Nakayla's shoulder. Three students sat close together on a plaid blanket near the shore of what looked like Lake Eden. Paul wore baggy bathing trunks; the women were clothed in one-piece swimsuits. Paul had an arm draped across the bare shoulders of each. All were smiling.

The caption read "Lakeside fun—summer 1948. Dancer Eleanor Johnson with two unidentified classmates." Eleanor Johnson was evidently the woman on the left. The black woman.

Nakayla gasped. "Oh, my."

"What is it?" I asked.

"In 1948, a black woman would never have gone swimming with whites, especially a white man."

"That's true," Violet Baker agreed. "But the college followed its own set of rules."

"And maybe flaunted them in the faces of the surrounding locals," Nakayla said. "You know Montreat?"

"The Presbyterian conference center?" Violet asked.

"Yes. Even though there were African-American Presbyterian churches, black members weren't allowed to stay in the inn or use the recreational facilities until the nineteen-sixties. That's how ensconced segregation was back then."

I thought about our conversation with Harlan Beale and what he said would be the reaction to blacks and whites dating. What had been a theoretical possibility now became a reality photographed in black and white.

It was also a lead.

I took the book from Violet to study the picture more closely. "If this woman was well-known enough to be identified, then we should be able to trace her."

"She was probably a student of Merce Cunningham's," Nakayla said. "He founded a dance company here that went on to achieve international acclaim in New York City."

"Then that's our starting point."

Violet took the book back. "Paul might be in other photographs. I should check them all."

Violet spent another twenty minutes meticulously scanning each page. She found only one additional photograph, a group of students around Buckminster Fuller and a partially collapsed geodesic dome made of Venetian blind strips. Neither the black nor white woman was in the frame.

The photograph was dated Summer 1948. No one other than Fuller was identified.

"Well, it looks like Eleanor Johnson is our best bet," Nakayla said.

"If she's still alive," Violet said. "Even if she was only eighteen in 1948, she'd be in her late eighties today."

"Plenty of people are in their late eighties," Nakayla said.

Violet laughed. "Yes. I forgot where I now live." Her moment of levity passed. "But if the woman is dead?"

"Then we find what enrollment records exist in the Black Mountain College Museum and start tracking down former students." Nakayla hesitated, and then looked at me.

"But that could get expensive," I advised. "Especially if we have to travel in person to interview them. And I'd recommend doing that rather than a phone call or Internet correspondence."

Violet nodded. "I understand. You've made good progress today. Let's at least follow through with Eleanor Johnson." She glanced at her watch. "I promised you dinner. I've heard good things about Bouchon. Would that be fine?"

"More than fine," I said. "Nakayla and I love it." The nearby restaurant was known for good French comfort food, and I admit I'd rate their cuisine over barbecue.

• • ● • •

The three of us were finishing after-dinner coffee when my cell phone vibrated. I ignored it, but Violet evidently heard the low hum.

"Answer it if you need to. You must get important calls all hours of the day and night."

Not wanting to disillusion an impressed client with the truth that it was probably some credit card offering, I made a pretense of looking at the screen. The number wasn't blocked nor was it one of those 800 area codes. 213. That was Los Angeles. The only people I knew from Los Angeles were on the movie set in Black Mountain.

"It's not important," I said.

Nakayla gave me the look that showed she'd seen my surprised reaction. She said nothing. If it had to do with our case, we wouldn't want to hear information in front of our client without having the chance to evaluate its implications.

We walked Violet Baker to her car. When the taillights had been lost in traffic, I pulled out my phone.

"I think we got a call from someone based in L.A."

"Really? You think it's the film people?"

"Either that or Claire Danes is stalking me again." I had one voicemail. I pressed play and speaker so Nakayla could hear.

"Sam. Hey, man, it's Marty. Marty Kolsrud. Can you come to the set at seven tomorrow morning? You and Nakayla both. I want you in my movie."

Chapter Eight

If we were going to meet Marty Kolsrud on location at seven the next morning, Nakayla and I decided spending the night in our separate residences was a pragmatic idea for a fresh change of clothes and an early start. And, frankly, I needed some time alone to process what we'd learned.

"So we beat on, boats against the current, borne back ceaselessly into the past." That last line of F. Scott Fitzgerald's *The Great Gatsby* came to me as I drove home. I'm not a Fitzgerald scholar. Far from it. But the first case Nakayla and I had worked as partners in our detective agency had involved historical elements entwined with the renowned author's visits to Asheville, and, as a consequence, I'd taken an interest in his writings.

The quote summed up the majority of our investigations. Something thought long dead and buried in the past reemerged with tsunami power that swept down the decades to explode into the present. And too often those initial turbulences involved race and racism.

To some degree, Nakayla and I fought that current as an interracial couple. And though we lived in a more enlightened time, like Fitzgerald's boat, we seemed to be ceaselessly pulled back into the sins of the past. Could Paul Weaver, arm around a black woman, smiling into a camera, have fueled such violent bigotry that it cost him his life? Harlan Beale had warned the times held such hostility. If Eleanor Johnson was still alive, she might confirm it.

I took those thoughts to bed, depressed that Violet Baker's search for the truth might yield an answer so indicative of the racist times, that her brother died because he befriended and perhaps even loved a woman whose skin was a different color. Seventy years ago, I would have been Paul Weaver.

At six-thirty the next morning, I picked up Nakayla in front of our office building. There was no sense driving two cars, plus after the meeting with Marty, we'd get back to our case. The drive to Lake Eden wouldn't be a waste of time because our first priority was to take the photos of Paul Weaver to Harlan Beale. He was the one person we knew who might identify other students in those pictures.

The same stocky guard was on duty when we arrived a few minutes before seven. He stepped in front of my CR-V and greeted us with a stern face of authority. I rolled down my window and he walked to my door.

"Good morning, Officer," I said. "Looks like we've got a brighter day than yesterday."

"Yep," he replied unenthusiastically. "You're Blackman and Robertson, right?"

"Correct. We have an appointment with Martin Kolsrud."

"He drove in nearly two hours ago. Check in at the production office." He waved us on.

"Not even a 'Have a nice day,'" I said.

"Remember, he's in a costume." Nakayla laughed. "Maybe that's why we're here. Kolsrud has security guard costumes for us."

The production office was a beehive of activity, like the staff had never gone home. Camille Brooks, phone jammed against her ear, stood and signaled us to her desk. A man stood beside her, scowling at several sheets of paper in his hand. He wore a wrinkled sport coat a size too small for his pudgy body. He must have been pushing fifty in a sea of youngsters.

Brooks was talking rapidly, giving someone an ultimatum on a delivery date.

"If those materials aren't here by this afternoon, you're not getting one more piece of business from us. Is that clear?" She raised the phone over her head, not bothering to listen to the response. "Marty and Nancy are in a conference room on the second floor. It's the door opposite the balcony." She turned to the man beside her. "They're giving me the runaround, Raymond. Nancy wants you to hold up any payments."

We left Camille Brooks and the crisis of the moment and retraced the way we'd gone with Arnold Osteen the day before. The door was closed, so Nakayla knocked gently.

"Come in," came the sharp reply. I recognized Osteen's voice.

He, Marty Kolsrud, Nancy Pellegatti, Nicole Madison, and Grayson Beckner were seated around a long folding table. Yellow script pages littered its surface.

"Please have a seat." Marty gestured to two empty chairs close to the door.

Nakayla and I sat and said nothing. It wasn't our meeting.

Marty gathered the yellow pages into a stack. "Sam, I want you to know you kept me up all night."

"And then Marty dragged the rest of us here at five-thirty," Osteen complained.

"So…I'm guilty of what?"

Grayson Beckner sat opposite me. The actor leaned across the table. "Creating conflict. Developing character. One fuels the story, the other drives the performance."

I didn't know what the hell he was talking about.

"You put flesh on the bones of Robbie Oakley. Added dimension to the role, which, frankly, I was struggling to infuse with life."

I saw where Grayson was headed. "You're making your character an amputee?"

Marty Kolsrud beamed. "Exactly. When I heard your story yesterday, I thought, 'Now that's what this script lacks. A layer of inner conflict, the challenge to become whole in body and soul.' It's *The Best Years of Our Lives* for this generation."

"Is that a soap opera?"

Kolsrud looked at me like I was insane. "Hell, no. It's a cinema classic. Fredric March, Dana Andrews, seven Academy Awards. Three servicemen return from World War II. But the drama isn't about the war, it's about the aftermath. And one of them is a double amputee with hooks for hands."

I shook my head. "I'm not a poster child."

"No, you're not." Nancy Pellegatti focused her fierce eyes on me. "You're a veteran whose life was altered by war. You're not a poster child. You're a successful man who happens to be an amputee. But you're not going to sit there and tell me you haven't gone through a struggle. Maybe you still are."

"I deal with it."

"And there are men, hell, boys really, coming back from Iraq and Afghanistan today who are maimed and facing a future of pain and hardship. Is that your advice? Deal with it? War doesn't create victors. It creates wounds and scars, widows and orphans, victims on all sides. I don't want people to forget that. I want them to see courage after the battle, a battle that never really ends for so many. A past that haunts their present."

So we beat on, I thought. Fitzgerald's boat against the current. Like it or not, I was pulling one of the oars, and this little obnoxious woman had forced me to see it.

"What do you want from me?"

"We want you to work with Grayson," Marty said. "Tell him your story. He's not going to play you, but he can take your emotions, your experiences, and incorporate them into his character."

"All right, if it doesn't interfere with my casework."

Marty patted the pile of yellow pages. "Good. We need to start immediately. We have a few scenes we'll need to re-shoot." He looked at Osteen. "Not that many, Arnold. Just enough to create the continuity of Grayson's body movement. Fortunately, we're not that far into filming."

"What does Roland Cassidy think of these changes?" Nakayla asked.

With synchronized motion, all heads turned to Osteen.

"I'll handle Roland. I paid for rights to the book and I can alter it any way I want. Marty's sold me on this new approach or else I wouldn't approve a nickel be spent on re-dos." He looked at Pellegatti beside him. "But it's not carte blanche, Nancy. Understand?"

"Of course. And we'll save money on visual effects."

Marty gave his producer a sideways glance and slight shake of his head.

"What visual effects?" I asked.

"Well, what would be really helpful…" Marty hesitated as if groping for the right word.

I suddenly understood why he'd been measuring me against his star yesterday. "You want my leg, don't you? For close-ups?"

"If you would. We really can't do it otherwise. Painting out Grayson's leg in special effects is cost-prohibitive. It would just be a few scenes. You're a great stand-in physique wise."

"No nudity. I don't want to upstage Grayson."

Everyone laughed.

"Marty, you included Nakayla in last night's phone message," I said. "What's that about?" *And it had better not be nudity*, I thought.

"Right," Marty said. "Nakayla, I'd like you to be one of our extras. You can pass for a college student, you represent the diversity of Black Mountain College, and you have the natural movements of a dancer. We'll have some rehearsal scenes and a performance, but nothing complicated and you'll be part of a group."

Nakayla's lips tightened, a sign that she resisted the idea. "I told you I haven't danced since I was twelve."

"It's like riding a bicycle," Marty argued.

"Fine. Let me ride a bicycle."

Again, Nancy Pellegatti spoke up. "How about you agree to be an extra. And when our choreographer rehearses the dance scenes, you rehearse with the troupe, but if you're uncomfortable, or she doesn't feel like you're a believable student, then you're not in the scene."

I nudged Nakayla with my elbow. "If I can be in it, you can be in it. You can't be any worse."

"That's true," she conceded too quickly.

"It's settled then." Nancy slid back her chair and stood. "Grayson, why don't you and Sam find some place quiet to talk? Nakayla, go with Nicole. She can introduce you to wardrobe and makeup. Marty might want you for a scene later."

"Time out." I made the signal with my hands. "Nakayla and I aren't doing anything till we follow up on our case."

"How long's that going to take?" Nancy asked.

"If Harlan Beale's here, then maybe thirty minutes."

"Why him?" Osteen asked.

"I need him to identify some pictures from 1948. He's the only one here who goes back that far, right?"

"You think Harlan can shed some light on your suspicious death?"

"We won't know till he sees the photographs." I turned to Grayson. "I'll look for you when I finish with Beale."

"And I'll play it by ear," Nakayla told Nicole. "If I can't find you, I'll check in with Camille."

Nancy Pellegatti picked up a backpack. "Then let's go, people. We've got a movie to make."

Nakayla and I found Harlan Beale on the lawn near the lakeshore. He was laying out thin, narrow strips of white metal that looked to be a good ten or fifteen feet in length. The old mountaineer was being assisted by a man I took to be in his fifties. His white hair was close-cropped in contrast to Beale's ponytail, and instead of bib overalls, he wore a white shirt and gray pants. Both men stopped their work and turned to face us.

I started to speak, but the words froze in my throat. The man was Dustin Henry, an actor I recognized. He'd played Captain Jefferson in *Star Fleet Commander,* a sci-fi TV series and movie franchise that I'd watched religiously as a boy. He was clearly more than twenty years older than when he'd roamed the galaxy, and his loose shirt and baggy trousers appeared more suited to the nineteen-forties than the twenty-third century.

"Can we help you?" Dustin Henry's baritone voice held such familiarity that the wrinkles and gray hair became some sort of disguise concealing the hero of my childhood.

"Captain Jefferson," I managed to blurt out.

Nakayla looked at me like I'd lost my mind.

Beale shook his head. "No, this here's Dustin Henry, though we're all callin' him Bucky."

"I'm playing Buckminster Fuller," the actor explained. "The first man to call this world Spaceship Earth. Captain Jefferson couldn't hold a candle to him."

"I'm Sam Blackman." I started to say that I watched him as a kid, but that was obvious from my star-struck paralysis.

"And I'm Nakayla Robertson." She had the presence of mind to offer her hand.

I wanted to give the intergalactic sign of a raised palm with splayed fingers, but I retreated to the protocol of a firm handshake.

"Sam and Nakayla are detectives," Beale announced. "But they need you to invent a dome that's a time machine, cause they're lookin' into a death back in 1948."

"Really? During Bucky's time here?"

"In the fall," Nakayla said. "I believe Buckminster Fuller was only here during the summers."

Dustin Henry nodded. "That's right. But Harlan was here. He's helping me get the feel for what happened." The actor slowly spun in a circle, pointing at the metal strips as he did so. "Harlan says these were Venetian blinds, longer strips before the finishing factory cut them to an ordered size. He and the students bolted overlapping segments together, but the dome just lay there, sagging like a partially deflated ball."

"We know," Nakayla said. "We have a picture."

She reached in her purse and retrieved the book we'd shown Violet Baker the previous evening. She flipped it open to the first of two bookmarked pages. "Here's one of the students and Fuller working on this dome."

Dustin examined the photo. "Yes, I saw this one in a research packet. That's the scene we're going to re-create."

Nakayla angled the book toward Beale. "This is Paul Weaver." She tapped the boy with a forefinger. "Do you recognize him?"

Beale cocked his head. "Yep. He looks familiar, but I wouldn't have been able to recall his name. He wasn't around that long."

"Because in a few months, he'd be dead," I said. "How about the other students in the photo? Ever see him hanging out with any of them?"

Beale tried to focus on the small faces. "I need my magnifying glass. If I could borrow this book, I'll give it a good goin' over."

Nakayla flipped the pages to the second bookmark. "How about these women? Remember them?"

"Oh," Beale said with a low whisper. "There's trouble in the makin'."

"Because he's swimming with the black woman?" Nakayla asked.

"It wouldn't have set well in some parts, that's for damn sure. Don't make me no never mind nor anyone else at the college." He looked to the edge of the water. "I reckon from the looks of the background, they were sittin' right over there." He pointed to a spot about twenty yards away.

We stood in silence for a few seconds, as if the three students might materialize in front of us.

"Show me that picture again?" Beale asked.

Nakayla let him take the book.

He studied it and nodded to himself. "The colored girl was a dancer, just like it says. But we didn't call her Eleanor. She was Ellie. And when she danced, it was like she was about to break loose off the ground. If she wanted to float like a dandelion seed, she'd just need a breeze."

"And the other girl?" Nakayla prompted.

"Yep. I seen her around." He looked across the lake, eyes blinking rapidly as if clearing some blur. "She was here that summer, but she weren't here at Christmas."

"How do you know?" Nakayla asked.

"Because we had a holiday social. Didn't call it Christmas 'cause we had a lot of Jews. Not that they bothered me none. I was invited and got to dance with all the girls. This girl weren't one of them."

"Did you dance with Ellie?" I asked.

"Yep. Though I was afraid I'd break her. If I'd told my Pa I danced with a colored, he'd a probably whupped me." Beale looked at Nakayla and then shrugged. "But it would have been worth it." He tucked the book under his arm. "I'll take this book,

Missy, and give it some thought." He turned to Dustin Henry. "Let me run this to my truck. I'll be right back."

He'd taken only a few steps when a voice bellowed across the lawn.

"Hey, Harlan, what the hell do you think you're doing?"

We turned to see Roland Cassidy storming across the lawn. He'd traded his tweed sport coat for a stiffly starched denim shirt that made him look like a first-day tourist at a dude ranch.

"Takin' a book to my truck. What's it to you?"

Cassidy ignored Nakayla, Dustin, and me and zeroed in on the old man. "I paid you for research, and this movie continues to pay you. You have no business talking to Sam Blackman about Black Mountain College or any of your experiences."

Between the white beard and bushy eyebrows, Beale's wrinkled skin flushed crimson. "You little piss-ant. I'll talk to whoever I want about whatever I want."

I heard Dustin Henry chuckle. Cassidy must have heard the actor as well because he glared at the man.

"This is between Harlan and me."

"No, it's not," I interjected. "You don't talk about me. You talk to me. I asked Harlan to identify some students in old college photographs. That's all."

"Yeah. And then what? Weasel back to Marty with more ways to get in this film?"

So, Cassidy had heard about the script revisions. With Osteen backing his director and producer, the pompous writer could only vent his wrath at me.

"None of the script changes were my idea," I shot back. "If you've got a problem, take it up with the people making the decisions."

Beale waggled a finger at Cassidy. "And keep your stuck-up nose out of my business or I'll knock it so flat you'll be breathin' through your ears."

"What script changes?" Dustin asked. For the first time the actor appeared more than bemused by the scene before him.

Cassidy glared at me. "Thanks to Blackman, Marty's turning Robbie Oakley into a goddamned amputee. If he was supposed to be an amputee, I'd have made him an amputee."

"That your idea?" Dustin asked me.

"No. But I'm an amputee, and if Grayson's playing one, I want to help make it real."

"The thousands of my readers will revolt," Cassidy warned. "They're very loyal."

Dustin Henry walked over and gently placed a hand on Cassidy's shoulder. "Roland, if they didn't revolt when they read your drivel, they're certainly not going to revolt when a character becomes more interesting and sympathetic. Why don't you run along and pose for an author photo somewhere? Pretend to think deep thoughts."

Cassidy turned purple. He seemed to have stopped breathing. Then he managed to choke out, "What do you know, you has-been?"

I expected Captain Jefferson, *Star Fleet* commander, to deck Cassidy.

Instead he nodded and smiled. "Guilty as charged. I'm in your movie. But, thanks to Mr. Blackman, maybe it's being converted from shit to fertilizer and all our careers will grow, yours included." Dustin turned away and began placing the Venetian blind strips in crisscrossed patterns.

Cassidy stood there, not sure what to do.

"You heard the man. Shoo." Harlan Beale waved the writer away like he was scattering a gaggle of geese. "The rest of us have real work to do."

"You're going to regret this, Harlan. All of you will." And with that toothless threat, Cassidy pivoted and headed for the main building.

Beale laughed. "If I knew this was goin' to be so damn entertainin' I would've sold tickets." He raised the book. "It'll be my pleasure to go through this and recall as many names as I can."

"Have you still got my card?" Nakayla asked.

Beale patted the top pocket of his overalls. "Yep."

The thought struck me that if some kind of interracial relationship had been going on between Paul Weaver and Ellie, Beale might be reluctant to discuss it with Nakayla. I pulled out my wallet. "Here's my card, too, in case you can't reach her."

"Okay. But I'm sure I'll be seein' ya around, if you're goin' to be an advisor like me." He set off for his truck.

"What now?" Nakayla asked.

"Show biz beckons. I'll meet with Grayson and you check with Marty if there are any big scenes needing your talents. Between the two of us, we can save this film."

At five o'clock, after a long afternoon of shooting the collapsed geodesic dome reenactment, Camille Brooks released Nakayla and me for the day. My conversation with Grayson Beckner had gone well, and we'd talked through lunch. I got the sense that he would incorporate his amputee condition in subtle ways and not milk it for overt sympathy.

Nakayla had been used in multiple group shots as the students worked with Bucky. Harlan Beale stayed close to the spot, working with the prop master between shots to make the 1948 event as authentic as possible. Dialogue and close-ups with Grayson and Nicole were scheduled for the next morning, and then Marty hoped to start filming scenes of the students constructing their own classrooms and dormitories, depending upon the delivery of the materials replacing the ones that had been stolen.

As we pulled out onto the main road, a flatbed truck carrying lumber and tarp-covered cargo was turning in. The logo on the driver's door read "Phillips Building Supplies."

"Looks like you'll have another glamorous day of life in front of the camera," I said.

"Yeah. The glamour part faded on about the sixth take. How about you? When's your first stand-in for Grayson?"

"I'm what they call a weather cover. If we get another miserable day like yesterday, then they'll shoot some scenes with Grayson and me. Grayson's a good guy. I like him."

Nakayla patted my leg. "Think I have a shot at sleeping with a stand-in for the stars?"

"Maybe. If you buy me dinner first."

Dinner was takeout from the deli section of Ingle's grocery store. Nakayla picked up a rotisserie chicken, Caesar salad, and a broccoli casserole and we had a quiet dinner at my apartment. We were on our second glass of a dry rosé when my cell phone buzzed. I'd left it on the kitchen counter and wasn't inclined to move from my chair.

"Shouldn't you get that?" Nakayla asked.

"It can go to voicemail. You know my policy during meals."

"Yeah. Never let a phone call interfere with your drinking."

I clinked her glass. "Words to live by."

Nakayla and I cleaned up my kitchen around nine. She handed me my phone. "Remember, you have a message."

I retrieved it. "Sam. It's Harlan. Harlan Beale. Listen, it might be nothin' but I don't like it. Can you meet me at the college first thing in the mornin'? I got somethin' I want ya to see." I heard a background shout that was unintelligible. "Okay," Beale yelled at someone. "Over here." Then he spoke softer. "Gotta go. See ya tomorrow."

I played it again on speaker. "What do you make of that?"

Nakayla shrugged. "Maybe he found something in the book. Some photograph without Paul Weaver that meant something to him."

"Why didn't he just tell me?"

"He's in his eighties, Sam. Probably not a big phone talker. And besides, it sounded like he was meeting someone."

"We ought to have him meet Violet Baker. If they start talking about the old days, maybe it'll spark some memory."

"Like old grudges?"

"Maybe. I'd like something more solid to work with. This case is like Bucky's Venetian-blind dome—not quite able to support itself."

"Well, maybe Harlan Beale's about to change that." Nakayla grabbed my hand. "Come on, stand-in for the stars. The sooner we're in bed, the sooner it will be morning."

"Why rush it? Morning, that is."

Somewhere down in the depths of sleep, I heard my phone ring. I would have worked it into a dream, but Nakayla elbowed my side.

"Better get that. It's three o'clock."

"Oh, shit," I mumbled. "Nothing good happens at three o'clock." I looked at the screen. Five letters. Newly.

I answered and spoke the written word. "Newly?"

"You know Harlan Beale?" the homicide detective asked.

"Yeah. Is he in trouble?"

"You could say that."

"Did he tell you to call me?"

"We found your card in his pocket. Nakayla's too."

I felt the ice crystallize in my stomach. "Please. Don't say it."

"Sorry, Sam. He's dead."

"Are you at his house?" I fought to clear my head. Harlan Beale's house was out of Newly's jurisdiction. So was the movie location.

"No. I'm at the Black Mountain College Museum in town."

"Then stay there. I'm coming."

Chapter Nine

The old mountaineer lay under a fallen bookcase in a back room of the small museum. His upturned face was partially exposed beneath the heavy wooden shelves that had crashed onto his body and cut into his forehead. Blood stained his white hair and beard. Books of all sizes were scattered across the floor. Many appeared to be college catalogues, more like pamphlets than books. Other larger volumes had titles like *The Black Mountain Experiment* and *The Arts at Black Mountain College*.

Newly and his partner, Tuck Efird, knelt on either side of the body. I could see the open pocket on Beale's chest where one of the detectives had extracted our business cards.

Nakayla and I had put on shoe-coverings and been admitted to the scene.

"What do you think happened?" I asked.

Newly got to his feet and peeled off his latex gloves. "First indication is he tried to climb up the shelves to reach a book on the top. The case was attached to the wall by lightweight brackets. They broke away and he fell backwards."

"First indication? What's a second?"

"Well, there's a two-step stool in the back storeroom. That should have been adequate to reach the top shelf. We'll remove the body and bring the museum director in to see if anything's missing."

"Why would you think that?" I asked.

"I don't. But if something's gone, then we have a pretty good indication that Beale wasn't here alone. You and Nakayla are here because two days ago you asked for my help on a 1948 Black Mountain College murder. Your business cards tie you to the deceased and the deceased meets his maker in the museum tied to your case. What was he looking for, Sam?"

"We'd asked him to identify some students in one of the Black Mountain books Nakayla got from the Pack Library. I guess Harlan was trying to match pictures to others where names might be listed. He called last night saying he had something to show us."

Newly glanced at Nakayla and back to me. "Show you here, in the museum?"

"It was a voice message," Nakayla said. "He asked us to meet him at the movie location this morning. He didn't mention the museum."

"Maybe he planned to take something from here and bring it to you," Newly mused. "Do you remember exactly what he said?"

"Better than that." I pulled out my cell phone and retrieved Beale's voicemail. "Sam. It's Harlan. Harlan Beale. Listen, it might be nothin' but I don't like it. Can you meet me at the college first thing in the mornin'? I got somethin' I want ya to see." We listened to a muffled voice a distance away from Beale, then Beale shouting, "Okay. Over here." And then, barely above a whisper, his final words, "Gotta go. See ya tomorrow."

Tuck Efird stood. "The museum is open to the public. What was so goddamned urgent that this old man tried to scale a bookcase like a monkey? You could have just met him here."

"I don't know. He didn't say anything about coming to the museum, during or after hours. How'd he get in?"

Efird jerked his head toward the back hall. "Broke in through the rear door. Jimmied the deadbolt. He dropped the crowbar just inside."

"No alarm?" I asked.

"He disabled the power box on the exterior wall," Efird said. "Killed the whole system. If there was battery backup, it didn't kick in."

"So, who reported the death if there was no alarm?"

"A call came in a little after two. Someone passing by heard a crash inside. Called 911 but didn't leave a name."

"You get a trace?"

"Too soon," Newly said. "The 911 operator said the caller sounded drunk. And young. Could have been a kid out after his curfew."

"Who was first on the scene?"

"My nephew, Ted," Newly said. "He was on overnight and got here within ten minutes."

Newly's nephews Al and Ted Newland were identical twins. Both were patrolmen.

"Ted called me direct," Newly said. "I got here about two-thirty. Tuck was ten minutes behind me."

I weighed the intervals. "So, not much time could have elapsed between the 911 call and Ted's arrival."

"Correct," Neely said. "M.E.'s on his way, so we should be able to confirm that with a body temp."

"Were the lights out when Ted arrived?" Nakayla asked.

"Yes," Efird said impatiently. "We told you the power had been cut."

Nakayla walked the perimeter of the room, studying the scattered books.

"What?" I asked.

"If the museum was dark, then where's Harlan's flashlight? I doubt he disabled the power and then tried to crawl up a bookshelf in hopes of feeling the right volume."

Newly and Efird stared at each other. Both looked embarrassed that neither had made that connection. I hadn't either, but I moved closer to Nakayla as if I could share the credit for her observation.

"There's your missing item," I said. "Not something taken from the museum but something that should have been brought here by Harlan."

"Maybe it's with him under the bookcase," Efird said.

"Maybe," I said. "You'll know after the M.E. checks and releases the body."

Ted Newland came in from the front room of the museum. He clutched his two-way radio in his hand. "Uncle Newly."

We all gave him our full attention. Ted only used "Uncle Newly" when he was excited. "Dispatcher said you might want to know there's a fire at Lake Eden. It's on the Black Mountain College movie set."

Newly looked at me. "Out of our jurisdiction." He emphasized "our" and I got the message.

"Nakayla and I will head there now."

"Your choice," he said. "I'd like to see those pictures Mr. Beale was trying to identify."

"I don't see the book here," Nakayla said. She gave Newly the name and description of the cover. "He might have left it in his truck."

"His truck…" I repeated. "Is it here?"

"In the alley." Efird said. "We ran the plate, and we'll give it a thorough search."

"The book could be at his home." I flashed back to our conversation in Beale's living room. "Oh, crap. He's got a dog. Someone needs to check on him."

"Out of our jurisdiction," Newly repeated. He looked down at the body. "But I'll give you his next of kin once they've been notified. And if anything seems interesting at the fire scene, you know how to reach me."

Nakayla and I arrived at Lake Eden to find volunteer fire department trucks surrounding what was more of a giant campfire than an out-of-control blaze. Fireman sprayed water on a stack of lumber that lay between the production offices and the lakeshore. It didn't take Sherlock Holmes to deduce that the burning material was the re-order of the supplies that had been stolen only two days earlier.

I saw Arnold Osteen silhouetted against the orange glow of the flames. He was in an animated discussion with one of the firemen and his arms were in constant motion as he gestured from the burning wood to the production offices.

"This whole project is turning into a goddamn nightmare." Nancy Pellegatti made the pronouncement as she stepped between Nakayla and me.

"Were you here working?" Nakayla asked.

The producer wore the same black jeans and turquoise T-shirt from the day before.

"No. Arnold called me about half an hour ago. I threw on clothes and Marty and I sped over. He's in his office trying to decide what to shoot. We can get the close-ups of Grayson and Nicole from the dome scene, but we were supposed to start the construction sequence this afternoon. I've got twenty extras scheduled for noon." She looked across the lawn to Osteen. "Arnold's going to have a coronary. His Midas touch has flipped. Everything he touches turns to shit."

"How'd the fire start?" I asked.

"The firemen haven't said. I spoke with the guard. He claims he was making rounds by the grip and lighting trucks on the other side of the building. He came around the far corner and saw flames. He says there were cans of paint and thinner beside the lumber. They'd been used in some touch-up work in one of the cottages."

"Is he a smoker?" Nakayla asked.

"Yes. I've seen him puffing his cancer sticks at his checkpoint."

"Was he the guard who got called off the night the supplies were stolen?" I asked.

"I don't know. But he's from the same damn temp company. These guys aren't even rent-a-cops. I had to get the uniforms from a local costume shop."

"We heard," I said. "See if you can get Arnold to switch to Armitage Security Services. I know the owner. His people are top-notch."

Pellegatti spun around to face us. "That's who I wanted from the beginning. I knew we couldn't bring in L.A. security, but I'd gotten good references on Armitage from other crews who'd shot in the area. No, Arnold said we had to save money wherever we could, and that Black Mountain had zero crime. Now he's going to have to buy the same materials for the third time."

"Have you fired any disgruntled employees?" I asked. "Anyone who might be wanting to sabotage the film?"

"No. Crew chemistry is good. Department heads are level-headed. We're employing a lot of locals, and they're grateful for the work, given the boneheaded moves by your legislature that have all but destroyed the industry. The biggest challenge is Arnold. He's not a movie person and he thinks this is a glorified real estate deal. But he's teachable. Wish I could say the same for his nephew."

Her reference to Roland Cassidy sparked the memory of his outburst at the script changes.

"Could Roland be so petty as to do something like this?" I asked.

"I'd say no. A halfway decent film will increase book sales." She turned back to the fire. "But this started somehow. So, who knows? I just hope this is the last setback. It's hard enough when everything's working smoothly."

Nakayla looked at me and arched her eyebrows. I understood her unspoken question. Should we tell Nancy Pellegatti about Harlan Beale?

As if she sensed our silent conversation, Pellegatti turned again to face us. "But why are you here? Who called you?"

"We have a friend who's a police detective in Asheville. He knows we're involved with the film."

"So he called you in the middle of the night?"

"Yes. But not about the fire." I looked beyond Pellegatti to where Osteen was still talking to the fireman. "We need to speak with you, Marty, and Arnold together. Can you get them to the conference room where we met yesterday?"

She eyed me suspiciously. "What's going on?"

"I'm telling everyone at once, or you can wait and hear it from the Asheville police."

At the mention of the police, she gave me a hard stare. Through gritted teeth, she said, "The building's unlocked. Go ahead. I'll bring Arnold and Marty as soon as I can."

I sensed she wanted Nakayla and me away from Osteen when she gave him my ultimatum. Otherwise, he would have wanted an immediate explanation, something I didn't want to happen in front of the first responders.

We waited in the small conference room about five minutes before Nancy Pellegatti herded in Marty and Osteen. The director had deep blue circles under his eyes from lack of sleep. Osteen's eyes were bloodshot from the sting of the smoke. Soot streaked his stubbled cheeks.

Osteen took the chair beside me. "Why are you bringing in the Asheville police?" he asked curtly.

"I'm not. They'll be here on their own." I paused, making sure I had their full attention. "Harlan Beale was killed last night."

Nancy Pellegatti drew in a sharp breath. Marty Kolsrud's eyes widened. Arnold Osteen slid back his chair as if to put distance between himself and the messenger with bad news.

"How?" Osteen asked. "He was fine when I last saw him."

"What time was that?" I asked.

"Six-thirty or seven. The crew was wrapping for the day. He was helping the carpenters get the building materials together." Osteen looked at Pellegatti. "The materials that are now a heap of smoldering ruins."

"How did he die?" Marty Kolsrud asked.

"His body was found in the Black Mountain College Museum in Asheville. It looks like a heavy bookcase fell on him."

"Why would an accident in the museum bring the police here?" Osteen asked.

"Because the museum is clearly tied to research for the movie. And they believe Harlan disabled the alarm system and broke in."

"To rob it?" Marty asked. "Roland took us there. Couldn't be more than forty dollars in their donation jar."

"No. He was looking for something else. Possibly something to help us with our case."

"The student who died under suspicious circumstances," Marty said.

"Yes. Paul Weaver. Harlan called us last night to say he wanted to show us something. Something he said wasn't right."

"A clue about the student's death?" Osteen interjected.

"Possibly."

Marty leaned forward. I got the feeling the director was eager to explore where this unfolding story was going. "Did he call you from here?"

"I don't know for sure. It was a voice message. But I was to meet him here this morning."

"Can we hear it?"

"The Asheville police have it," I lied. I didn't want anyone other than the police to hear it, especially if there were voices in the background that could be identified.

I looked at Nakayla, offering her the lead.

"When we heard from the police that there was a fire, we came over to see if we could help," she said. "And we know Harlan was an important part of your team as local historian and advisor."

"Yes," Osteen said. "His death's a terrible loss. He worked closely with Roland."

"Were you aware that Harlan and Roland got into a shouting match yesterday?" Nakayla asked.

"No. But my nephew was upset that I'd agreed to change those elements of the film Marty recommended. Roland was pissed and primed to shout at any and everyone."

"You don't think he'd take any spiteful action?"

"Like what? Kill Harlan? Start this fire?" Osteen shook his head. "Roland may be my flesh and blood, but he's basically gutless. And if he was going to be spiteful to anyone, it would be me. He came whining to my house last night about the script changes, and I told him not only were we shooting Marty's revisions, but I was changing the name of the film."

"What?" Marty said in surprise.

"Yes. I was going to tell you this morning. I know the film's based on Roland's book, but *Love Among the Ridges* sounds too damn sappy. We're going to call it *Battle Scars*. It fits both the physical and psychological dilemmas of the characters."

"Damn, Arnold," Marty exclaimed. "I like it. I like it a lot."

"I can have a good idea once in a while."

"But that further distances Roland from the film," I said. "Unless they read the credits carefully, the audience might not know it's based on his novel."

"Then he can re-title his novel," Osteen snapped.

"You told him that?" I asked.

"Yes. And he didn't like it. But I don't see him committing murder or arson. He'll sulk for a few days at most, and then show up on set probably wearing some outrageous ascot and carrying his book under his arm." Osteen turned to Marty. "Let him rewrite a few lines of innocuous dialogue and he'll be fine. Believe me, I know him."

"All right," I said. "Unless anyone has an idea of why Harlan wanted to see us this morning, we'll let you get back to work."

"Will our call time be the same?" Nakayla asked Nancy Pellegatti.

The producer looked at Marty Kolsrud. "What do you want to shoot?"

"We've got to get that smoldering debris out of here. I was going to film close-ups from yesterday, but I can't have smoke drifting into the shot." He turned to me. "I'll probably work with you and Grayson." He glanced at his watch. "It's four-thirty. Can you be back here at nine?"

"I can if you can," I said.

"Well, I'm going to crash on my office floor, not for the first time. Try to get some sleep." He looked to Osteen. "We'll do the best we can, Arnold."

"I know," Osteen said softly. "And I'd like to have a short meeting with the crew. Reassure them that nothing's going to stop us from making this picture. And also say a few words about Harlan. He was well liked and people are going to be upset. Nancy, when funeral arrangements are complete, maybe we can schedule the shoot day to allow as many as possible to attend his service."

"We'll work on it," Pellegatti said.

"Go ahead," Osteen said. "I have a few more things to discuss with Nakayla and Sam."

When the two filmmakers had left, Osteen said, "I'd like to hire you."

"To do what?" I asked.

"See if there's any possibility that someone's deliberately sabotaging this project." He glanced at the door. "I didn't want to get into it in front of Marty and Nancy because I don't want them distracted. We lose this location when summer camp preparations begin in mid-May."

"Do you have enemies?"

"I'm a real estate developer. Of course I have enemies. I've gotten property rezoned that pissed off neighborhoods. I've undercut competitors. But to commit theft and arson is such an extreme action, that I'm clueless as to who would do such things."

"We already have a case."

"A seventy-year-old death," he said. "How's that a conflict of interest?"

"I don't know. But Harlan Beale's death occurred less than three hours ago, and until we determine there's no connection to whatever he was going to show us, we're not taking other assignments. My advice, hire Armitage Security Services and get rid of these jokers you've got running around in costumes."

Osteen clenched his jaw. He didn't like my refusal to work for him. Then he relaxed. "All right. But if you come across something that connects to my problems, would you at least tell me?"

"That's why we came here before the police."

He nodded. "Fair enough." He shook our hands. "See you in a few hours."

When we were in the car, Nakayla said, "We'll get back to your apartment just in time to get ready to return."

"We're not going to my apartment."

"Where then?"

I started the engine. "I want to get that Black Mountain College book from Harlan's house. And someone's got to break the news to Ol' Blue."

Chapter Ten

Driving down the one-lane road to Harlan Beale's house was like driving through a narrow canyon. Clouds covered the moon and stars, and in the dark, the trees on either side became a black wall, illuminated only by the fleeting throw of my headlights.

I knew Nakayla and I would be on thin ice going into the home of a deceased man whose death was currently the focus of a police investigation. The potential charge of trespassing would be even more flagrant if Beale had locked his house and we broke in. But, if someone had been with Beale in the museum, then that person might have attempted to stop him from connecting some picture or document to Paul Weaver. That involved our case, and I would risk the wrath of Newly in order to be first to examine whatever notes Beale might have left.

As we neared the house, I slowed until the engine noise diminished to little more than an idle. If someone had been with Beale in the museum, there was the possibility he or she might be here, perhaps destroying any trace of involvement.

As the dark shape of the house appeared, I killed the headlights and parked about twenty yards away. "Let me approach first," I told Nakayla. "I'd prefer you remain out of sight."

"And if there's trouble?"

"Get the hell out of here and speed-dial Newly. I'm leaving the keys in the ignition."

"No way." She lifted her handbag from the floor and extracted her pistol. It was a Colt twenty-five caliber semiautomatic, perfectly sized to be an extension of her hand. She racked the slide, loading a round into the chamber.

I knew arguing with her would be futile. And she was an excellent shot. If trouble lay inside, Nakayla and her pistol would be welcome backup.

"All right," I conceded. "Keep to my left. I'll stay right." I didn't want to block Nakayla's line of fire if things really went off the rails.

She trailed me by about fifteen feet. I kept my hands visible and my Kimber tucked in the small of my back.

I stepped up the cinder blocks and onto the porch. The creak of the old boards sounded like thunder. Immediately, a mournful howl arose from the other side of the door. Ol' Blue was on duty. I relaxed. If anyone waited inside, I doubted they'd left Blue free to roam.

"Blue," I cried, hoping he'd remember how Harlan Beale had welcomed me into his home.

The howls became baritone barks of excitement, free of menace.

"It's me, boy. Sam."

"What? Did you give him a business card?" Nakayla's wisecrack told me she, too, was relieved to hear the dog.

I tried the door. It was unlocked. I opened it and then crouched down on the threshold where Blue could see me face-to-face. He sniffed my shirt and neck, then slobbered a drooling lick across my cheek.

"Come up and let him greet you," I told Nakayla. "And lose the pistol. He might take that as aggression."

Blue gave Nakayla no more than a cursory sniff and then walked to the edge of the porch. He stared into the darkness.

"He's looking for Harlan," I said. "Let's get him inside. We might not have much time before Newly or the Buncombe County Sheriff's Department show up."

I gave a whistle, entered the living room and felt along the inside wall for a light switch. Two bulbs in an overhead milk-glass fixture burned with low-watt intensity. Harlan Beale had probably paid his electric bill with loose change.

Blue went over to his rug and flopped down on his side. Even in this hound dog repose, his brown eyes remained wide open and fixed on the front door. He was watching for his master.

"What are we looking for?" Nakayla asked.

"The book you gave him. I'm hoping he saw something that led to his middle-of-the-night run to the museum."

The living room yielded only a few back issues of *Field & Stream*. In the kitchen, we found the Black Mountain College book open on a small dining table covered with a plastic, red-checked cloth. Beside the book lay a blunt pencil and a note-pad bearing a Holiday Inn logo. One of the out-of-town crew members must have given it to him.

Beale had started a list of names: Ellie Johnson, Merce Cunningham, Bucky Fuller, Harold Green, Martha Kepler, Arthur Penn, Josef Albers, and Anni Albers. Some I recognized; some may have been students. Each name had single or multiple page numbers scrawled beside it. It appeared Beale had gotten about two-thirds of the way through. The photograph on the open right-hand page was of Buckminster Fuller, students, and the collapsed dome, the scene re-created for the movie the day before. Beale had drawn a faintly penciled circle around Paul Weaver. His name appeared in bolder letters at the bottom of the list. Beale had written "Weaver and ???" I examined the photograph more closely and noticed a penciled circle around a woman whose back was toward the camera. She wore a horizontally striped blouse and dark shorts. The black-and-white picture showed she was a white woman, probably a student.

We moved on. Beale's kitchen was spotless, although the porcelain sink had stains that suggested mineral-rich well water. Fake marble linoleum covered the countertops and floor. A tri-angle of worn paths showed the countless footsteps from sink to stove to the old Frigidaire in the corner. To the right of its base were two matching cereal bowls, one with water, the other empty but obviously Blue's food dish. A cabinet under the sink held a fifty-pound bag of Jim Dandy dog food.

The only other item of interest in the house was a white, empty iPhone box atop Beale's bedroom dresser. I remembered he said Roland Cassidy had given him the phone when they were collaborating on research for Cassidy's novel. But that had to be a while ago because the book must have taken at least a year or two to bring to publication.

I lifted the box. "This might be the answer to the missing flashlight. He probably had an app on his phone."

"Newly didn't say they found a phone."

"No. But it could have been under the bookcase."

"So could a flashlight," Nakayla said. "But you're probably right. Remember to ask him."

I didn't have to wait long. My cell buzzed a few seconds later. I read the screen. "It's Newly."

"Better answer and fess up."

"What's happening?" I asked without bothering to say hello.

"When Harlan Beale called you last night, where was he?" Newly asked.

"I gathered he was still at the movie location. You heard him yell to someone. Why?"

"We're finished at the museum and there's neither a flashlight nor phone with the body. Either would have shown how he could have navigated in the dark."

I mouthed "No phone" to Nakayla. She pointed to the empty box on the dresser.

"Newly, we're at his house," I said.

"What? Why?" The detective clearly wasn't happy.

"I came to check on the dog and see if Beale left the book here we'd asked him to examine. Don't worry, we've been careful. The house was unlocked and we haven't disturbed anything."

"Did you find the book?"

"Yes. And he wrote down some names on a pad next to it. He stopped on a photograph that depicted a scene the crew shot yesterday. Two of the people in the photograph are circled in pencil. One is Paul Weaver, the other is a woman who's not facing the camera."

"Leave everything as it is," Newly ordered.

"Okay. I know Beale had a cell phone. The empty box is still in his bedroom."

"Then he either didn't take it from his house, or he left it somewhere at the location. I'll request the call record from the wireless company to see if he phoned anyone after you."

"Do you want us to look here?"

"No. Take the dog and get out of there. I'll want my forensics team going through it and I don't want to explain why your fingerprints are there."

"I've been in the house before, so what are a few more?"

"Sam, don't make me play the hard ass. If you want to stand in the yard, fine."

"What should I do with Blue?"

"Who?"

"The dog. Why's he have to leave?"

"Because with my luck he'll either chew up or pee on a clue. I'll give you the book and the notes as soon as we can release them. I know they're important to your case and your client. But for now I can't rule out that Harlan Beale's death was a homicide. You know the drill as well as I do."

I did, and I didn't argue. "Okay. We're leaving." I ended the call.

"Sounds like Newly's giving you a new friend."

"You and me. Joint custody is only fair."

She shook her head. "Not if he howls."

"At least you've got a house. I'm on the fourth floor."

"With more dogs in your building than people."

Nakayla had a point. I lived in the Kenilworth Inn Apartments, a huge old resort hotel that had also been a military rehab hospital and a mental institution before the conversion to rental units. And life in Asheville revolved around dogs. Blue would just be one more.

"All right. We'll take him to my apartment. Have you seen a leash?"

Nakayla laughed. "I doubt if Blue's ever been on a leash in his life. Surely Harlan has some rope somewhere."

I found a coil of quarter-inch rope in the tractor shed and knotted it through Blue's collar. The hound just lay on his bed without protest. "Come on, Blue. Let's go for a ride. You want to flip Nakayla for shotgun?"

She came from the kitchen carrying the two bowls. "I'm not sitting in the back for a dog. Put his rug on the seat so something smells of home."

Blue hopped in the CR-V with surprising ease. Nakayla took the bowls with her to the front passenger seat.

"I should bring that bag of food," I told her.

"Put it in the rear or Blue might eat half of it between here and Asheville."

I returned to the kitchen and pulled the nearly full bag out of the cabinet. Before lifting it on my shoulder, I looked around the kitchen to make sure all was as we'd found it. The bowls and food were the only missing items. I glanced at the table, wishing I could take the book and notes. Then the obvious dawned on me. Newly ordered me not to take them, but he didn't tell me not to photograph them. I pulled my phone and took several shots of the notepad and open page. If the library had a second copy, then we wouldn't have to wait for Newly to release this book to pursue potential leads.

Blue settled down on his rug and rode without so much as a whimper. Dawn was breaking when I parked behind the apartment building, opting to bring Blue through a back entrance rather than the lobby. He peed on every bush and shrub between the car and door, claiming the territory of his new surroundings.

My apartment is one bedroom with a full kitchen, single bathroom, and a living area that's furnished as a combo den and dining area.

Nakayla dropped Blue's rug by my recliner. "I figure you men will want to be together. You can bond while I take a shower."

Two hours later, Nakayla and I were changed and ready to return to Lake Eden. Blue sat staring at the door.

"Should we leave him here?" Nakayla asked.

Blue looked back at us, big brown eyes scanning our faces.

"I don't know. What if he starts howling?"

The dog stood and stepped closer to the door.

"Well, he obviously senses we're leaving," Nakayla said. "What's the high temperature today?"

I pressed the weather app on my phone. "Sixty-eight. Not too bad if we crack the windows."

So the three of us pulled into the movie lot a few minutes before nine. Smoke still hung in the air and the roar of a diesel engine told me Marty Kolsrud wasn't directing any scene with sound.

We parked in the shade of a white pine, rolled down the windows enough to keep Blue from sticking his head out, and walked toward the production office.

"No guard this morning," Nakayla remarked.

"What good are they? The boy scouts would have done a better job."

We rounded the corner of the main building and discovered the source of the engine's noise. A Caterpillar front-loader was clearing the burned debris, lifting scoops of the wet mess into the bed of an Osteen Developments dump truck.

Arnold Osteen stood near the truck's cab talking to a silver-haired man in a blue suit. Nathan Armitage, a good friend and owner of Armitage Security Services. He spotted us from the corner of his eye and waved us over.

Osteen turned to greet us. "Well, I'm doing what I should have done two weeks ago, hired professionals. Nathan says he can have his first two-man team in place this afternoon—one to watch the gear, the other to check people in and out."

"And overnight, two guards can patrol a wider perimeter," Nathan said. He glanced at the pile of charred rubble. "And none of my guys are smokers."

"Is that the prevalent theory?" I asked. "Someone tossed a match or cigarette?"

Osteen shrugged. "What else could it be? Paint and thinner cans were beside the lumber. The carpentry crew did some touch-up work in one of the cottages yesterday. They left brushes and cleaning rags with the paint. Flammable enough, the firemen said." Osteen shook his head. "Only one likely to make any money out of this movie is the lumber company." He turned to Nathan Armitage. "Thanks for responding so quickly. Let's go to my office and I'll sign the contract."

As the two men started to walk away, I grabbed Nathan's arm. "Can we talk a few minutes before you go?"

"Sure. Where?"

"I'm parked under a white pine on the other side of the building. The CR-V with the coonhound in it."

Nathan looked at Nakayla. "He serious?"

"Yes. I guess you could call us foster parents."

"Okay," Nathan said. "I'll meet you in about ten minutes."

When he and Osteen were out of earshot, Nakayla said, "You're going to ask Nathan about the museum's security system, aren't you?"

"Yes. I'd like to get his opinion on how hard it would be to disarm and why a backup battery wouldn't have kicked in."

We returned to the CR-V. Blue was sitting up on the backseat, his nose against the window. With each breath he fogged the glass. When he spotted us, he started barking.

"He might have to go," Nakayla said. "I'll walk him up in the woods since we don't have any poop bags."

"I'll go with you. Nathan will wait if we're a few minutes late."

I'd kept the rope attached to Blue's collar so that I could grab it as he hopped out. He sniffed the air a moment to get his bearings. Nakayla started walking up the hill toward the trees and Blue tugged on the makeshift leash to follow. I gave him some slack and let him proceed at his own pace. His quivering nostrils went to the ground as if it were easier to follow Nakayla by scent than sight.

Suddenly, he stopped, looked back at me and barked as if I would understand. Then he looped around the spot, keeping his nose to the grass.

"What's he doing?" Nakayla asked.

"Tracking something. Maybe a deer. More likely a raccoon, if that's what he's trained to hunt."

Blue took one more circle and then pulled hard to the right, determined to pursue whatever had crossed his path. I tried to restrain him, but he started choking from the pressure of his collar.

"Let's go with him a little while," I told Nakayla. "I'll rein him in if he goes too far."

Blue lunged forward and I jogged to keep up. Instead of veering up into the woods as I'd expected, he headed toward the enclave of vehicles and tents in the grassy field across the road. We wound between two eighteen-wheelers and paralleled the actors' trailers. On the most level terrain stood a large white tent with heavy power cords snaking under its sides. The front was open and inside were the tools of a carpentry shop. Two men worked building a wall that must have been part of a shooting set. They were attaching a wooden chair rail over a line of demarcation between an upper section painted pale yellow and the lower section of vertical pine paneling. Blue ignored them and made straight for a folding chair by the rear wall. A used paint can and brush were on the ground in front of it. Blue sniffed all three and then gave three sharp barks.

The men stopped working and walked over.

"That there Harlan's dog?" asked a tall man wearing sawdust covered jeans.

"Yeah," I said. "His name's Blue."

The other older and shorter carpenter shook his head slowly. "Poor thing. Harlan would talk about his coonhound. You his kin?"

"No. Harlan was helping us out with some history research. Like he did for Cassidy."

"So how come y'all got his dog?" the taller man asked.

"The police have to go through his house."

Nakayla stepped closer. "We thought it would be too upsetting for Blue."

"Yep," the taller man agreed. "I reckon Blue would be right anxious." He approached Blue slowly, let him smell his extended hand, and then stroked his side. "Harlan used to sit in this chair. He'd come round and chew the fat just about every day."

"Sometimes he'd help us even though he weren't on the clock," the shorter man said. "He liked to paint."

"We didn't let him lift nothin' heavy like this." The taller man pointed to the wall flat. "He was an old-timer, but he knew some tricks and he didn't hesitate to give advice."

Both men chuckled and then turned somber.

"Terrible thing," the shorter man said. "Any idea why he was up at that museum in the middle of the night?"

"No," I said. "But he must have wanted something pretty badly. Did you see him yesterday?"

"Yep," the shorter man said. "We knocked off about six. He was hangin' around while the lumber truck was unloadin'." He looked at the paint can and brush.

Dry light blue paint streaked the can's side. The broad brush had a mix of colors on the base and handle, but the bristles were clean enough.

"He must have given up and gone home," the man said. "Set his things out for today."

"But today never came," his buddy said. "Goes to show ya never know."

"Do you know where Harlan parked his truck?" I asked.

"Yep," the taller man said. "Up by the pine trees. Most folks don't like to park where the sap could drip, but Harlan said it was better than paying for a new paint job."

We took Blue to the CR-V and he hopped in the backseat without hesitation. Nathan Armitage arrived a few minutes later.

"You and Osteen get things straightened out?" I asked.

"Yes. My guys start at four this afternoon."

"Have you dealt with him before?"

"Not directly. We've had contracts with some of his tenants in his retail developments and a few ongoing contracts with a lease management subsidiary, but never with Osteen himself."

"You ever hear talk about anyone who carries a grudge against him?"

"No. As far as I know, he greases the right palms, serves on the right boards and gives to the right charities."

"Your by-the-numbers corporate executive," Nakayla added.

"He wanted my assurance my staff is all local," Armitage said. "He wants as much of the movie budget to stay in the area as possible."

"Then why didn't he hire you in the first place?"

Armitage laughed. "Because he also wants as much of the budget to stay in his own pocket as possible."

I changed the subject. "You've heard about the death at the Black Mountain College Museum, haven't you?"

"Yeah. Osteen told me."

"Did you install their security system?"

"I don't believe so. Why?"

"Because Harlan Beale or someone cut the power and disarmed it. I thought those systems had battery backup."

"Not all of them," Armitage said. "Or if power's been lost previously, say a thunderstorm outage or a transformer malfunction that took a while to fix, then the battery could have drained and not been rechargeable. It's rare but it can happen."

"I doubt if the museum had the money for an elaborate system," Nakayla said.

"Well, give me the make and model and I'll check it out," Armitage offered.

"Thanks," I said. "Newly shouldn't have a problem sharing that information."

Armitage left. I looked at my watch. Nine-thirty. "What do you say we bail out of here? I'll tell Marty I'll work with Grayson another day. If you want to stay for a possible dance rehearsal, I'll come back for you."

Nakayla opened the passenger door. "Are you kidding? I want to check on those names Beale listed. But first I'd like breakfast and a few hours sleep."

"Damn. I forgot to feed Blue. What's the recipe for Jim Dandy?"

"Pour in the bowl, Iron Chef."

Blue retraced his scent to the rear entrance of my building.

A few other dogs were walking with their owners, and the little ones barked the loudest. Blue ignored them.

Once in the apartment, the coonhound flopped down on his rug and watched us. I pulled eggs and bacon from the fridge and then turned low heat on a frying pan. Nakayla bent over the bag of Jim Dandy and read the directions.

"My apologies," she said. "You can also moisten with water."

"I was thinking more like bacon drippings. I bet that will get Blue out of bed."

"It looks from his weight, he should get one cup twice a day." She went to a cabinet and pulled down a set of plastic measuring cups. She selected the proper one and took it to the bag of dog food leaning against the side of the refrigerator. I heard the crunch as she dug it into the dry kernels.

"Sam," she shouted. "Come here."

She opened the bag wider. I looked over her shoulder.

Half exposed amid the pebble-sized pieces of food lay a black iPhone.

Chapter Eleven

"Did you touch the phone?" Newly stared into the bag of dog food while Tuck Efird donned a pair of latex gloves. The four of us stood in my kitchen.

"No," Nakayla said. "When I scooped up the food, I uncovered it. Sam called you immediately. My fingers didn't even graze it."

Newly turned to me. "I told you to take the dog and that was all."

"Come on. The dog had to eat."

We looked at Blue sleeping on his rug.

"Yeah," Newly said sarcastically. "I can see how he burns the calories."

"And you're going to stand there and tell me that you and Tuck would have searched through a bag of dog food?"

Efird laughed. "Damn straight. Newly sticks his nose in any bag that has the word food written on its side."

Newly didn't dignify the comment with a reply. He stepped back and gestured for his partner to dig out the cell phone. Efird extracted the iPhone with two hands, his fingers minimally touching the top and bottom.

"Is it on?" I asked.

"The screen's dark," Efird said. "Might be hibernating. We'll lift prints before we go trying to break his passcode."

"He might not have had one," Nakayla said. "Harlan Beale didn't strike me as a high-tech kind of guy."

Efird shook his head. "Well, if this is one of those phones that only gives you a set number of tries before destroying the data, I don't want to be the guy who squandered one of the attempts."

"Tell the techs to repeat the number of the number of password numbers," I suggested.

"You want to say that in English?" Newly said.

"It's simple. If it's a four-numeral code, then enter four, four times. If it's six, repeat the number six. See? That would be easy for Beale to remember."

"Yeah, I see," Newly said. "Sounds like I just learned the pin for your ATM card."

Nakayla laughed. Newly had spoken correctly.

Efird dropped the phone into an evidence bag. "We'll pass your sophisticated mnemonic theory along to the geeks. They'll probably want to meet you."

He and Newly headed for the door.

"Wait," I called. "Anything turn up in the museum?"

The men looked at each other. Newly shrugged. "No phone, no flashlight, no lead as to what he was seeking. We tagged the books by where they fell, figuring those farthest from the bookcase would have been hurled from the top. Those were the shelves that Beale had to climb to reach."

"By himself in the dark," I said.

"There's that," Newly said. "And, for your ears only, the M.E. thinks there was too little blood at the scene, especially for a head wound."

"He was killed elsewhere?" I asked.

"Not necessarily. The trauma of the fall could have killed him instantly. Heart stops, blood only seeps. But the body temperature was low for the time of death."

"By how much?"

"Maybe a couple hours. It was cool last night, both outside and in the museum."

"Well, we know he went home," Nakayla said. "He had the Black Mountain College book at the movie location and then we found it in his kitchen."

"And he called me and then hid the phone in the bag." I had another thought. "Maybe that's why he left the iPhone box on his dresser. A clue that he had a phone."

"Or maybe he was looking for operating instructions," Nakayla said. "Apple touts its phones don't require a manual, but Beale wouldn't be so technologically intuitive. He wanted to perform some function but didn't know how."

"So, tell me how this fits with your case?" Newly asked.

"I have no idea," I admitted. "But we have a few leads to follow and I'll share if it's a two-way street."

"Okay," Newly agreed. "A two-way street. Just don't stand on the center line when you don't know what's coming. You could end up as roadkill."

As soon as Newly and Efird left, Nakayla emptied the cup of food into Blue's bowl. The sound of the dry nuggets hitting the dish roused Blue from his rug. He sauntered over, took a few bites, and then walked to the apartment door.

"We forgot to ask Newly about Beale's next of kin," Nakayla said.

"I'll check with him this afternoon. Give him time to collect more information." I walked to the stove. "You still up for breakfast?"

"It's the only reason I'm still awake."

We had double portions of scrambled eggs with three strips of bacon each. Then we went to the bedroom and took off our outer clothes. I laid my prosthesis, shoe attached, at the base of my dresser.

Blue saw it from the hall and barked. He ran to the bedroom, nails clicking on the hardwood floor. He skidded to a halt beside the artificial leg, clearly bewildered by the detached limb. I sat on the foot of the bed, my left stump covered by the fitted sock that aided against irritation. Blue came over to me, sniffed the point of amputation below the knee, and whined. Then he started licking the severed end.

"Aw," Nakayla said. "He's trying to heal what he thinks is a wound."

I patted Blue's head and gently pushed him away. "It's all right, boy. There's nothing wrong." Other than I'm sitting in my underwear trying to reason with a hound dog.

I slid back on the bed and lay down. Nakayla rested her head against my shoulder. We heard the click-click as Blue left. Then he returned, dragging something behind him.

We both sat up. Blue had his rug in his mouth and pulled it next to my prosthesis. He circled three times, then lay down with his head on the shoe.

Nakayla squeezed my hand. Her eyes were moist. "You've got a new friend and he's got your back."

We awoke four hours later. Blue sat with his head cocked watching me re-attach my prosthesis. When I stood, he barked his approval and ran to the apartment door, ready to go, even though I wore only my underwear.

"He might need a walk," Nakayla said, not yet rising from the bed.

"Do you want to go out?" I asked.

She yawned. "I think I'll do a search of the names Harlan Beale wrote down. Forward me the pictures you took."

I picked up my phone from the nightstand and thumbed to the photographs of the book and notepad on Beale's kitchen table. I heard Nakayla's phone ping as they were delivered.

I slipped on a pair of jeans. "I might swing by the museum and check it out in the daylight. I want to get Nathan the name of the security system they used."

"You taking the dog?"

"Yeah. He seems fine in the car."

I found a parking spot in a lot off Walnut near the museum. Despite what I'd told Nakayla, Blue didn't like the unfamiliar city surroundings and started howling as soon as I opened my door. Asheville is one of the dog-friendliest cities in the country so I took him with me rather than leave him where some overzealous animal lover might be tempted to free him.

The rope leash gave Blue a rustic distinction—a mountain dog at home on a busy sidewalk. Men nodded appreciatively.

Women fawned with comments like "he's beautiful," or "how well trained."

Blue stayed close to my left side, and I became aware that he constantly angled his body between me and approaching pedestrians. He was protecting what he must have thought was a vulnerability, my missing leg.

A man who couldn't have been out of college more than a few years himself stood in the doorway of the Black Mountain College Museum. Blue and I walked up just as he told a group of four tourists that the museum was closed for the afternoon, but hoped to reopen at ten the next morning. The people moved on and the man started to retreat inside.

"Excuse me," I said. "Are the police still here?"

"No, they left around half an hour ago."

"So, they've released the scene?"

The young man swallowed hard and nodded, as if the connotation of the word "scene" made it difficult to answer.

I reached for my wallet and showed him my P.I. license. "Have they ordered you not to reopen until tomorrow?"

"No. But we have no power and the reference room is a disaster. They boxed all the books and articles and took them. We've been promised they'll be returned as soon as the police conclude their investigation."

Good, I thought. They probably numbered each item and matched it to the position it occupied on the floor. Newly was looking to establish what materials had been on the higher shelves.

"If there is no police restriction, then might I come inside? I'm working a case connected to the victim."

The man looked at Blue sitting next to me.

"I'd prefer not to tie the dog outside," I said.

"No, of course not. He's welcome." The man's tone suggested that Blue was more welcome than I was.

He held the door open as we stepped past him.

"I'm Josh Crater." He offered his hand. "How can I help you?"

Before I could respond, Blue whined and yanked the rope

out of my hand. He loped from the front room of exhibits into the next where Beale's body had been discovered.

"Blue!" I cried.

His whines reduced to whimpers. Crater and I found him prone on the floor in the spot where Beale had lain. A lump formed in my throat.

"What's the matter with him?" Crater asked.

"He was the man's dog." I didn't try to force Blue to move. He was clearly distraught, behaving entirely differently from when he picked up Beale's scent at the movie location. Somehow, he knew his master was dead.

I looked around the room. The bookcase had been righted, but its shelves were bare. Newly had taken everything for review in an effort to determine what Beale had considered so important.

"Can you tell me what would have been on the top two shelves?"

"Lighter books and pamphlets. We didn't want the case to be top heavy."

"Were they materials contemporary with the college or things written later?"

Crater looked at the upper empty shelves as if trying to visualize what had been there. "Some college catalogues, spiral notebooks with minutes of staff meetings, and miscellaneous enrollment records. Nothing really valuable like the artwork we have in the exhibition room."

"What do you know about the alarm system?"

Crater shrugged. "Just the code to turn it on or off."

"How many others use it?"

"We have a small staff and volunteers. Around ten people total. It's known by anyone who opens or closes the museum. But the police said no one turned off the alarm. Power was cut to the building."

"Can I see the alarm and the power box?"

Crater led me through the back hall where a keypad was mounted just inside the door. The logo read "CopBeat" and I didn't recognize the manufacturer.

"Where's the brain and power supply for this device?"

He opened a closet door and swept aside a few reams of printer paper from a central shelf. On the inner wall hung a gray metal box with a black power cord and thinner wires that must have connected various motion detectors or window and door alarms.

"And the battery?"

"I don't know," Crater said. "I guess it's built in."

I used the flashlight app on my phone to read the model number and then took a photo to send to Nathan Armitage.

"Where's the power box for the building?"

"Right out back. The on-off handle was thrown, but whoever did that also cut the wires going from there into the building. Plus they severed the phone line."

The main panel was mounted beside the meter. Whoever had disrupted power had been thorough, not simply trusting the main switch. I thought about Harlan Beale's handyman experience, how he'd built his own house, which probably meant he did his own electrical wiring.

"Do you need to see anything else?" Crater asked.

Again, Blue preempted my response with a series of deep, throaty barks. I hurried inside to see what had set him off.

Roland Cassidy stood in the doorway from the exhibition room, his hands away from his sides like Blue was a police officer demanding him to freeze.

"It's just me, Blue." Cassidy stepped back when he saw me.

"We're closed," Crater said curtly. "Didn't you see the sign?"

"Your door was unlocked." Cassidy pointed at me. "What's he doing here?"

"I'm helping the police." I figured my two-way-street arrangement with Newly kept the statement from being a total lie.

Cassidy turned to Crater. "I'm the author of *Love Among the Ridges*."

Crater folded his arms across his chest. "So?"

Cassidy reddened. "So, my book put Black Mountain College in the homes of thousands of readers. Surely you've seen an increase in your visitors."

"Yes. But why are you here?"

Cassidy looked around the room. "I was a friend of Harlan. We spent a lot of time talking together." He paused and moistened his lips. The phony author persona began to disintegrate. "I can't believe he's gone. I'd have no book without him." He shifted his gaze to Blue lying on the floor. "Is this where it happened?"

"Yes," I said.

"I heard a bookcase fell on him."

"Who told you that?"

"My Uncle Arnold. The police were out to the movie set after you left. When they told him, he suggested they speak with me."

"Do you have any idea what Harlan could have come here for?"

Cassidy shrugged. "I assume it was something for you. He was just sharing mountain stories with me. I'd pretty much mined everything to do with the college." He looked at the bare shelves. "Did the police take the books?"

"Yes," Crater said. "If you're interested, I can let you know when the materials are returned."

Cassidy nodded. "Okay. Sam, are you about finished?"

"I guess."

"Then let me buy you a drink. I feel badly about the way I acted yesterday. I know Marty's changes weren't your idea. And I deeply regret that my last conversation with Harlan was…" he paused, struggling for the word "… was confrontational. What about LAB? We can sit outside so Blue can be with us."

LAB was short for Lexington Avenue Brewery, one of my favorite spots. I wasn't thrilled to spend time with the writer, but I'd learned a long time ago that you never know where you're going to find vital information, so you hang out with all sorts of characters.

"All right. Why don't you get a table? I've got a few quick phone calls to make."

"Want me to take Blue?"

I handed him the rope. Cassidy gave it a gentle tug but Blue refused to get up. Cassidy whistled and then called the dog's name in a soft, friendly voice. Blue got up, shook himself, and then walked over to stand by me.

Cassidy dropped the rope. "Looks like he prefers your company. I'll go ahead. What do you want to drink?"

"A porter."

Cassidy left and I picked up the makeshift leash. "I don't want to take any more of your time," I told Crater. "I'll use the back door so I can make my calls without bothering anyone."

I thought perhaps Blue wouldn't want to leave the spot where Beale's body had lain, but he responded to an easy pull and walked by my side. I stopped at the damaged power box next to the meter and took a photo with my cell phone. Then I sent both that picture and the one of the security alarm to Nathan Armitage with a note asking if the damage would have been sufficient to put the alert system out of commission.

Blue and I looped around the back of the building toward Lexington and a cold beer. A Duke Energy truck passed us going the opposite direction. The museum would soon be powered up.

I found Cassidy at a table in the open-air front of the brewery. He sat at a table for two with his back to the sidewalk. The afternoon was chilly and only a smattering of patrons ate outside. I suspected the vain author would normally opt for a table of greater visibility in hopes he would be recognized, but whatever he wanted with me must not have involved publicity.

Like many Asheville restaurants, bowls of water were scattered on the floor for their customers' canine companions. I gave Blue enough rope to reach one beside Cassidy's chair while I took a seat opposite him. The pint of porter was already served, and Cassidy had ordered a pale ale.

"So, you and Harlan got to be pretty close?" I took a sip from the glass as if the question was nothing more than a casual conversation-starter.

"It took me eighteen months to write the book. I went to his house about ten times during that period."

"And there's the cell phone you bought him."

Cassidy nodded. "Yeah. Questions would come up on the spur of the moment. You see, everything doesn't have to be historically accurate, but it does have to be historically plausible.

I'd get an idea and I'd want to bounce it off Harlan while it was fresh in my mind." He glanced down at his ale and twisted the glass in a circle. "That's why I wanted to talk to you."

"About an idea?"

"Yeah. I'm not so blind that I can't see there's something strange going on with Harlan's death. An old man climbing a bookcase in the middle of the night?"

"You want to write a mystery?"

Cassidy's mouth turned down in disdain. "Who killed Colonel Mustard with a candlestick in the library? Please. I write literature."

I didn't say anything. As a detective, mysteries were my business.

"I'm interested in what stirs the human soul," Cassidy said. "What drove Harlan to do whatever he did? Or what motivated someone else to do him in? I'm about the psychology of the process. And I know you're about the solution."

I wanted to say what the hell's the good of the process if you don't find out who killed Colonel Mustard, but I knew Cassidy was up on his elitist literary high horse and wasn't worth the breath of an argument.

"What's that got to do with me?"

"I want to help you. And, as it's appropriate, you can share details with me. I'd like to follow the investigation step by step. This could be for me what *In Cold Blood* was for Truman Capote."

"You have to understand I'm a private investigator. I represent a client's interest and that might be for the client to remain anonymous."

"I know." He raised his ale in a toast. "Here's to your integrity. All I'm asking is a little reciprocity for whatever I can do for you."

I realized I had nothing to lose and the blowhard had spent a lot of time with Beale. "Then let me ask you a few questions. As an old-timer, did Harlan have any trouble operating the cell phone?"

Cassidy laughed. "He wasn't Steve Jobs, if that's what you're asking. He could make a call and retrieve his messages. That's all I ever showed him. He never asked what else it could do."

"How about taking photographs?"

"Well, yes. I did show him the camera icon. It was one of the apps that came with the phone. Biggest problem was the reception at his house. He could only get one bar, and sometimes he'd have to walk up his driveway to get a more stable signal."

That was interesting. The message he'd left on my voicemail the previous evening had been crisp and clear. That reinforced the theory he'd called me from Lake Eden.

"Was there any idea you suggested that Beale said was implausible?"

Cassidy thought a moment. "Not directly."

"What do you mean?"

"He has a cousin named Nadine. Nadine Oates. She's over ninety and lives out Fairview way."

I recognized the area to be where Paul Weaver and his sister Violet had grown up.

"I mentioned that I'd like to talk to her," Cassidy said. "See what she remembers. He told me not to bother. She was nutty as a hickory tree and she'd send me off on a wild goose chase."

"Did Nadine attend the college?"

"No. She'd go up when they had a dance or were putting on a show. Harlan said she stopped going before he started working. But he'd heard her talk about the college, which was why he went looking for a job in the summer of 1948."

"What kind of wild goose chase?"

Cassidy smiled and leaned across the table. "Communists," he whispered. "Behind every tree and rock."

Chapter Twelve

Blue and I left Roland Cassidy a little after four. Next on my agenda was to see Newly in person rather than talk over the phone because it would be harder for him to evade my questions. But, Blue wasn't going to pass for a K-9 police dog so I decided to swing by the office, leave Blue with Nakayla, and then see if Newly or Tuck Efird had anything to share. That plan fell apart a few seconds after I loaded Blue in the car. My cell rang and I recognized Newly's number.

"Where are you?" he asked.

"I'm leaving the museum. I went back and spoke with one of the staff."

"Josh Crater?"

"Yeah. He didn't seem to know anything. But you might be interested in who showed up while I was there."

"Enlighten me."

"Roland Cassidy. The writer who used Harlan Beale as a research source for his book."

Newly grunted dismissively. "Tuck and I spoke with him this morning. He seemed clueless."

"He is. But he wants to follow the investigation. He envisions a literary masterpiece-in-the-making."

"So, first you're in a movie and now a literary masterpiece. Remind me to bow next time I see you."

"Just honoring our two-way street, my friend. And guys like

Cassidy sometimes know things they don't realize they know. Now, what can you share?"

I heard the squeak of Newly's chair as he shifted his weight.

"Tuck and I just came back from visiting Beale's next of kin. Nadine Oates."

"Did she say the Communists killed him?"

The phone went silent a moment. Then Newly said, "How the hell did you know that? Yes, she said the Communists had been stalking her cousin for years."

"Cassidy said that Beale told him his cousin was nutty as a hickory tree and to avoid her. Sounds like he wasn't exaggerating."

"I don't know if she's certifiable, but I think she's a few apples short of a full bushel."

"Anything more from the M.E.?"

"No. And with tomorrow being Saturday, I might not get a preliminary till Monday."

"How about the phone?"

"Sent a request to the carrier for all activity. But we did catch a break on the code. Four fours. I guess it proves even a dumb ass can stumble across a good idea."

I laughed. "Then you should take hope your day will come. So what did you find?"

"Most calls in the log came to and from Roland Cassidy's number. Last one was to your cell. There were some photos he took at the movie location. Some were of the actors. Some of the construction work and that dome thing they were trying to re-create. Nothing looks very promising."

"I'd like to see them."

"I'm headed out, but if you come by Monday morning I'll show you what we pulled off. You going to see the Oates woman?"

"I guess I should. I've got Beale's dog that needs go to someone."

"I don't think Nadine Oates is an option," Newly said. "She's already got a pet."

"Blue's laid-back. Another dog or even a cat might not be a problem."

"Not in this case." Newly gave a deep, throaty laugh. "Her pet's a raccoon. Even you wouldn't be dumb enough to put a raccoon and a coonhound in the same room. Or would you?" He laughed again and hung up.

Nakayla was at her computer when Blue and I arrived at the office. The hound, unperturbed by the new surroundings, rested his head on Nakayla's thigh as a canine hello.

She scratched behind his ears. "How did you two do?"

I gave her the summary of my conversation at the museum and then the surprise encounter with Roland Cassidy and his request to shadow our investigation.

"I don't see how that will work," Nakayla said. "No telling what he'll do with the information."

"I agree. But he did spend a lot of time with Beale, and Newly confirmed the description of Nadine Oates as a nut job. I don't think it will hurt to keep a line of communication open. As for Nadine, I think we should see her tomorrow."

Nakayla got up, walked to the printer and retrieved several pages from the tray. "You might want to delay her for a more promising lead."

She handed me the papers. The top sheet was a *Wikipedia* entry for Eleanor Patricia Johnson that described her as a stellar dancer of the nineteen-fifties and nineteen-sixties, most prominently with Merce Cunningham's dance company. She then went on to teach and her list of pupils was a veritable Who's Who of Performers, at least, according to the article. My knowledge of dance was only slightly ahead of my knowledge of nuclear physics. Eleanor Johnson had worked into her seventies before retiring to her native Brooklyn. The brief bio reported two marriages and one daughter. There was no date of death, and from her birth date, I learned she was ninety.

The second printout was an article published in an online magazine called *The Art in Heart.* Its mission seemed to be to highlight artists who were engaged in humanitarian efforts or giving of themselves to support the arts. The headline read *Keeping Dance in Motion.* Beneath were two photographs side by side, one featuring an elderly African-American woman seated in a rocker, and the other, the frozen leap of a female dancer on a stage with a colorful backdrop of geometric shapes. Centered underneath both pictures was the name Eleanor Patricia Johnson. The article told how Eleanor opened her four-story brownstone to dancers and dance students who needed inexpensive housing while actively pursuing their art. "Dance is a journey," she was quoted as saying. "You are never done, and even if physically you can no longer move like you once could, the dancer's mind spins forward, capturing the motion and energy around you. It's the young people around me who keep me young."

The publication date was two months earlier.

"She sounds pretty sharp," I said. "We need to talk with her."

"There's an early flight connecting through Charlotte that arrives at LaGuardia at eleven-fifty tomorrow morning. I've got her Brooklyn address."

"Phone number?"

She shook her head. "There's not one listed. I sent an e-mail to *The Art in Heart*, but haven't had a response."

"They should be leery of giving us personal information. I think we should just go. She's ninety. Where else will she be?"

"Do you want to clear the ticket expense with Violet Baker?" Nakayla asked.

"Do we have the photographs to take with us?"

Nakayla picked up a copy of the book now in police possession. "Pack Library had two. This one was in the reference section but I begged a librarian friend to let me take it out for the weekend."

"Then call Violet and bring her up-to-date. If she's good, then book the flight. See if you can get an evening return."

Nakayla looked down. Blue sat between us, looking back and forth at our faces.

"What about our friend here?" she asked.

I picked up the leash. "Come on, Blue. Let's take a walk."

Outside our office, Blue turned left back toward the elevator, but I pulled him down the hallway to the next suite. "Hewitt

Donaldson, Attorney at Law" was engraved on the frosted glass. I opened the door and let the dog enter first.

A face peered around the back of a computer monitor. I say, face, but it was more a white mask of heavy makeup with dark mascara eyes and spirals of jet black hair framing cheeks and temples.

Blue froze, unsure if he was confronting a person or a beast.

"Well, look what the dog dragged in." The woman rose from her desk. Shirley the Strange. Today, she wore a black shirt with pearl buttons, black jeans, and black boots. Death comes calling on a motorcycle.

This specter was Hewitt Donaldson's office manager and probably the smartest person in the firm, if not our entire building.

"Did you finally qualify for a service animal?" Shirley asked. "Does he make sure you come in out of the rain?"

I decided to derail the "make fun of Sam" monologue with a surefire counterattack. "Shirley, this is Blue. His master died this morning and he's having a tough time."

Shirley's shoulders slumped. She knelt down. "Poor baby." She patted her knees. "Come to Momma Shirley."

Blue trotted over and lay down in front of her, chin resting on his front paws. Shirley ran her hand along his side. "How old is he?"

"I don't know. But I suspect he's lived with his master since he was a pup. We just came from where the man died and Blue could sense it."

"The dog wasn't with him?"

"No. And this isn't for broadcast, but I think the man was murdered. I know it's hard to believe but Blue's bonded with me."

Shirley sat on the floor and lifted Blue's head in her lap. "The poor thing must be in shock. Is he hungry? Hewitt's probably got a bag of pork rinds stuffed in a desk drawer."

"We've got food. Is His Highness here?"

Shirley laughed. "No. He came in late so he said he'd make up for it by leaving early."

"Do you know if he was heading home?"

"You think he'd tell me? I'll be lucky to get notice of his funeral. Is it business? Maybe I can help."

I looked at the dog. "It's Blue. Nakayla and I need to leave town tomorrow on a case and I was hoping Hewitt could take him for the day."

She looked aghast. "Hewitt with a dog? The man can barely take care of himself."

Hewitt Donaldson was the top defense attorney in Asheville, and although he mastered juries and prosecutors alike, his free-spirited nature had been forged in the nineteen-sixties. Hewitt liked nothing better than taking on the establishment, but taking on personal responsibility, like caring for a dog, or, God forbid, a child, could be a life skill beyond his capabilities.

Shirley was reacting exactly as I'd hoped.

"It's just for tomorrow. We have to fly to New York for the day. We'll be back late, but we can pick up Blue so he doesn't stay overnight."

She looked up. "What about me? I could take care of him."

"That's generous of you, but I couldn't ask you to give up your Saturday. We'll probably have to leave early in the morning."

She laid Blue's head aside and stood. "Then you definitely don't want Hewitt. He doesn't know the world exists before ten on Saturdays. I can be at your apartment as early as you like. Leave me the keys and I'll be there with Blue when you return tomorrow night."

"You're sure it's no trouble?"

"No trouble at all. I have an early evening meeting of the Asheville Apparitions, but they won't object." Her black-lined eyes widened.

Blue sat up, staring at her face. For a moment I was afraid he'd mistaken her for a raccoon.

"What?" I asked.

"We're having a séance."

The Asheville Apparitions was a group of paranormal activists who sought spirits and other manifestations of the supernatural.

Shirley was the club president, or Chief Ghostbuster, or whatever title such responsibilities bestowed.

"I'm sure Blue will be fine."

Her eyes sparkled. "How cool would that be? The spirit of Blue's dear departed master could be lingering near him. Give me the man's name."

"Shirley! You are not channeling a spirit for a coonhound."

"It could give Blue comfort."

"If he needs comfort, buy him some cookies and a squeak toy. I'll reimburse you."

Shirley chewed on her lower lip, trying to fool me into thinking she was considering my request. "You're right, Sam. Maybe some other time when Blue's not present."

"And any messages can be passed along to me. I'll see that he gets them."

She nodded her agreement, but I knew full well Shirley was about to do what she damned well pleased.

Chapter Thirteen

At twelve-forty on Saturday morning, a Yellow Cab dropped Nakayla and me on South Oxford a block up from Lafayette Avenue in Brooklyn. The street was lined with brownstones and we found Eleanor Johnson's address in brass numerals on a dark wooden door at the top of a stoop.

Nakayla carried the book with the Black Mountain College photographs and I had a small backpack containing a laptop and Wi-Fi hotspot so we could retrieve information off the Internet. If Ms. Johnson identified anyone and they happened to live in the New York area, we wanted to see them before returning to Asheville.

Nakayla took the lead up the stairs while I stayed on the sidewalk below. She rang the bell, stepped back, and leaned against a wrought-iron railing. She must have figured a ninety-year-old woman wasn't likely to bound out of a rocker and be at the front door in less than thirty seconds. To her surprise, the door opened inward almost immediately and a lean African-American woman around Nakayla's age stood on the threshold. She wore a light blue tunic over navy tights. Her brown leather boots were mid-calf and trimmed with tan fur. She looked at Nakayla and then down at me. She frowned as she noticed the book in Nakayla's hand.

"What are you selling?"

Nakayla flashed her engaging smile. "Nothing. My name's Nakayla Robertson and this is my colleague, Sam Blackman."

I gave a little wave. Always the charmer.

Nakayla lifted the book, showing the woman its cover. "We were hoping to speak with Eleanor Johnson. We're researching Black Mountain College, the institution Ms. Johnson attended. We hope to learn things from her first-hand experience and also have her identify some other students in the book's photographs."

The woman nodded. "Gramama Ellie's told me about the school. What are you planning to do with this research?"

Nakayla went into the cover story we'd invented to get by any gatekeepers. "We hope to speak with as many former students as possible. Unfortunately, the pool of attendees is shrinking rapidly. We know Ms. Johnson went on to have a wonderful career in dance. We hope to document the accomplishments and contributions of as many students as we can."

"I'm her granddaughter. Mercy Thompson."

"Were you named for Merce Cunningham?" Nakayla asked.

"No. For my mother. But Gramama named her for Merce."

"Do you think your grandmother would be willing to speak with us? I promise we won't stay long and you're welcome to sit in."

Mercy Thompson shook her head. "I was just about to walk to a class at the Brooklyn Academy of Music." She looked at me as if I were the unknown factor in a decision she was pondering. "Where are you from?"

"Asheville, North Carolina," Nakayla said. "This is a local story for us, but we're only here for the day."

"All right. I'll introduce you." Mercy stepped out, closed the front door, and locked it behind her.

I was confused. "Is your grandmother someplace else?"

She laughed. "She has the lower floor. The entrance under the stoop. I'm on this level and we rent out the upper two floors."

I remembered Eleanor Johnson's bio stating she rented rooms to students. Nakayla followed Mercy down to the sidewalk and I stepped aside as the two women went to the lower door. Mercy knocked once and then used a key to open it.

"Gramama might be napping in her chair. She often does when she's finished her lunch. Let me check."

Nakayla and I waited while Mercy entered.

"Gramama. You've got company."

A reedy voice answered. "Company? Was I expecting someone?"

The high volume of the two voices led me to believe Eleanor Johnson might be hard of hearing.

"A woman and man from Asheville, North Carolina. They want to talk to you about Black Mountain College."

"All the way from Asheville?"

"Yes."

"Then, for Lord's sake, get my teeth. They're by the bathroom sink."

I looked at Nakayla.

"Just like my granny used to do," she said. "Except she would have told me to fetch 'em."

I thought about my own Nana, now gone for ten years. She would have been wearing fuzzy slippers and a housecoat over a slip. "Don't be surprised if we have to wait for her to change clothes."

I was wrong. Mercy returned to the front door in less than a minute and ushered us in. We were met in the living room by a woman as slender as her granddaughter. Her wide brown eyes were full of life and instead of a housecoat she wore a green jogging suit with yellow trim.

My grandmother Nana's living room had been furnished with a velvet sofa and matching chairs. There were even arm doilies that had been crafted by my great grandmother. Eleanor Johnson's room had chrome and gray leather furniture, a brushed aluminum coffee table, and wall hangings in bold, colorful, abstract designs. The only concession to what I considered the style of her generation was a dark oak corner curio shelf holding a collection of figurines. All were dancers, some white porcelain, some painted ceramic.

The face of the elderly woman was lined with wrinkles like the palm of a hand. She didn't appear frail, but rather as someone who had allowed herself to age naturally, secure enough in her own appearance to avoid the extreme cosmetic surgery and Botox treatments that so many celebrities embraced.

Nakayla and I introduced ourselves and she gestured that we should take a seat on the leather couch.

"Would you like some tea?" she asked. "Mercy can brew a pot."

"No, thank you," Nakayla said.

"And we don't want Mercy to be late for her class," I added. "No sense in our causing problems with her teacher."

Mercy laughed.

"She is the teacher," Eleanor Johnson said.

"Music?" I asked.

The grandmother's wrinkles deepened. "Oh, no. Dance. The body's music."

I glanced again at the multiple figurines. Some detective.

"Ms. Johnson," Nakayla said, "why don't you sit by me so that I can use the coffee table to show you some pictures in this book?"

"Call me Ellie, dear."

"Ellie, we'd like your help in identifying some of your fellow students."

"Oh, my, that's so long ago. Nearly seventy years."

"Gramama, you know your mind's sharp as a tack," Mercy said. "But if you get tired, just say so."

"Yes," Nakayla agreed. "And I promise we won't take long."

Mercy turned to leave and then paused. "Make sure you hear her lock the door when you go."

Ellie waved her granddaughter away. "I remember when we could leave the house unlocked."

Mercy walked over and kissed her grandmother's cheek. "And bread was twenty cents a loaf. Those days are gone, so I'd better find that door locked when I return."

Mercy left and Nakayla and Ellie sat down. I pulled one of the chairs closer to the coffee table where I would be able to see the book on its surface.

"Your granddaughter seems very nice," I said. "You're lucky to have some of your family so close."

"She is my family. My daughter was taken with breast cancer five years ago. My son-in-law died in that first Gulf War. Mercy was their only child. I keep telling her to find a good man, but between teaching and performing, she hasn't the time to be serious with anyone." She chuckled. "Can't complain. I was just like her."

Nakayla set the book on the coffee table. "We appreciate your taking the time to talk with us. Just for our clarification, when were you at Black Mountain College?"

"From 1948 to 1953. I studied four years and then helped Merce when he formed his dance company there in 1953. Then I moved back to New York and stayed involved with Merce till he died. He was still active at ninety. What a spirit! I wish I had half the energy of that man."

"Did you like your years at Black Mountain?"

"Like them? They were exhilarating. Not just because of the dance but because of all the artistic talent in so many disciplines. When I pass over, I won't be surprised to find heaven remarkably similar to Black Mountain."

Nakayla opened the book to the page where Paul Weaver and the unknown woman were with Ellie in the photograph by Lake Eden. "This is you, isn't it?"

Ellie adjusted her glasses and leaned closer to the picture. "My, my. I remember the day that was taken." She shook her head. "Poor Paul."

"What happened to Paul?" Nakayla asked.

"He loved to hike. They said he went out one night and slipped off a trail. Not long after this picture was taken."

"Do you believe that's what happened?"

Ellie looked up at Nakayla and then turned to me. "Are you all saying that's not what happened?"

"We don't know," I said. "We're here seeking your help. Paul Weaver's younger sister wants to be certain. It's a long time ago, but it's weighing on her. She saw you and Paul together in this book and thought you might have some insights. Were you and Paul friends?"

She nodded. "Yes. He was quiet. Very serious. That was common among the returning veterans. But there were times," she tapped the photograph with her slender forefinger, "there were times like this when he came out of his shell and could be very funny. And that was happening more and more frequently."

"Do you know of anyone he might have argued with?" I asked.

"At the college? No. Like I said, he was quiet. Architecture wasn't, shall I say, one of the more flamboyant areas of study."

"And away from the college?"

Ellie bit her lower lip. Her eyes moistened. "He was local, although he didn't talk much about his family. I remember he did talk about his little sister. He was worried about her growing up in that environment."

"The mountains?"

Ellie clutched her hands together in her lap. "Once we stepped out of that magical world at the college we entered the Jim Crow South. Whenever we went off campus, Paul insisted on accompanying us."

Again, I thought about Paul Weaver's fight over the admittance of black veterans to the Asheville American Legion post. Had that carried through to the black students in a segregated South?

"Were there confrontations with the locals? Did Paul try to protect all the African-American students?"

Ellie pointed to the picture again. "Just Leah and me. When we went into town together. He joked that he was our interpreter. My Brooklyn accent was pretty thick back then. Leah was a German immigrant and her English was limited. And then the locals had that mountain twang."

"Was there ever any trouble with the locals that justified his concerns?" I asked.

Ellie sighed. "Yes. The first time Leah and I went to town some men loitering by the drugstore yelled at us, 'Go back to Africa' and mean things like that."

"And Leah?"

"They called her 'Jew girl' and 'Yankee bitch.'"

"And you told Paul about it?"

"No. Leah and I agreed it would just upset him. The men were punks. Leah said she'd faced worse."

"So, who told him?" I asked.

"There was some kid in town who worked at the college doing odd jobs. He witnessed what happened."

"Harlan Beale?"

Ellie sat up straight. "I believe you're right, sir. I haven't thought about him in years. He was a nice boy. Rather shy, but he would show up at all our events. Do you know him?"

"Yes. I'm sorry to say he's deceased." I left it at that.

Nakayla lifted the book from the table and examined the photograph more closely. "What was Leah's last name?"

"Rosen."

"Was she a dancer?"

"No. She wanted to be a writer. Since English wasn't her native tongue, she had to put her thoughts down in German and then craft it into English. She worked very hard. We all admired her determination."

"Do you know what happened to her?" Nakayla asked.

"Yes. We stayed in touch. She left Black Mountain shortly after Paul's accident and returned to New York. She worked in a department store and attended classes at Brooklyn College. Sometimes she would come to see me dance. We would meet for coffee. She earned her undergraduate degree and then an MFA from the Iowa Writers' Workshop. And she went full circle—back to North Carolina, where she wrote and taught."

"Back to the mountains?" I asked.

"No. The University of North Carolina at Chapel Hill. I have one of her books on a shelf in my bedroom. Would you like to see it?"

Nakayla stood. "Yes, if it's not too much trouble. Can I get it for you?"

Ellie pushed herself up from the couch. "You'd never find it. I'll be right back." She disappeared down a hallway.

Nakayla leaned closer to me. "What do you think?" she whispered.

"Well, if Paul Weaver was seen off campus a lot with Ellie, he could have set himself up as a target. The Klan was pretty active in North Carolina at the time."

"Maybe," Nakayla mused. "Or maybe he simply fell. Violet Baker was a kid who idolized her older brother and still can't accept he made a careless mistake."

"Yes, and then there's Harlan Beale, both then and now. And there's the missing documents—the official coroner's report and Paul Weaver's death certificate."

"How much more should we press her?"

"Look through the pictures during the years she was at the college and get more names. I'll set up the laptop and enter them."

Ellie returned carrying a slim volume with a frayed dust jacket. "Here it is. She wrote other books, but this is my favorite." She handed it to Nakayla.

Nakayla looked at the cover and passed it to me. The title was written in cursive script, blue ink on a sheet of translucent notepaper cocked at an angle. *letters from camp* all lowercase. At first glance I thought the underlying picture was some industrial city. Then I saw the wire fence and the smokestacks, and the wagons loaded with corpses—"letters from camp," a Nazi death camp.

"Ms. Ellie," I said, lapsing into my childhood manners. "Do you think the people outside the college would have thought you and Paul Weaver were more than friends?"

"They had no reason to. We were never in town as a couple, if that's what you mean."

"And Paul and Leah?"

She hesitated, choosing her words carefully. "I'll just say they had a special bond. You'll have to ask Leah for any more than that."

"Where is she?" Nakayla asked.

"At a retirement community near Chapel Hill. I got a letter from her two weeks ago, but at our age, you'd better not assume anything. I can give you the address, but then you're on your own. Talking about Paul might be painful, and I don't want to cause her more pain. That woman has endured enough."

I looked down at Leah Rosen's book. The smoke from the ovens formed the texture of the notepaper.

What were a few punks yelling epithets to someone who had come face-to-face with such evil?

Chapter Fourteen

We spent another twenty minutes going through the photographs in the book with Ellie. She identified ten other students, but I had no luck in finding any of them on the Internet. Odds were, most, if not all, were deceased. We thanked Ellie for her help and listened outside the door as she threw the deadbolt.

Our return flight got us back to Asheville a little after eight. Nakayla and I entered my apartment to find Shirley stretched out on the floor of the living area sound asleep. Blue lay perpendicular to her with his head on her abdomen. He rose, gave a short bark, and loped over to us. Shirley blinked awake and her face turned red underneath her white makeup.

"Sorry. Just a catnap." She stood.

"Cat and dog nap," I said. "Did Blue wear you out?"

"We had a long walk on the Biltmore Estate. I have an annual pass so we hiked along the French Broad as far as the trail ran. I didn't think about having to walk back. How was your trip?"

"We saw the person we needed to," Nakayla said. "She was interesting."

"Interesting? That's what Hewitt usually says after interviewing a client who's guilty as sin."

"I doubt she'll ever need the services of your illustrious boss." I set my backpack on the kitchen counter and noticed a coiled leather strap and a brown paper bag. "What's this?"

I unwound the strap to discover it was a dog leash with silver studs running the length of the fine grain leather. The workmanship was better than the belts hanging in my closet.

"We also walked uptown and stopped at Three Dog Bakery," Shirley said. "I didn't want Blue led on a rope like some farm animal."

"And the bag?"

"Cookies. You just don't go into a bakery with Blue and not buy something. That would be cruel."

"Yes. I imagine the ASPCA would press charges."

Shirley scowled at me. "I'm just saying he has feelings. You're the one who told me he was upset."

I flashed back to Blue whimpering over the spot where Harlan Beale's body had lain. "You're right. Thanks for taking such good care of him."

Shirley brightened. "Any time." She picked up her handbag from a corner of the sofa and fished out my spare apartment key. "Just call."

I looked at Nakayla. We'd spoken on the plane about next steps and the logistics of moving forward.

"Would it be too much trouble if we left Blue with you tomorrow?" Nakayla asked. "Sam and I might need to drive to Chapel Hill."

Shirley dropped the key back in her handbag. "What time should I be here?"

"First, we've got to confirm that the person can see us," Nakayla said. "If you wait a minute, I'll try to find out now." Nakayla headed for the bedroom where she could make the call in private.

Shirley knelt beside Blue. "What do you think will happen to him?"

I shrugged. "That's more a question for your legal-eagle boss. Maybe there's a will."

"The only way Hewitt would touch a will was if one beneficiary murdered another."

Her statement gave me pause. At this point, for all I knew, Beale could have been killed for some personal family matter. I needed to speak with his cousin, Nadine Oates. Leah Rosen could wait. Paul Weaver had been dead for nearly seventy years; Harlan Beale, less than forty-eight hours.

"Nakayla," I yelled down the hall to the bedroom. "Hold off."

She came out with her cell phone against her ear.

"We need to see Nadine tomorrow," I said.

Nakayla held her forefinger to her lips, signaling she had reached someone. Then she turned her back to us. "Yes," she said. "A mutual friend asked us to visit her when we were in the area. Tell her we're bringing greetings from Ellie Johnson in Brooklyn." Nakayla pivoted and cupped her hand around the bottom of the phone to cover the microphone. "Leah's gone to bed already," she whispered. "They want us to check back in the morning."

"Fine. Let's not go till Monday."

Nakayla nodded that she understood. She removed her hand. "Yes, that will be fine. I'll call around ten. We won't be coming till Monday at the earliest. Thank you for your help."

She disconnected. "Since we don't have Leah's direct number, they won't put us through. The woman took our information and the morning shift will check with Leah at breakfast."

"Good. You can confirm that tomorrow while I see Nadine Oates."

Shirley ran her hand down Blue's back. "Then you won't need me to dog sit?"

"No," I said. "We won't go to Chapel Hill till Monday. We'll find a kennel."

Shirley's black eyes narrowed. "Ridiculous. I can watch him Monday. He can come to the office. Hewitt probably won't notice and Cory's a dog person."

Cory DeMille was Hewitt Donaldson's paralegal. She and Shirley kept Hewitt in line as much as anyone could. If they both wanted Blue in the office, I doubted Hewitt would object.

"All right," I said. "If we go Monday, we'll drop him off on our way out of town."

Shirley gave Blue a parting hug and admonished us to take good care of him.

Nakayla left a few minutes later, deciding clean clothes and a check of her mail outweighed spending the night with me. Blue and I padded back to the bedroom. I didn't know if he dreamed, but I spent a restless night trying to keep Harlan Beale from climbing a gigantic geodesic dome—shouting "you'll be killed"—to no avail. I tried to follow but my prosthesis kept tangling in the Venetian blind strips that bent beneath my weight but didn't collapse under Beale. At the top of the dome stood Violet Baker, scanning the horizon for her brother. I looked down at the base where the metal strips touched the ground. A body lay in the same position as Beale's had been in the museum. But this wasn't Beale. Even though I couldn't see the face, I knew it was Paul Weaver, trapped in Buckminster Fuller's failed dome of 1948, and I didn't know if he was dead or alive.

I tossed and turned till eight when I decided sleep was going to be futile. I realized there was a good chance Nadine Oates would attend her church Sunday morning and that at her age, someone might take her there and back. I wanted to speak to her alone so there was no sense rushing. Early afternoon would be my target time.

I took a cold shower, drank two cups of black coffee, and walked Blue around my apartment building in an effort to clear the fog from my sleep-deprived brain. While Blue ate breakfast, I downed scrambled eggs and toast. At twelve-thirty, I called Newly and got the address for Nadine Oates in Fairview. Then I swung by Nakayla's to hand off Blue, new leash attached, before circling back to take Old Highway 74 out of town.

The valley around Fairview was a farming community that appeared to be transitioning into a series of housing developments. The new neighborhoods were marketed to second-home buyers and retirees, homes that few locals could afford. I drove through acreage that might have once belonged to the Weavers—the farm that Violet's parents sold so soon after Paul's death. And now Nadine Oates, Harlan Beale's closest relative, brought me to the same area. I couldn't help wonder what connection might link the two families.

I left the main highway for a side road, narrow but paved, that ran along a bold stream. A quarter mile farther, I spotted a rusty mailbox with the faded name *Oates* written on its side. The gravel driveway curved through a thicket of rhododendron to end in a small turnaround in front of a white, single-story clapboard house. A maroon Ford Taurus sat under a metal carport that looked more like a funeral tent than a sturdy protective structure.

A sad and sagging three-cushion brown sofa was pushed up against the outside front wall of the porch to get as much shelter from the overhanging tin roof as possible. On the opposite side of the house from the carport were two outbuildings constructed from the same materials as Harlan Beale's sheds. I suspected her cousin had made them for her from materials left over from Black Mountain College.

Newly had told me Nadine Oates lived alone so it was a logical deduction that the Taurus was hers. On a sunny spring day, why would a guest use the carport?

I parked, grabbed my notepad and pencil from the passenger's seat and made a quick check of my face in the rearview mirror. No errant hair strands; no food stuck between my teeth.

As I stepped up on the porch, a voice called out from the other side of the front door. "Whatcha want?"

"My name's Sam Blackman. I'm here to see Nadine Oates. It's about her cousin Harlan."

"Harlan's dead."

"I know. He tried to reach me the night he died. I'm hoping to learn why."

"You the law?"

"No," I said.

"Then why you sticking your nose in my family's business?"

The woman behind the door wasn't being unreasonable. I was a strange man who showed up on her doorstep. After a death, all sorts of hucksters descended upon the survivors. I needed to make a personal connection.

"Miss Oates, I'm actually helping Violet Baker."

"Don't know her."

"She used to be Violet Weaver."

Silence. I waited for a response and heard only a squirrel chattering in a tree somewhere behind me. Then, a click as the latch sprung and the door swung inward.

A tall, lean white woman with a gaunt face that looked more like cracked leather than skin stood in the gap. She wore a long, faded brown cotton dress and a misbuttoned blue sweater. A single-barrel shotgun rested in the crook of her left arm. Her steel gray hair was pulled into a bun the size of a pin cushion, a yellow pencil pierced through it like a stiletto. Behind her lay only darkness as if every window had been shuttered tight.

She eyed me up and down. I held my arms out to my side, the Black Mountain College book the only object in my hand.

"How do you know what happened to little Violet?"

"She's returned to Asheville. I'm a private detective and she's hired me to look into her brother's death."

Nadine Oates lowered the shotgun to her side. "I don't know how I can help, but you might as well come in for a spell." She stepped back and opened the door farther. "Take the wicker rocker."

I walked past her, and then waited until my eyes adjusted to the dim light. The wicker rocker she indicated was near the far corner with an empty TV tray set up on one side and a floorlamp on the other. On the wall behind stood a breakfront with glassed-in shelves containing knickknacks and framed photographs. In addition to the wicker rocker, two armchairs that once matched the sofa on the front porch were angled so that all three chairs were like points of a triangle. I didn't see a television, although one could have been in a back room.

Nadine Oates stood the shotgun by the door in a wicker basket with an assortment of walking canes. "You can turn on that lamp as soon as I take Ricky to the back." She reached in the pocket of her sweater and brought out a small pellet. She held it up and made kissing sounds.

I heard the click of small claws as a rotund raccoon lumbered from beneath one of the armchairs. The masked bandit eyed me as he followed Nadine Oates down the hall. Sunlight from the open door sparkled on rhinestones decorating a leather collar like Ricky the Raccoon was a poodle going for Best in Show.

I didn't know if and how Nadine Oates could help me, but it was clear Blue wouldn't be coming to this house.

I switched on the floorlamp and used my moment alone to examine the photographs in the breakfront. Most had to be at least seventy years old. The vintage automobiles and wardrobes depicted an era in which Nadine would have been a young girl. I studied one group photo of some family celebration. I recognized Nadine as a laughing teenager with long black hair. Behind her stood young Harlan Beale, eyes closed as the camera shutter caught him in mid-blink. To the right of that picture stood an oval pewter frame encompassing a soldier and a woman standing in front of a black car I guessed to be from the late nineteen-thirties. I leaned close to the breakfront glass for a better look. The woman was Nadine Oates. The soldier was Paul Weaver. In one hand, he held a duffel bag. In the other, he clasped Nadine's fingers.

"Ricky doesn't like the light." Nadine spoke as she entered the front room.

I stepped away from the picture, hoping to mask my surprise at what I'd seen. "Have you had Ricky since he was a...?" The question died as I couldn't remember what you called a baby raccoon.

"Cub. Yes. A pack of dogs killed the mother and her other cubs. Ricky was the only survivor. By the time I nursed him back to health, he was too old to follow instincts of the wild." She sat in a chair and I took the rocker. "But he's still nocturnal. We go on night walks together."

"You were good to take him in," I said. "Does he get along with other people? Like when Harlan came to visit?"

She frowned. "Harlan wouldn't go anywhere without that damn coonhound." She sighed. "Blue had to wait in the truck, and he'd howl 'cause he knew Ricky was in the house. Still, Harlan was good to help me if my well needed priming or there was handyman work too tough for me to handle. Don't know what I'll do now."

"Harlan was helpful to Violet and me." I raised the book from my lap. "He identified some people at the college, people who might have known her brother."

"What's that got to do with me?"

"Did you know Paul Weaver?"

She shrugged. "The Weavers were the next farm over. We knew each other as kids."

"How about when you were older?"

"Just to say hi. Then he went to war and I heard from someone, maybe Harlan, that Paul was up at the college after that."

"Did you ever go there? To see Harlan? To see Paul?"

Her bony jaw clenched and she spoke through gritted teeth. "I didn't know none of them. They weren't my kind of people."

"What kind of people were they?"

"Germans. Yankees. Jews. Communists. Take your pick."

"How about African-Americans?" I asked. "Did you ever hear about Paul being especially friendly with them?"

"No. You think they killed him?"

"I don't know that anyone killed him, Miss Oates. That's what I'm trying to find out."

"Well, if you ask me, look no further than the Communists." She leaned forward in her chair. "But my advice is not to look at all. You're stirring up a mess of trouble. No telling what's been let loose."

"I don't understand. What could possibly be let loose after seventy years?"

"Things that should be forgotten. Harlan knew and they killed him, too. That's all I'm saying, Mr. Blackman." She got to her feet. "I don't know nobody in that book. Now I'm a busy woman with things to do and little time left to do them." She walked to the front door and opened it. But not before picking up her shotgun.

Chapter Fifteen

I left Nadine Oates and her nocturnal friend, Ricky, to return to Nakayla's. Her car wasn't in the driveway and there was no note explaining where she and Blue might have gone.

The world was quiet on a late Sunday afternoon. I lay down on Nakayla's sofa to think about what we'd learned over the past few days. Harlan Beale had known Paul Weaver back in 1948. He had agreed to review the photographs in the library book and had tried to reach me Thursday evening. From his shout to someone else during his voice message, I assumed he was still at the movie location, but that would need to be verified from the cell tower records that Newly was requesting.

But why would Beale call me and then continue to work on the old photographs at home? Had he made an initial discovery and then done due diligence by going through the rest of the book? And yet he hadn't finished. His notes only went up to the photograph of Buckminster Fuller's collapsed dome and the penciled circles around Paul Weaver and a woman facing away from the camera.

Ellie Johnson had confirmed that tension existed between the Jim Crow culture of the town and the culture of the college, but she denied that she and Paul were a romantic couple. However, she didn't make the same assertion regarding Paul and Leah Rosen. Our trip to Chapel Hill the following day could be either pivotal to the investigation or a dead end. We had no more leads. *No*, I thought. *I was wrong.* The photograph I'd seen of Paul and Nadine belied her claim that she only knew him well enough to say hello. Perhaps Harlan Beale also knew Paul better than he'd said. And now he was dead.

Somewhere in the midst of these thoughts I drifted off to sleep.

A wide, wet tongue slurping across my mouth and nose jolted me awake.

"Working hard?" Nakayla stood behind Blue. She held a large brown cushion.

I sat up and rubbed my eyes. "Just thinking."

"Poor baby. That is hard for you. Blue and I went shopping and he has a new bed."

"What was wrong with his rug?"

"It's at your place." She dropped the bed on the floor near the end of the sofa.

Blue didn't have to be given any instructions. He sauntered to it and lay down.

"You and Blue can go back to thinking, if you like."

I patted the cushion beside me. "Sit down. I need to tell you about Nadine Oates."

I gave Nakayla a detailed account of my visit, including Nadine's categorization of Black Mountain College as a nest of Germans, Yankees, Jews, and Communists, and her claim that she really didn't know Paul, but I'd seen a framed picture she evidently treasured of the two of them together.

"When do you think the photograph was taken?"

"I'm not an expert on antique automobiles but I'd guess the one in the background was mid- to late-nineteen-thirties."

"Paul didn't go into the war until 1943."

"I doubt if those farm people could afford new cars, especially during the war. I believe it was 1943 and Paul was shipping out."

"Why would she lie about her relationship?"

"Why, indeed? Maybe she wrote him a 'Dear John' letter and didn't want to admit it." I thought of another possibility. "Maybe he wrote her a 'Dear Jane' letter because he met someone overseas. He was probably stationed in Europe after the surrender. There were a lot of G.I. romances with French and German women."

Nakayla nodded. "We haven't checked his service record. We only know what Violet Baker told us."

"A good point," I admitted, "but I don't know how much that can tell us."

"It might shed some light on his relationship to Leah Rosen." Nakayla got up and retrieved her iPad from the dining room table. She returned to the sofa and showed me the image on the screen. It was the dust jacket for *letters from camp,* the book written by Leah Rosen that Ellie Johnson kept in her bedroom.

"It was available as an e-book," Nakayla said. "Let me pull up the last letter." She swiped the screen and brought up the index. She touched the final entry.

The chapter heading was "letter from Paul."

"Read it," Nakayla said. "It's not very long. I'll start some pasta boiling and we'll have supper here."

I read it, and then read it again. I scrolled through the other chapters, each a letter from an individual who was in the death camp. The letters served as a literary motif that not only shared camp experiences but the hopes and dreams of those who would be gassed or shot and then incinerated by the Nazi war machine simply because of their ethnic heritage or religious beliefs. Some were men, some women, some even children. The letters never mentioned a specific camp like Treblinka or Auschwitz, but, rather, encompassed all of them in what the writers simply referred to as "the camp."

Except for Paul's letter. His was addressed "To Those Who Will Not Believe," and the author was an American soldier liberating Dachau. He described the horrors he witnessed and the inhumanity of humanity that portended more letters would be written from camps of the future, both physical and psychological, camps that would be created by hatred and bigotry.

The last paragraph was short yet powerful.

What is the difference between life and death? One breath. The final intake, the final exhale. And then not another. The air in this place is full of final breaths. How many were a prayer? How many were a release of pain? How many a quiet surrender to oblivion? I breathe them in, even as they scar my lungs. Those breaths, those last gasps. I feel them now inside me. So many that I cannot breathe. So filled with them that there is no room for my own breath. I live on that threshold between life and death, breathless from the hidden wounds that others refuse to see.

Chapter Sixteen

The drive from Asheville to Chapel Hill took about three and a half hours. Nakayla had arranged for us to meet Leah Rosen in her apartment at one o'clock, giving her plenty of time for lunch. We'd left Blue with Shirley at the law office. She'd bought matching food and water bowls as well as a cushion identical to the one Nakayla had purchased. Blue was acquiring real estate faster than Donald Trump.

The Carol Woods Retirement Community was a mix of cottages, apartments, and recreational and health facilities. Leah Rosen lived in a ground-floor, one-bedroom unit in one of three buildings all interconnected by enclosed walkways that insured residents could access dining and amenities, whatever the weather.

At three minutes after one, Nakayla knocked on a door displaying a carved wooden sign that read "Enter With Joy."

"Coming." A woman's voice sounded warbly but strong.

The door opened and Leah Rosen greeted us with a smile. She had to be an inch or two below five feet and made me feel like an NBA star. Her gray hair was wavy and pulled off her wrinkled brow with a single gold clasp. She had thick glasses that magnified her brown eyes to the size of quarters.

"Welcome. Welcome. Any friend of Ellie's is a friend of mine."

She motioned with her cane for us to step through a small foyer into the living room. Except it really wasn't a living room. Bookshelves lined the walls and held so many volumes I should more accurately describe the room as a library. A small burgundy love seat was positioned to allow access to the books behind it. An antique secretarial desk was opposite it. A reading lamp threw bright light onto a lined-page journal with an open fountain pen lying diagonally across it. I realized her life's passion was as evident in her surroundings as Ellie Johnson's passion for dance had been expressed through her figurines.

"Take the sofa," she instructed, and then went to the desk chair and turned it to face us. She capped the pen, started to sit, and then said, "Where are my manners? Would you like a cup of tea?"

"I'm fine, Ms. Rosen," I said.

"We grabbed a bite of lunch," Nakayla lied. "But if you'd like something yourself, please don't hesitate."

Leah Rosen eased into the chair. "No, nothing for me. And you must call me Leah. I bet Ellie didn't like Ms. Johnson."

"She didn't," Nakayla said. "She's quite a lady. Still living in her brownstone. We met her granddaughter, Mercy. Ellie's fortunate to have someone check up on her every day."

Leah nodded. "We're both at that age when we need assistance. If I don't show up at breakfast, five people will knock on my door within fifteen minutes." She shifted in her chair and laid the cane across her lap. "How long have you known Ellie?"

I looked at Nakayla. We'd agreed she'd take the lead in explaining why we'd come.

"Actually, we just met her on Saturday," Nakayla said. "She's helping us with some background research on Black Mountain College."

A visible tremor ran down Leah Rosen's body and ended with her hands tightening around the shaft of her cane. "What kind of research?" she whispered.

"We're working for Violet Baker. She's Paul Weaver's sister. We saw a picture of Ellie and Paul together at Lake Eden. There was a third student in that particular photograph and Ellie confirmed that you were that person."

Leah took a deep breath. The eyes behind the thick lenses moistened. "What picture?"

Nakayla had set her handbag at her feet. She retrieved the library copy of the Black Mountain College book and opened it to the correct page. She walked over and knelt beside Leah, holding the book just above the woman's lap.

Leah raised one hand from the cane and ran her fingers over the photograph like reading Braille. "So long ago. I remember the day—yesterday to me." She looked at Nakayla. "I've never seen this before because I couldn't bear to see any photos from that time. Ellie is my link. We share memories, not pictures."

Nakayla flipped to the second of the marked pages—the photograph of Buckminster Fuller's failed dome where Harlan Beale had used a pencil to circle Paul and an unknown woman facing away from the camera. Nakayla pointed to her. "We see Paul, but who is this?"

Leah Rosen bent over, her thick glasses coming closer to the page. "Me. I was heading back to my room. Paul followed." She stopped and looked at me. "We didn't have a lot of time to be alone."

I tried to visualize this elderly, diminutive woman as the young, smiling girl by the lake. The girl that Ellie said had a special bond with Paul Weaver. The woman who had written "a letter from Paul."

And I thought of Harlan Beale, the source of Roland Cassidy's stories. What was fact? What was fiction?

"You were in a concentration camp, weren't you, Leah. Ravensbrück." It was a statement, not a question.

She only nodded.

"And Paul told you he liberated Dachau. He'd seen the horrific conditions you experienced."

"No. He and his battalion liberated Gunskirchen. I changed that for the book. Paul and I didn't talk much about our experiences. We didn't need to. We shared a unique perspective and so we carved out life for ourselves. A life that hoped for a better world."

"What happened to Paul?"

Tears sparkled beneath her magnifying lenses. "I don't know. He said he was going to meet someone. To set her straight. An old girlfriend who had confronted us in town. There was quite a scene between them. But he didn't come back that night. The next day some deputies came and told us Paul was dead. That he'd fallen while hiking. I tried to tell them he'd gone for a meeting." She paused long enough to wipe her cheek. "Then the men in the suits came and told me no one had seen Paul since he left the college. That I should stop saying otherwise or there would be problems with my papers."

"Your papers?" I asked.

"I was an immigrant, a refugee sponsored by my aunt after the war. My parents and two brothers didn't survive the camps. You don't understand what the phrase 'problems with your papers' meant to someone who had endured the Nazi reign of terror."

"Is that why you left the college?"

"Yes. I returned to New York to live with my aunt under her protection until I could gain my American citizenship."

Nakayla closed the book. She stood and turned to me. She mouthed "Roland Cassidy" and I knew she referred to the similarities between what Leah was telling us and the characters in Cassidy's novel.

"Tell me, Leah," I said. "Was the woman Paul was supposed to meet Nadine Oates?"

Leah's mouth dropped open. "Yes. How did you know?"

I ignored her question and asked another. "Did you ever see her after Paul's death?"

"No. I'd been warned off. I left the college a few weeks later."

"And when you wrote the 'letter from Paul' in your book, was that presenting some of Paul's feelings he'd shared with you?"

"Yes. One of the few times he'd opened up about his war experience when he spoke of witnessing the Gunskirchen horror. He said his breath caught in his chest. He realized that a single breath was the difference between the living and the dead." Leah Rosen leaned forward and pointed a finger at me. "And, Mr. Blackman, in that moment of telling me, Paul couldn't breathe. We were walking around Lake Eden in the evening and he suddenly sat down. He was able to wheeze the word 'inhaler' and

I ran to his room and found it in his shaving kit. It took about thirty minutes before his breathing eased enough for us to return to the college. That conversation and Paul's physical reaction formed the 'letter from Paul.' It was my way of keeping him alive." She stared for a few seconds at the bookshelf behind me. "William Faulkner said, 'The past is never dead. It's not even past.' Here you are today, bringing the past to me. At age ninety, even I can't outlive it."

I thought of F. Scott Fitzgerald's boats beating ceaselessly against the current. Leah Rosen had tried to pull against the current, and Nakayla and I had pushed her back into those waters churned by a fascist dictator so many years ago. Waters from which Leah Rosen could never row free.

• • ● • •

"Do you think Nadine Oates could have killed Paul Weaver?" Nakayla asked the question as we merged onto I-40 headed west to Asheville.

"She could have. And she has the family tie to Harlan Beale. Maybe he knew her secret."

"Or even helped her," Nakayla offered. "Paul Weaver could have died elsewhere, been transported to the site along the Blue Ridge Parkway, and then his body thrown from the trail."

"Newly suspects Beale's body could have been moved as well. But it's hard to believe that a ninety-year-old woman could orchestrate that maneuver. As for 1948, we have no proof that Paul Weaver actually saw Nadine on the day of his death. I'm sure she'll deny it and there's no one to state otherwise."

"And what about the missing death certificate and sheriff's report? How did Nadine manage that?"

"She didn't," I said. "This is more than a jilted lover. I don't know what we're stirring up, but we've got only one option."

"What's that?"

"Keep stirring." I kept my eyes on the road and handed her my cell phone. "Speed-dial Newly. Tell him we should be back before six and we'll come straight to headquarters. Tell him we've got some traffic for our two-way street of communication."

Newly agreed to meet but not at police headquarters. I suspected he didn't want to appear too cozy with private detectives at this early stage of his investigation. We were to call him when we reached our office and he would walk over.

Nakayla returned my phone and I clipped it to my belt.

"Tell me about the plot of *Love Among the Ridges*," I said. "How much does it mirror what we've learned from Ellie and Leah?"

"The main female character, Sacha Molter, is a concentration camp survivor like Leah. But she wants to be a dancer like Ellie. That makes dramatic sense as the action of dance is more interesting than scribbling in a notebook. The male lead, Robbie Oakley, is an artist who paints what are described as angry abstracts. In the book, the horror of the war fuels his drive. He was part of the U.S. troops that liberated Buchenwald. That's a change from Gunskirchen, but maybe it's only Cassidy's thin attempt to fictionalize what he'd heard, like Leah Rosen did."

"Heard from whom?" I asked. "Harlan?"

"I guess. Unless he also talked to Nadine, but didn't want to credit her as a source."

I thought about how Roland Cassidy had advised me to stay clear of Nadine Oates. Did he think she was a nut or was she someone who would undercut his claim to have invented his characters and story?

"And there's no violent death in the book?"

"No. The plot's a slow revelation of the two characters' backstories. It's like *Dirty Dancing* meets *Love Story*. Sacha turns out to be dying of tuberculosis contracted in the camp."

Those old movies were before my time, but Nakayla liked nothing better than a classic cinema tear-jerker.

"That's interesting," she said.

"What?"

"Tuberculosis. Both the fictional Sacha and real Paul had breathing difficulties."

"Anything else? Any small detail or subplot could be relevant."

"I hadn't made the connection before, but you said Nadine spoke disparagingly about the people at the college."

"She called them Germans, Yankees, Jews, and Communists."

"Then we need to have another conversation with Roland Cassidy," Nakayla said.

"Why?"

"In the book Sacha is a member of the Communist party. Where did Roland get that idea? Maybe we should have asked Leah Rosen about her politics."

Chapter Seventeen

Newly, Nakayla, and I sat in the conversation area of our office with cups of freshly brewed coffee. Newly had arrived with an unmarked manila envelope, but did nothing more than drop it on the table in front of his chair. It was like the ante in a poker game. Nakayla and I would have to give him something in order to play.

I decided to go ahead and lay out my cards. "Since Friday, we've seen three people who might have a bearing on Harlan Beale's death. Ellie Johnson in Brooklyn, New York; Nadine Oates, whom you know; and Leah Rosen in Chapel Hill. Johnson and Rosen were students at the college with Paul Weaver. Nadine Oates was Weaver's old girlfriend who got dumped for Rosen. Nadine might be the last person to have seen Weaver alive."

Newly raised his hand. "Whoa. You're moving too fast. Slow down and connect the dots."

I walked him through the history we'd uncovered and that Nadine Oates had clearly lied about her familiarity with Paul Weaver. Harlan Beale appeared to have known more about Weaver as well, evidenced by what he shared with Roland Cassidy that wound up in Cassidy's novel.

"So, you're going to talk to Cassidy?" Newly asked me.

"Unless you want to."

"No. I don't have the cause. Stories about Paul Weaver are just that. Old stories. Bring me a present-day motive that I can act upon. And Cassidy has an alibi for the time of Beale's death. He was dining with the actress Nicole Madison. She confirmed they didn't leave the restaurant till after ten."

"And you know Beale was dead by then?"

Newly picked up the manila envelope and slid out several pages. "The M.E. report determined Beale died between eight-thirty and ten-thirty. And he died elsewhere. Hypostasis confirms it."

Hypostasis or livor mortis was the discoloration of the skin as gravity affected the non-circulating blood.

Newly continued. "Beale's body had lain on its stomach for several hours before being placed in the museum and the bookcase toppled. He'd died from a blow to the head, but not from hitting the floor. He was struck by a hard, rounded object like a tire iron."

"Any speculation as to where he was killed?"

"No. Although he had to have made it home from the movie location if he'd been reviewing that book of Black Mountain College photographs."

"What line of inquiry are you following?"

"We're interviewing cast and crew to see if there was any trouble on set. Your Weaver connection is intriguing, but with Cassidy alibied, that leaves only three ninety-year-old women, not a promising suspect pool."

"What about Beale's phone?" Nakayla asked. "It didn't just happen to wind up in Blue's dog food bag."

Blue looked up at the sound of his name. He lay by my feet on the bed Shirley bought him.

Newly set his coffee on the table and pushed the M.E. report to the side. Underneath were several photographs. "We pulled these off of Beale's phone. Looks like he took pictures of some of the sets. Plus a picture of the construction materials they had to restock."

"Can I see them?" I asked.

Newly slid them across the table.

I recognized the cottage where we had watched Grayson and Nicole film the house of cards scene. There were other interiors—the dining hall, a library, and a classroom where Dustin Henry as Bucky Fuller taught a group of students. Another photograph showed Fuller and the class standing in front of a stack of lumber. The last picture was just the stack, although I wasn't sure if it was the stolen material or the replacement lumber that had later been set ablaze.

"Can I have these?" I asked.

"All this is for you. Off the record, of course. I'm not proud. I'll take help from anyone."

I dropped the photos and reports back in the envelope. "Then you won't mind if we seek some outside help as well."

He cocked his head and looked at me suspiciously. "Who?"

"The U.S. Army. And the FBI."

Newly laughed. "Hey, they're not coming out of my budget. So, knock yourselves out."

After Newly left, Nakayla telephoned Violet Baker to update her on our progress. Blue and I took the opportunity for a walk around the block.

The country hound was quickly developing an interest in city life, especially the multitude of other dogs sharing the sidewalk—every breed from toy poodle to great dane.

We were coming up Biltmore Avenue near the Diane Wortham Performing Arts Theatre when my phone buzzed. I expected it was Nakayla wondering which pub had captured Blue and me.

The 213 area code signaled Hollywood was calling.

"Benedict Cumberbatch," I said in a bad British accent.

A brief pause and then a woman laughed. "Thank God. I was afraid we were going to have to settle for this local yokel named Sam Blackman."

"Sam taught me everything I know."

"Then he's forgotten a lot."

I recognized the voice. "What's up, Camille?"

"We just got an updated weather report. Tomorrow's supposed to be rainy and chilly."

I didn't understand why the assistant director was calling me. Neither Nakayla nor I were scheduled to shoot the next day.

"I don't have a call time."

"You do now. Marty would like to use the day for prosthesis shots—you know, matching you to Grayson. Marty's compiled a list of close-ups needed throughout the movie. We can get most, if not all, tomorrow. No exteriors, no sound. We could shoot in a hail storm. It would really help us out."

I'd planned to spend the next day working our case. Roland Cassidy and Nadine Oates both knew more than they'd shared. And I wanted to make good on my pronouncement to Newly that I was contacting the U.S. Army and the FBI.

But being on set still offered the chance to confront Cassidy. Plus, I was bothered that Beale had hidden his phone, and yet the police had found only a few innocuous photographs on it.

"What time do you need me?"

"Seven. We'll want to get you and Grayson in matching wardrobe, and we have several prostheses from the World War II era we'd like to try."

"Then I'll see you at seven."

"Thanks, Sam. Come fifteen minutes early and report to catering for a hot breakfast."

"Do I get my own star trailer?"

"No. But you can eat in your car and use your imagination." Camille disconnected.

When I returned to the office, Nakayla told me that Violet Baker remembered Nadine Oates living at the farm next door. Although Violet had been young, she understood her big brother and Nadine had been boyfriend and girlfriend, and that the relationship had changed after the war. Violet wasn't aware of any animosity or hostility between them.

I told Nakayla about my movie role for the next day and we agreed to divide up the work. She would research the Weaver family, check the Registrar of Deeds, tax records, and other information that might provide insight as to when they sold the farm and to whom. She would also look into any records she could find that mentioned the political leanings of Eleanor Johnson and Leah Rosen. My opinion was Nadine Oates, jilted lover, was fabricating accusations, but we needed to check it out.

Meanwhile, I'd seen enough of the film business to know there would be downtime between shots. I planned to call a former Army colleague who worked in personnel records at Fort Bragg and see if he could access any data on Paul Clarence Weaver's service, particularly the circumstances of his discharge. My gut told me there was a connection between Weaver's military experience and the college. But I didn't know who wanted him dead in 1948, and how that tied into the undeniable murder of Harlan Beale. As Newly pointed out, when our only suspects were three ninety-year-old women, we weren't exactly hot on the killer's trail.

• ● ● ● •

Parts of disembodied mannequins. That's how I viewed the three left legs lying on the table in the large room dedicated to prop storage. Marty and Grayson flanked me as we looked at the vintage devices. All three were variations of the same design: a wooden lower leg attached to a leather sleeve that laced around the thigh like a heavy-duty corset.

Marty ran his hand along the surface of the closest one. "What do you think, Sam?"

"I think I'm glad I'm living in the twenty-first century." I circled the table, examining the choices. "The key will be finding one that's the correct length."

"We asked for a man five-foot, nine or ten inches," Marty said.

"That's a general indicator." I looked at Grayson. "We might be the same height but not the same leg length."

"True," Grayson said, "but I actually don't have to wear it. Marty will detach the upper sleeve and show me lacing it up without filming below the knee. That's when your close-ups will be used."

"Will I just be shown putting it on or close-ups of the leg in use?"

"Probably just putting it on," Marty said. "But I would like you to walk with it so that Grayson can mimic the gait."

I picked up the middle prosthesis that had the shortest sleeve. "I'll need to take my pants and prosthesis off. Is there a place I can change?"

Marty signaled to a woman arranging clothes on a portable rack. "Crystal, bring the wardrobe for Grayson and Sam for our first scene." He turned to me. "Grayson will take you to a makeshift dressing room down the hall. Things are rather primitive here."

I laughed. "You call this primitive? Remember, I was in the Army."

I followed Grayson and Crystal to a smaller room that must have once been a dorm space. Crystal hung two outfits on another portable rack. I noticed she wore a utility belt chockfull of pin cushions, spools of thread, scissors, and tape. In her early forties, she was a little overweight and had the edge of a red-and-yellow tattoo peeking out from under the short sleeve of her right arm. The design looked intricate.

She eyed me like measuring me for a suit. "What kind of underwear are you wearing?"

"I beg your pardon?"

Grayson made an unsuccessful attempt to stifle a laugh.

"Boxers or briefs? You've got to have your pants off for the close-up of the prosthesis. We can't have you wearing some leopard-skin Speedo. You should have been told to wear plain boxers if you have them."

"Sorry. I'm wearing gray underwear that's a brief but with material part way down my thigh."

Crystal frowned. "I'm sure they're very comfortable and very anachronistic. I'll see what I can find. In the meantime, try the leg and the pants and shirt. Marty will just have to shoot around your underwear till I can find something more appropriate." Crystal gave both of us a hard stare. "And, for God's sake, don't either of you spill anything on the clothes. Since I'm trying to fit both of you with the same outfit, we don't have any backups."

She left, closing the door behind her.

"Wow!" I exclaimed. "She's a tough cookie. And you're a star and she cuts you no slack."

"You'll learn in the movie business you're only as good as your crew. Crystal knows her job and she'll always make you fit your britches no matter how big you think you are."

"Or fit your briefs and boxers."

Grayson laughed. "True. Now show me how that antique leg works."

I stepped out of my pants and pulled my left stump free of my prosthesis. The World War II device was awkward to manage. The socket wasn't nearly as form-fitting and the leather sleeve that laced around the thigh chafed my skin. I stood and took a few tentative steps around the room. As I feared, the length of the leg was about an inch longer than my right.

"The other legs will be either too short or too long," I said. "I'll have to go with this one. The hinge lets the lower leg move with my below-the-knee action, but I have to swing my left leg a little wide for the stride."

Grayson studied my motion. "It's not bad, but it's enough to signal something's amiss. I think the best way for me to duplicate the walk is to have my left shoe built up about an inch. Let's go ahead and change and then ride a golf cart up to the shooting cottage. That's where Marty wants to start."

I left my good prosthesis tucked away in a corner. "Can we swing by my car on the way? I need to pick up something."

The predicted rain began to fall. I'd had the foresight to bring a poncho that not only kept my clothes dry and spared me the wrath of Crystal but also protected the envelope I'd retrieved from the CR-V, the envelope containing the prints Newly had made from the photos on Harlan Beale's cell phone.

Marty loved the look of the leg. He shot close-ups of me putting it on, then taking it off. We changed angles in the cottage and propped the room to look like another. Marty explained it was easier to move furniture than transport the lights and cameras to another interior.

We filmed most of the shots in my underwear. The crew was as indifferent to my semi-nakedness as the staff at my doctor's office. Grayson and I often exchanged places. I'd be filmed when the missing leg needed to be seen; Grayson would be in the same setup when they shot from the thigh up. He wore a pair of old boxers authentic to the period. At one point, Marty suggested we share the underwear so that the camera wouldn't be so confined on the close-ups. Grayson and I nixed that idea and Marty didn't push it.

We were setting up for the final shot before lunch when Mick Ritchie came over. We'd said hello earlier, but his electrician duties kept him running back and forth from the set to the generator.

"You know, Sam, if you catch pneumonia, you can sue their pants off."

"Actually, under your lights, I'm probably the most comfortable person in the room."

"Aye that. These HMIs do put out the heat." He stepped closer. "Listen, are you doing anything about Harlan's death?"

"What do you mean?"

He lowered his voice. "Rumor is Harlan was doing some work for you. Looking into the death back in forty-eight when he was a boy." He raised his hands palm out. "I'm not saying you're responsible. It's just that Harlan was a friend and if there was some sort of connection, I think you'd want to get to the truth. Everybody knows you'd do a better job than the Asheville police or Buncombe County deputies."

"What do you think happened?"

Ritchie stroked his beard. "That's the thing. I don't know. He must have thought something was important in that museum."

"Did you spend much time with Harlan?"

"Sometimes we'd sit together at lunch, but he didn't say anything that would lead me to believe something was troubling him." Ritchie paused. "Other than Roland."

"Roland?"

"Well, you know what a pain in the ass he can be. Mr. 'I'm an Author and You're Not.' I heard about the shouting match between him and Harlan. But Roland doesn't have the guts to do anything but spout off." Ritchie looked at me quizzically. "That is, if there's any talk about Harlan's death being more than an accident."

"No talk." And that was true. We were way beyond talk, but the case was Newly's to discuss, not mine. "There is one thing. Harlan happened to send me some pictures from his phone. We were talking about his duties here. Could you take a quick look and tell me why they'd be important?"

"Sure. Glad to."

I unwrapped my poncho from around the manila envelope and extracted the photos. Fortunately, Newly hadn't identified the prints as police property.

Ritchie quickly flipped through them. "Harlan probably took these for continuity. In case we had to come back and reshoot something. These group shots of the actors also show wardrobe."

"And that was part of Harlan's job?"

"Nah. He was just super conscientious. He was an advisor to Roland and the film, but also a good handyman. Even at his age, he put in a good day's work. I had to tell him to cool his jets a few times. He wasn't union and he'd take on a task he wasn't authorized to do."

"Did other members of the crew resent that?"

"Nah. Nobody felt threatened by Harlan. It's just that we have a very definite system of responsibilities."

"And why the shot of the lumber?"

Ritchie looked at that photo again. He shrugged. "He liked to check what was delivered. In case something went missing or an order was incomplete. He'd paint the ends of the boards as an identifying mark. He said it's what they used to do back during the days of the college. So the materials the scene shop purchased were not only to be used for construction but also to be used in an authentic way."

I looked at the photograph of cast members in front of the materials. "Was this for the construction scene?"

"Most likely. These roles would all be part of the construction scene."

"But you never shot it. The lumber was stolen, right?"

"Yes, but we shoot out of sequence. All of these actors might have already appeared in other scenes taking place the same day of the story, so continuity must be maintained when they come together."

"Got it. Thanks." Another thought crossed my mind. "You said Harlan knew a lot about handyman work. Did that extend to electricity?"

"Oh, yeah." Ritchie winked. "Sometimes I'd ignore the union rules and let him pull some power cables or top off the fuel in the generator. The man loved to work."

We wrapped the last shot of the morning and the crew broke for lunch. I decided to ditch the old leg for my good one and change back into my own clothes so I could spill as much food as I wanted. As I headed back toward the wardrobe room, I heard the producer Nancy Pellegatti shouting in her office.

"Goddamn it. I told you to leave her alone. The woman wants nothing to do with you. If you don't stop harassing her, I'll have you barred from the set."

"You can't do that. I have a contract."

I recognized Roland Cassidy's voice.

"A contract doesn't trump a restraining order," Pellegatti countered. "And that's what she'll get. I'm trying to be your friend here, Roland."

"Yeah, right. With friends like you and Marty, it's a wonder I don't have knives sticking out of my back. None of you would be here without me and my book."

"How can I forget? Now please leave before Nicole and I both get restraining orders."

I ducked into an empty room on the hall to avoid Cassidy and waited until his footsteps faded. Then I went to Pellegatti's office and knocked.

"What is it now?" she snapped.

I cracked the door and stuck my head in.

"Sorry, Sam. I thought you were somebody else." She stood behind a desk that was covered in four inches of paperwork. "What's up?"

"I'll just take a minute. I couldn't help but hear you and Roland. Were you talking about Nicole Madison?"

She shook her head. "I never discuss personnel matters."

I stepped into her office and closed the door. "I only ask because I know Nicole and Roland were supposed to be at dinner the night Harlan Beale died."

"That's true."

"I'm working with the police since Harlan was helping me with my case, and in light of what I heard, I wonder if that dinner was as amiable as Roland described."

Her eyes narrowed. "You think Roland had something to do with Harlan's death?"

"No. But if Nicole's not the friend Roland claims her to be, then it actually makes his involvement less likely. Why would Nicole lie about a dinner date for someone she doesn't like?"

Pellegatti walked around the desk. "This is not to leave my office, but Nicole felt sorry for him. She went to dinner only to show an interest in his writing. Roland had been hanging around her like a love-struck sixth grader. Since then, he's been insufferable, practically stalking her. She's my star. I can't have her upset, and if it takes a restraining order, then so be it."

I decided I'd leave Cassidy off my inquiry list for the day and hope the pain of his spurned affection would ease before I confronted him about the connection between his novel and Paul Weaver.

"Anything else?" Nancy Pellegatti asked.

"Yes. Harlan had called me the evening before he died. I think he was still here. Would he have clocked out that night?"

"The police already asked that. Harlan kind of kept his own schedule. Half the time he wasn't officially working. He just liked to be part of the team. Why?"

"He left me a message saying he had something to show me the next day." There was nothing to be gained by telling her about the phone in the dog food bag, so I kept my lie consistent with what I'd told Ritchie. "He did send me a couple of pictures. We'd been talking about his work on the film. I'm told these are for continuity."

"Possibly. I'll take a look."

I handed her the photographs one at a time. She studied each. Only two held her attention for a longer period: the cast in front of the construction materials and the stack of lumber.

"And he wanted to show you something?"

"That's what he said. Anything there seem odd?"

"We don't usually take photos of supplies, but they were also props for a scene. The others can be explained as continuity and nothing seems out of the ordinary. Let me see them one more time."

She examined the prints, again stopping on the photos with the lumber. Then she shrugged. "Sorry. Wish I could be more helpful."

"Thanks anyway. And I'll keep our conversation confidential."

Marty wrapped my scenes a little after two and I drove back to the office through a steady downpour. I checked in with Nakayla by phone and she told me she'd gotten Cory to help her search the property records for the Weavers. The farm had been sold in December of 1948 to Violet Baker's uncle. Tax stamps confirmed the price had been five thousand dollars, which seemed low for one hundred acres and a house. Nakayla also reported Eleanor Johnson and Leah Rosen had championed liberal causes in the nineteen-fifties and nineteen-sixties, but neither had ever been accused of Communist activities or even leanings. They were not subjects of Senator Joseph McCarthy's zealous anti-Communist actions or the House of Representative's infamous Committee on Un-American Activities. Neither woman was ever blacklisted.

I told Nakayla I'd managed to reach my buddy at Fort Bragg between scenes and he'd agreed to check records for Paul Weaver. I expected to hear from him in a day or two.

"How's Blue?" I asked.

"I don't know. He's been next door most of the day. When Hewitt came in this morning, Shirley told him he had to meet

the new employee at Blackman and Robertson. She didn't tell
Hewitt that employee was a dog. We were invited down for coffee.
I took his bed so Blue would have a place to lie down. Hewitt
laughed but didn't seem particularly impressed. He went back
to his office, and then Blue pulled his bed next to Hewitt's desk.
That was all it took. Blue made Hewitt the center of attention. He
got Hewitt's number pretty damn quick. How'd your shoot go?"

"I'll tell you when I get there."

"You had the early call. If you want to go straight to your
apartment, I'll wrap up here and bring Blue. Any ideas on what
you and I can do on a rainy afternoon?"

"We could discuss boxers and briefs," I said.

"Or neither."

"I think you got my number pretty damn quick."

• • ● • •

My cell phone rang on the nightstand. I heard it only a split-
second before Nakayla punched me in the ribs.

"This can't be good," she said.

I sat up in bed and hesitated only long enough to check the
time. Twelve-forty.

"Sam Blackman," I answered, my voice husky with sleep.

"Did you see Nancy Pellegatti yesterday?" The caller was
Newly.

Nakayla had been right. This couldn't be good.

"I did."

"Figures. She's dead. Throw on some clothes. Here's the
address."

Chapter Eighteen

Police tape had been strung across the driveway and angled to the edge of the main house on the left and a small guesthouse on the right. Three patrol cars, one unmarked cruiser, and an EMT vehicle were pulled up perpendicular to the tape. A group of curious neighbors in coats and pajamas stood in the middle of Rosewood Avenue in the Montford section of Asheville. They spoke in subdued murmurs.

Nakayla and I approached the perimeter and caught the eye of a uniformed officer. He was either Ted or Al Newland, the twin nephews of Detective Newland.

"Uncle Newly wants to see you."

I read "Al" on his name badge. "Can we cross?"

"No. Crime lab's on its way. Uncle Newly will be over shortly."

I looked beyond him to where a cluster of people stood outside the door to the guesthouse. The police were only letting in essential personnel.

"Have you been inside?" I asked Al.

"No. But my brother has. He was the first responder. The Farmers called it in."

"Farmers?"

"That's their name. Woody and Mickey Farmer. They live in the big house and were renting the guesthouse to the movie."

"They found the body?"

Al shrugged. "This isn't official. Ted said Mickey Farmer, she's the wife, heard an argument around ten when she took some garbage from her kitchen out to the bin. Then, about an hour later, she thought she heard a shot. I guess they went inside to check."

"Sam!"

I heard my name and turned back to the street. A silver Mercedes stopped in the middle. Marty Kolsrud jumped from the passenger's side and ran to us. In the flashing police lights, I could see tears streaked down his face.

"Tell me it's not true." He started to duck under the yellow tape, but Al stepped up and blocked his path.

"I'm sorry, sir. You need to stay here."

Marty clutched my arm. "What happened?"

"We don't know. Nakayla and I just got here. Detective Newland called me. The home owners heard an argument and then a shot. That's all the information I've got and that might not be accurate."

He released my arm and balled his hands into fists. "That goddamned Roland Cassidy."

"Was he here?" Nakayla asked.

"Probably. He and Nancy had a fight today. She told me he was pretty upset and that he'd go whining to Osteen."

I looked back at the Mercedes. Osteen was sliding out from behind the wheel.

"How did you hear?" I asked.

"The guy who owns the place phoned Arnold."

"You were with him?"

"Yes. Arnold called me earlier this evening and wanted to talk. He sent a car and I've been at his house since eight-thirty. We were going over some shooting options that could save some money."

"When did you last speak with Nancy?"

"Right after Arnold called. Usually we have a next-day planning session every evening, but when your executive producer summons, you go."

"And that's when she told you about Roland?"

"No. That had come up earlier." He wiped the tears off his face. "Actually, she was more pissed at Raymond Braxton."

"Who?"

"The state-approved CPA we have to work with. He has to examine all of our expenditures as to whether they qualify for the state's incentive program. The twenty-five percent return that Osteen's counting on to help fund the production."

"This isn't the time to worry about money." Osteen made the statement as he joined us. He looked at the guesthouse and sighed. "I can't believe it. Poor Nancy. And we'll finish this movie come hell or high water."

"We're not shooting tomorrow," Marty said.

"Of course not. Delay the rest of the week if you need to." He turned back to the house. "First Harlan and now Nancy. I wish I had more confidence in the police."

We stood in silence for a few minutes. Then Osteen said, "Would Blackman and Robertson be interested in working for me if the police aren't making progress?"

"Detective Newland's a good man," Nakayla said.

"But I'm sure he's got lots of cases."

"Let's give it forty-eight hours," I said. "Then we'll see where they are."

A few minutes later, Newly came down the driveway, stopped about ten feet away, and beckoned Nakayla and me to join him. Al lifted the crime scene tape and we ducked under. Newly slowly walked toward the main house, allowing us time to catch up.

"Did Osteen have anything to say?" Newly asked.

"No. Marty said Roland Cassidy and Nancy Pellegatti had a heated argument this afternoon. He doesn't know I overheard it. Cassidy has the hots for Nicole Madison. She considers him a stalker."

"Cassidy's the writer, right?"

"Yeah. Osteen's nephew."

Newly nodded as if that explained everything. "Writers. I've never met one yet who was in touch with reality. We'll pick him up for questioning."

We came to the back door of the main house.

"The Farmers have given us a room to use." Newly opened the

door and we followed him to a spacious den. Newly's partner, Tuck Efird, was sitting on a sofa, flipping through his notepad. A couple I took to be the Farmers were seated in armchairs. Everyone rose to greet us.

"Woody Farmer," the man said. He was around six feet tall and wore jeans and a blue flannel shirt. His hair was salt and pepper, heavy on the salt. I pegged him for late sixties.

"This is my wife, Mickey."

She appeared to be several years younger. Her black jogging suit looked more comfortable for relaxing than running, and I assumed they had been spending a quiet evening at home until…

"Sorry to meet under these circumstances," Nakayla said. Then she introduced us.

"Nakayla and Sam are working an overlapping case," Newly explained. "Normally, this would be an exclusive police matter but at this point we're looking for any connections." He glanced at Efird to make sure his partner was on board.

Efird flipped open his notepad. "If you wouldn't mind, I'd like you to repeat what you told me about tonight's events."

"All right," Woody said, "but would anyone like some coffee? Or something stronger?"

I must confess I could have used a stiff drink, but I said, "Coffee will be fine."

We all took seats and Efird walked the Farmers through their story. Mickey Farmer had carried out some garbage around ten and heard Nancy Pellegatti in a loud argument. The producer must have been close to the front door. She was telling someone to "stay the hell away from her." Mickey heard those words distinctly but not anyone else. She couldn't be sure if someone was there, or if Pellegatti was shouting into her phone. Mickey felt like she was eavesdropping so she went back into the house without listening further.

Newly and I exchanged a quick glance. The scenario fit a continuation of the argument she'd had with Cassidy in the afternoon.

"I mentioned it to Woody, but he was engrossed in one of his history books."

"You weren't concerned, Mr. Farmer?" Efird asked.

"Well, obviously I should have been. But, everybody knows these Hollywood people are high-strung. I thought someone had probably delivered the wrong brand of bottled water. Then about an hour later, we heard a shot. I told Mickey to stay here. I put down my book and slipped out the back door."

"Were you armed?" Efird asked.

"No. And as I was walking toward the guesthouse, I wished I had been. The lights both inside and out were off."

"Was that unusual?"

Woody nodded. "There's an exterior light by the front door that Ms. Pellegatti usually left on till eleven or later. And a small interior light burned all night. The sitting room is on ground level and the other rooms are up a short flight of six steps. I told her it was fine to leave it burning in case she got up in the middle of the night."

"Why didn't you call the police?" Efird asked.

"I didn't want to look like a damn fool. What if it was some prop gun that fired blanks? So, I listened at the door for a few minutes and when I heard nothing, I knocked. When I got no response, I tried the door and found it unlocked. I called out again, flipped on the main lights, and saw her body crumpled on the floor. Her eyes were open, unblinking. Blood pooled beneath her. I knew she was dead. I closed the door, ran to our house, and phoned 911. Then I waited in the driveway where I could both watch the guesthouse and meet the first responders."

Efird looked at Newly to see if his partner had any follow-up questions.

Newly said, "Have either of you heard similar arguments in the past?"

"No," Woody said. "I mean the lights are on late, like I said, and she'd have people in for meetings, but nothing out of the ordinary."

"So, you got along with her," Newly said.

I knew as a good investigator Newly had to rule out the Farmers as potential suspects. Too many times the perp turned out to be the person who claimed to have discovered the body.

"We rarely saw her," Woody said. "She worked fourteen- and sixteen-hour days."

"And as you waited for the first responders, did you see anything else?"

"No. I heard a car engine start down the block, but the vehicle didn't go speeding off."

"That's helpful," Newly said. "We'll canvas the neighbors to see if anyone heard or saw something unusual. My feeling is the killer turned off the lights in the guesthouse to make sure he wasn't seen leaving. He could have parked a block or two away and someone might have noticed him passing under a streetlamp." He turned to Nakayla and me. "Anything either of you would like to ask?"

I leaned forward in my chair. "Mr. Farmer, when did you call Arnold Osteen? Was it while you were waiting for the police?"

"No. I focused on the guesthouse. It was awful standing there knowing a body was inside. I called Arnold after Detectives Newland and Efird instructed us to wait in the house."

"Is Mr. Osteen a friend?"

"Not really. We know each other socially. No more than that. He approached me when looking for a place to house some of the movie people. He offered a fair rental rate and Mickey and I decided it would be fun to have a little Hollywood in our backyard."

"We have a daughter and son-in-law in the business in L.A.," Mickey said. "They produce documentaries for television. We know how stressful film production can be. Woody's even done historical research for some of their projects."

"Were you doing research for this film?" I asked Woody.

"No. I'm strictly on the sidelines."

"How much do you know about Black Mountain College?"

"I've read a few articles and visited the museum. I'm no expert."

I made a final attempt to find a link. "Do you happen to be an investor in Osteen's film?"

"No. Arnold only asked me about housing. That was the beginning and end of my involvement."

That was also the end of our questions. Newly and Efird thanked the Farmers for their cooperation.

Newly walked Nakayla and me to my car. "If you get any bright ideas, you've got my number."

"Tomorrow share what you can about the crime scene," I said. "There's got to be some connection to Harlan Beale's death."

"The only connection we know is your hot-tempered writer, Roland Cassidy, and we'll be grilling him soon enough."

I remembered Cassidy's desire to be kept close to Beale's murder investigation. He was certainly getting his wish.

Chapter Nineteen

At eight the next morning, Nakayla, Blue, and I arrived at the office. The day promised to be pivotal as we sought to re-interview Nadine Oates and Roland Cassidy. And Newly could have information regarding Nancy Pellegatti's death that might shed light on the killing of Harlan Beale.

"What would you think about taking Violet Baker with us when we see Nadine Oates?" Nakayla asked me.

We were enjoying a second cup of coffee, waiting for Shirley to arrive so we could hand off Blue.

"Why?"

"To encourage Nadine to be more truthful. When I updated Violet yesterday, she said she remembered Nadine well. There was talk among the families that Paul and Nadine might marry."

"And the war changed that."

"Maybe the war and Black Mountain College." Nakayla set her cup on the coffee table. "Leah said Nadine made a scene in town when she saw the two of them together. Paul Weaver's desire to attend college might have been the major factor for breaking up with Nadine. She might be fabricating other reasons that she'd have to abandon in Violet's presence."

"Sure," I said. "It's worth a shot. See if we can pick her up this morning."

Nakayla went to her office to contact Violet. I mulled over the core question that personally dogged me: What had Harlan Beale wanted to show me?

My cell phone buzzed. The ID screen flashed "Armitage."

"Nathan?"

"Hey, Sam. Hope I didn't wake you."

"Would you believe I'm in the office?"

"No." He paused. "Unless you were tied into the shooting of that film producer last night."

"We don't know what's a tie-in and what's a loose end. But, yes, that's why we're in early."

"I read the story in the online edition of the paper," Nathan said. "It reminded me I hadn't gotten back to you about the CopBeat."

"The what?"

"The security alarm at the Black Mountain College Museum."

"Right." I realized my mind was too scattered if I couldn't remember the disabled device. "Any explanation for why it didn't work?"

"It's a fairly decent brand. More for a consumer market than anything we would install. There are a couple of possibilities. An electronic relay could have failed and when the power and phone lines were cut, it didn't resource the battery. Or the charge could have been depleted. At some point earlier, the building lost power, the alarm drained the battery, and it didn't recharge."

"How much earlier?"

"Hard to say. Theoretically, it could have been any time after the installation. You could check Duke Energy for a record of power losses. Are the police conducting a forensic exam?"

"Probably nothing more than dusting for prints."

"Well, if the battery has a charge, then we rule out the power loss."

"Which leaves the faulty relay."

"Yes." Nathan paused again. "Of course, there's one other possibility."

"What's that?"

The alarm was deactivated by someone entering the code and then cutting the power and phone lines to make that look like the cause of the failure."

"Can you prove that?"

"No, but I can make it more probable if I examine the unit."

I mentally kicked myself for overlooking that possibility. I figured Newly had done the same. We saw a sabotaged alarm and looked no further.

"Thanks, Nathan. I'll be back in touch."

I started to dial Newly when a knock came from the hallway door. Blue lifted his head and gave a low growl. From his reaction, I knew it wasn't Shirley.

I grabbed Blue's collar. "Come in."

Dustin Henry entered. The actor carried himself like he was walking onto the bridge of his starship. I hadn't seen him since we'd both witnessed Roland Cassidy's rant against Harlan Beale.

"Sam, I hope you don't mind me dropping in unannounced. I was in the area."

Captain Jefferson was standing in my office. Of course, I didn't mind. "Not at all, sir. It's just me and Nakayla. She's on the phone. Would you like coffee?" I released Blue and he lay down, judging our intruder to be harmless.

"No, thanks. But I would like to talk a few minutes, if you have the time."

I motioned for him to take one of the leather chairs. Nakayla's door opened and Dustin turned to greet her.

"Please sit," she said. "Will you have coffee?"

"Thank you, but Sam already offered. I won't be here that long."

"We have time." Nakayla looked at me. "We're picking up Violet Baker at nine-thirty."

She sat on the sofa, knowing Dustin was too much of a gentleman to sit first. He and I took the chairs.

"What would you like to discuss?" I asked.

Dustin Henry's face was composed, but I noticed his hands were balled tightly atop his thighs.

"Do you have any information on what happened to Nancy?"

"No," I said. "Only that she was shot."

"Marty called me at two this morning and broke the news. He knew I'd grown fond of Nancy. She was an excellent, no-nonsense producer, and I've worked with quite a few in my career who weren't of her caliber. Marty said you were at the house with the police. I thought maybe you had more information than what was on the TV this morning."

Even though we did have more information, I didn't feel at liberty to share it. I would reinforce what I knew Marty must have told him.

"All I heard was that Nancy and Roland had a shouting match at the production office."

Dustin shook his head. "Roland Cassidy is all talk. She told me about it at dinner last night."

"You were with her?" I asked.

"Yes. At Rhubarb. We grabbed a quick bite at seven."

Rhubarb was a casual but superb restaurant on the ground floor of my office building.

"Nancy mentioned your address was the third floor and she was thinking of talking to you."

"About what?" Nakayla asked.

"Phillips Building Supplies."

The name sounded familiar. Then I remembered we'd seen their truck delivering the replacement lumber and materials to the movie location.

"Did she say why?" Nakayla asked.

"She said she wanted to see their invoices, but that Raymond Braxton wouldn't let her."

I recognized the name. "He's the accountant, right?"

"Yes. The state makes any film receiving incentives use a state-approved accountant to verify expenses qualifying for a grant. The receipts have to be from North Carolina companies or labor. Braxton claimed those invoices from Phillips Building Supplies had been paid and forwarded to Raleigh. And Braxton argued that Nancy had already approved them."

"Why did she want to review them?"

"I've been in the film business a long time, not only as an actor, but I've also produced a project or two. You know what's the most creative part of making a motion picture?"

I shrugged, but Nakayla said, "The accounting department."

"Correct. Nancy said she thought Arnold Osteen might be getting cheated and wanted to look at the receipts again."

"Where do we fit into that request?" I asked.

Dustin leaned forward and lowered his voice as if he thought our office was bugged. "She didn't say exactly. But you evidently showed her some photographs yesterday and she wanted to talk to you. She wouldn't tell me anything more."

The only photographs we had were from Harlan Beale's cell phone.

I stood. "Let me get something from my desk." I retrieved the manila envelope Newly had given me with the scans of the photographs. If Nancy was concerned with Phillips Building Supplies, then I needed to examine the photos of the construction materials more carefully. I pulled the one of the cast members beside the lumber stack and then the closer view of just the stack. I returned to the conference area and set the two pictures on the coffee table.

"There must be something here, Dustin. You're in the cast photo. See anything unusual?"

Dustin Henry lifted the picture and studied it closely. "No. We were discussing the first construction scene that was supposed to take place the next day. But, that night the materials were stolen." He laid the picture down and picked up the second. "This second picture must be Harlan photographing the new inventory. Maybe Nancy counted the boards."

I took it from him. You could count the boards by looking at the ends. Then, it struck me. "Let me see the cast picture."

Dustin handed it to me. The lumber pile was smaller in the frame. "Nakayla, do you have a magnifying glass?"

"In my desk drawer."

She brought me the old-fashion lens reminiscent of Sherlock Holmes. I held it over each picture and saw the difference. I also felt I knew what Harlan had wanted to show me.

Nakayla and Dustin Henry looked over my shoulder.

"See, the ends of the boards in the cast picture have white marks on them. Harlan had tagged the boards for the scene so they wouldn't be used in other set construction. Now, look at the second photograph. Some of the boards have a light blue tag, others are white, and the rest are unmarked. It's not the same stack of lumber."

"The second one is the replacement delivery," Dustin said.

"The stolen materials must have gone back to Phillips Building Supplies," Nakayla said. "Then some of the original boards were loaded into the replacement order."

"That's what Harlan wanted to show me," I said. "I saw the light blue paint where Harlan was working the afternoon before he was killed. Maybe he just grabbed whatever paint bucket was nearly empty. He started marking the new delivery and then he noticed the white markings."

Dustin Henry started pacing. "Would Nancy and Harlan be killed over a load of lumber? And Harlan was found in the museum. How does that fit?"

"It doesn't," I said, "so maybe we should stop trying to make it."

"We provided a ready-made diversion," Nakayla said. "Everyone on the movie set knew we were researching the college."

Dustin stopped. "You mean whoever killed Harlan tried to force a link to your cold case?"

"We have to consider the possibility," I said. "Both Nancy and Harlan could have asked questions about the stolen supplies. But, the lumber's been burned so we have no evidence. The building supplier will argue those boards with the white ends had been added on-site and didn't come with their replacement load."

"What do we do?" Dustin Henry asked.

"We do nothing right now," I said. "I'll speak to Detective Newland of the Asheville Police Department about what we suspect."

Dustin Henry stared out the window at Beaucatcher Mountain, the high ridge walling in the eastern side of the city. "How would the lumber company know about your interest in Paul Weaver?"

"They wouldn't," I said.

"So, the idea to relocate Harlan Beale's body had to come from somewhere else," Dustin said. "Someone familiar with your involvement with him."

"Yes. Someone involved with the movie." I gestured for Dustin and Nakayla to sit back down. "What's this Raymond Braxton like?"

"Typical bean counter," Dustin said. "He's probably early forties. He's pudgy, balding, and has the personality of a cucumber. He's from the eastern part of the state."

I remembered seeing the man he described with Camille Brooks as she chewed out someone from Phillips Building Supplies on the phone. "And he's state-approved?"

"Yes. My understanding is the Department of Commerce has a list of CPAs certified to conduct these audits on any film applying for a North Carolina Film Grant."

"So, if Arnold Osteen was being ripped off and deliverables were less than invoiced, or stolen materials were resold, Braxton should catch that as part of his review."

Dustin shrugged. "He would be one of the checkpoints. A department head could be another. And a sharp-eyed line producer like Nancy would be in a position to examine all outgoing expenses."

"And she and Braxton had an argument yesterday?" I asked.

"That's right," Dustin confirmed. "Braxton's worth checking out." He looked at me and then Nakayla. "You still want to do nothing?"

"With Phillips Building Supplies, yes," I said. "Because if they're confronted, everyone in the conspiracy could go to ground. Any evidence would be destroyed. Look what was done to the lumber."

Nakayla nodded. "It would be premature, Dustin."

"But," I added, "if we could get a look at Braxton's files, his reports and expense approvals might confirm our suspicions."

"Will you know what you're looking for?" Dustin Henry asked.

"Probably not. But I know someone who would. I just need to get her the records."

Nakayla arched an eyebrow but said nothing.

"Braxton keeps the key to the accounting office," Dustin said. "I don't think the cleaning crew even goes in there if he's not present."

"Who else would have a key?" I asked.

"There's a master that Arnold carries. Do you want him to know what you're doing?"

I remembered the first time I saw Osteen, roaring at the staff because of the theft of the construction supplies. "No. He'd blow up if he thought someone was stealing from him. Better to wait till we have definitive proof."

"So, does this mean breaking-and-entering?" Dustin asked.

"That would be breaking the law. If we knew about it, we'd be obligated to report such an action to the police."

Dustin Henry nodded. "They say ignorance is bliss. I'm feeling very blissful and would like to remain so."

As soon as the actor left, Nakayla fixed me with a disapproving eye. "Are you really thinking of breaking into the accounting office?"

"No. At least not as our first option. I'd prefer to be invited in."

"By whom?"

"By the person who can get me the key."

"Who's that?"

"I don't know. That's the temporary flaw in my plan."

Nakayla laughed. "Why don't you asked Roland Cassidy? He wants to be close to the case."

"Good idea. Who better to get Arnold Osteen's master key than his nephew?"

"I was kidding. For God's sake, he could be the killer."

"Do you believe that?"

"You're the one who heard Nancy and him arguing."

I pulled my cell phone from my belt.

"Who are you calling?" Nakayla asked.

"Newly. Let's see if Cassidy's still in his suspect pool."

I speed-dialed Newly's cell, not wanting to go through the police switchboard.

No hello. Just a gruff, "You solved my case yet?"

"Good morning to you, too. And I'm working on it. You have any luck with Cassidy?"

"He's off the hook," Newly said. "He was in the lower bar of The Thirsty Monk till midnight. Bartender vouched for him. Cassidy admitted calling Pellegatti around ten after a couple of beers. He claimed he was trying to apologize for a misunderstanding, but Pellegatti shouted at him and hung up."

"Did he admit she said the words Mickey Farmer heard— 'Stay the hell away from her?'"

"Yes. And that she had bigger problems than dealing with him."

"What kind of problems?"

"She didn't tell him. He sensed she was pissed about something and his phone call came at the wrong time."

I decided withholding what we'd identified on Harlan Beale's two photos was the wrong move. Newly needed to know.

"I think we've discovered why Pellegatti was upset." Newly listened to my explanation without interrupting. I didn't pass along Dustin Henry's comment that the CPA Raymond Braxton could be a member of a conspiracy over billing Osteen. I did suggest the Phillips Building Supplies theft could have been an inside job involving a production staffer.

"Take it slow, you're telling me," Newly said.

"I'd never presume to tell you how to run your case."

"Right. Well, it was damn good work spotting the board markers. But don't let it go to your head."

"One other thing. What kind of forensics did you run on the museum's security alarm?"

"Prints. Why?"

"Nathan Armitage suggests checking the battery to see if it was drained. That could help determine how the device was disabled. He offered to look at it."

Newly grunted. "Not a bad idea. I'll give him a call."

"What will you do about Beale's photographs?"

"Tuck and I will pay a visit to the set construction crew to confirm that Beale did mark the boards. Since all we have are ashes for evidence, we'll go to the supplier and find out who assembled the truckload and request copies of any invoices or itemized order lists."

"Would you get copies for me?"

Newly was silent a few seconds. "How could that possibly be related to your cold case?"

"I don't know. That's why I'd like to see them."

"Right. And how are you doing with those pals you've invited to the party?"

The question startled me as I thought he meant Roland Cassidy. "Who?"

"The FBI. The U.S. Army. You mean they haven't deployed teams of experts to help you?"

"Hey, they've had so many volunteers, they're still selecting the cream of the crop."

Newly laughed. "In other words, no word."

"In a word, yes." I disconnected.

I went to my desk, took a fresh notepad from the drawer, and began jotting down questions I'd ask Nadine Oates and Roland Cassidy. The main office door opened and I wheeled my chair to where I could see who had entered. I expected Shirley but was surprised to see Hewitt Donaldson.

"Hey, Blue. It's your pal, Hewitt."

Nakayla rolled her desk chair in her doorway, but Hewitt ignored both of us and whistled for the coonhound. Blue loped over to the attorney and sat. Hewitt patted him vigorously on the side. Only then did he acknowledge our presence.

"Shirley had some car trouble this morning. I can take Blue to my office."

Hewitt was dressed in his normal office attire—a brilliant Hawaiian shirt that looked like it was powered by batteries, faded jeans, and zip-up boots of brushed suede. His white hair hung to his shoulders, a sign that he wouldn't be in court today, otherwise his locks would have been pulled back in a ponytail.

"Thanks," I said. "We should be back mid-afternoon, if that's not a problem."

"No problem at all. Mind if I take Blue for a spin at lunch? The temperature's mild and I'll crack the windows."

Hewitt drove a Jaguar, a far cry from Harlan Beale's pickup. Ol' Blue was cultivating expensive tastes.

"That's fine." Nakayla handed Hewitt the leather leash Shirley had purchased.

An idea struck me. "Hewitt, I know you only do defense cases, but do you think Shirley or Cory could do a little corporate work for us? It's for a case."

"Sure. What do you need?"

"I'd like to find out about a local seller of construction materials. Phillips Building Supplies."

He repeated the name. "What do you want to know?"

"Whatever. Are their corporate filings up-to-date? Any liens or judgments against them? Who are the owners and what's the company structure?"

"Are they culpable for anything?"

"Maybe some invoicing irregularities. Right now it's just a due diligence test. But I want it done thoroughly and professionally. I know you're a hack, but Shirley and Cory are top-notch."

Hewitt tossed his head in mock indignation. "Come along, Blue. These people wouldn't know a *habeas corpus* from a haberdasher's corpse."

"Spoken by a haberdasher's nightmare," I said.

But Hewitt and Blue were already out the door.

Chapter Twenty

Nakayla and I were on our way to pick up Violet Baker when I got a call from Captain Bret Nolan, the officer at Fort Bragg I'd contacted regarding Paul Weaver. Nolan was a lifer and we'd served together in Iraq.

"Well, I've got some information for you," Nolan said. "I'd feel more comfortable just telling you rather than sending anything in writing."

I knew a paper trail could circle back to bite him since he'd undertaken the personnel search without an official request.

"That's fine, Bret. If I need something official, I'll come back through proper channels. Is it okay if I put you on speaker so my partner can hear?"

"Sure."

Nakayla pulled a notepad and pen from her handbag as I activated the phone's speaker.

"Okay, give me what you've got."

"Your information about Weaver's attachment to the Black Panthers really narrowed the search."

Nakayla looked at me quizzically. "Black Panthers?" she asked.

"Yeah," Nolan answered. "That was the nickname for their battalion. They had a black panther for a patch and the motto 'Come Out Fighting.' Weaver was one of a few white officers assigned to them. He would have been at the Battle of the Bulge. After the war, the unit was deactivated in June of 1946. Weaver had been given an honorable medical discharge a month earlier."

"Medical?" I asked.

"Yes. A diesel storage tank exploded at one of the occupational sites. Suspected sabotage. Weaver wasn't burned but he suffered severe smoke inhalation. He was transferred stateside to the VA hospital in Asheville."

"That's where I had rehab."

"He received some small disability payment for chronic asthma aggravated by the explosion and was receiving medication at the time of his death."

The inhaler Leah Rosen described, I thought. "If he was under the care of the VA, would they have received an official death notification?"

"Not in the records I have. But if the disability checks were returned, they would have eventually been discontinued. I also expect Weaver would have been required to see a VA doctor periodically to monitor his condition."

"You mean to see if he should still get his benefits," I said.

"Hey, you know the drill, Sam."

"All too well. Listen, I don't know much about the 761st. Were they involved in any liberations of concentration camps?"

"Yes. The satellite of Mauthausen, a smaller camp named Gunskirchen. One of the lesser-known but still filled with walking skeletons and littered with corpses. Must have been a hell of a thing to witness."

"Yeah," I agreed, "must have been."

I thanked Nolan and disconnected.

"What are you thinking?" Nakayla asked.

"That we need to learn more about Paul Weaver's medical condition. Everything Leah Rosen said checks out with what Nolan just told us. I think it's time for me to revisit my caregivers at the VA."

Violet Baker was watching for us from the bay window of her Golden Oaks cottage. She came out wearing a smartly tailored gray pantsuit, but with no jewelry. Her makeup was more lightly applied than when we'd first met for lunch, and I deduced she was trying to strike a balance between sophistication and her down-home roots. After all, we were headed to see a woman who was probably in a housecoat and talking to her pet raccoon.

We'd gone a few miles exchanging pleasantries when I said, "I've learned from Leah Rosen and U.S. Army records that your brother had a medical discharge from the service. Do you remember anything about that?"

I glanced at Violet in the rearview mirror and saw her stare out the side window as she searched her memory.

"Are you talking about the breath?"

"Yes. Did you ever see him have trouble breathing?"

"Paul usually carried an inhaler with him. He called it his breath. Told me he always kept a few extra ones in it."

"Did he use it often?"

"No. At least not in front of me." She hesitated. "I do remember one time that really scared me. We'd had three days of heavy rain, and the creek behind our house was transformed from a babbling brook to a roiling river. Paul had been home a few weeks and we walked out to survey the mountain runoff. The normally clear water was brown with soil swept from the hillsides. I ventured too close to the edge, not realizing the current had carved out the bank beneath me. The lip broke away and I tumbled in. The torrent propelled me downstream.

"I heard Paul yelling, 'Feet first,' and I swung around so that any collision with a rock or log would not be with my head. About a hundred feet downstream, the channel veered sharply right and I was able to latch onto an exposed tree root in the left bank. Paul called from above me to hold on tight. He lay down on the wet ground and reached for me. Clutching my wrist, he told me to let go of the root. He hauled me to safety.

"I was crying, but when I looked at his face, I stopped. He'd gone red as a ripe tomato and was breathing in short gasps. 'My breath,' he managed to say.

"I ran to the house as fast as I could in my soaked clothes and shoes. I'd seen the inhaler on his dresser. I screamed for mother and father as I tore through the house. They followed me back to my brother who crammed the inhaler's nozzle in his mouth and gave three hard pumps.

"It took several minutes before his gasps slowed to deep breaths. 'Thanks, Vi,' he told me. Then he laughed and tousled my wet hair. 'Bet I looked like a fish out of water. Good thing you were with me.'

"Then it struck me that he had pulled me from the water and if he hadn't been with me, I would have drowned."

"How old were you?" Nakayla asked.

"This was in August of 1946. Paul moved out of the house the next month when he started at Black Mountain College. So, I would have been nine."

In the rearview mirror, I saw her look out at the passing pastures. "Funny," she said, "I haven't thought about that day in years, but I can feel my heart racing just talking about it."

As we started down the road to Nadine Oates' house, I suggested that Nakayla and Violet stay in the CR-V until I'd spoken with Nadine. That way she wouldn't feel outnumbered until I explained why we were there. Actually, I didn't want either Violet or Nakayla exposed to a woman whose initial greeting included a shotgun.

The maroon Taurus was still in the metal carport. I parked farther away from the house than on my previous visit, and before I left the driver's seat, I noticed Nakayla bury her hand inside the handbag on her lap. She gave a slight nod and I understood her fingers were wrapped around the butt of her Colt semiautomatic.

I had walked about ten yards toward the house when Nadine burst through the front door, her shotgun barrel in the crook of her left arm.

"I thought I told you to stay the hell off my property. Can't you hear?"

I kept walking. "I heard. I also heard you say you hardly knew Paul Weaver, and we both know that's a lie."

She immediately jerked the shotgun butt to her shoulder and fired. The boom of the twelve-gauge sounded like a cannon. As the echo reverberated through the hills, pieces of shredded leaves from the tree behind me drifted past. I wasn't stupid. I stopped.

"Naydee!" The cry came from my car.

I turned to see Violet Baker running toward me, an eighty-year-old unconcerned that she was charging an armed lunatic.

"Naydee, stop!" Violet halted in front of me, placing herself in the line of fire.

Sam Blackman, combat-tested, thirteen-year U.S. Army veteran, was being shielded by an octogenarian.

"I'm Vi. Vi Weaver. Why would you deny my brother? What happened to him?"

I moved to the side where I could see Nadine Oates. In my peripheral vision I saw Nakayla step up on the other side of Violet Baker, her hand still in her handbag.

Nadine lowered the shotgun. "Vi? Is that you?"

"Yes, and you have no call to welcome us this way."

"I didn't know you were with them." The old woman's voice cracked as she stifled a sob.

"No. I'm not with them. They're with me. I want to know what happened to Paul. If you are hiding something by denying you knew him, then you are being cruel, Naydee. Cruel and complicit." Violet started walking toward Nadine. "And that's not who you are. Not the girl I looked up to."

Nadine's eyes dropped down to the shotgun. Her shoulders started shaking. Then she hurled the weapon into the weed-strewn yard and collapsed.

Nakayla and I lifted the sobbing woman onto the old sofa on her porch. Violet sat beside her but said nothing.

Between gasps for air, we heard her mumbling, "Communists. Somebody had to stop them. Somebody had to stop that Communist whore." Then she stiffened as if a steely resolve infused her backbone. She turned to stare at Violet as if trying to find the face of the little girl she'd known nearly seventy years ago. The initial shock of hearing what must have been her childhood nickname had worn off, and the hardened personality of the recluse reasserted itself.

"I did nothing to Paul. It was them."

"Who?" Violet Baker asked.

But Nadine ignored the question. Instead she eyed the shotgun lying on the ground. I could tell she was calculating how quickly she could retrieve it.

"Git off my property. Git before I sic the law on you." She stood. "Or worse. We'll see how you like the men in the suits."

Violet reached out and grabbed Nadine's arm. "Please, Naydee. What happened to my brother?"

But Nadine Oates struggled free, jumped from the porch, and hurried toward the gun.

"We're leaving," I yelled. "So you can take your conscience back into the dark with your raccoon. We'll find the truth without you."

I helped Violet from the sagging sofa and kept my eye on Nadine as I backpedaled to the car. She stood holding the gun by her side, her stringy, white hair blowing in the breeze like jellyfish tentacles. A Medusa who had turned her own heart to stone.

I strongly suspected she'd contributed to Paul Weaver's death. Now, I had to prove it.

Chapter Twenty-one

Our encounter with Nadine Oates led to a revision in our plans for the rest of the day. Since a connection between the death of Paul Weaver and the murders of Harlan Beale and Nancy Pellegatti continued to be elusive, we needed to treat them as separate events and not be limiting our interpretation of facts to what might be an invalid theory—namely, that our search for the truth about Weaver's death had unleashed a present-day murderer. Theories follow facts, not the other way around, although in several of our earlier cases, past murders decades-old had done just that.

We took Violet Baker back to her cottage. She was shaken by Nadine's hostility and extremely disappointed that the old woman appeared to be a dead end. I assured her we weren't discouraged and that the confrontation was merely a setback. We would keep her updated.

As soon as Violet disappeared through her front door, Nakayla asked, "What do you want to do now?"

"Split up. I'll drop you at the office. See if Shirley or Cory have had any luck with the background check on Phillips Building Supplies. And do you think you could find out if there was ever any conflict between Black Mountain College and law enforcement agencies?"

"What kind of conflict?"

"I don't know. I realize that makes it difficult to research any police records that might not be indexed in a way that any complaints or incident reports can be easily retrieved."

"What are you going to do?"

"See Roland Cassidy. And since I believe he's enamored with you, he might be more forthcoming, with less preening and posturing, if it's just me. Then I'll go after the common thread to both Violet's and Nadine's stories."

Nakayla smiled. "I wondered when you'd get to that."

"Get to what?" I asked, teasing her to prove she really had picked up on the significant point.

"The heart of our case. The men in suits."

Roland Cassidy lived in a moderately sized stone house on a side street off Macon Avenue, the road that wound its way up Sunset Mountain to the historic Grove Park Inn. I'd called ahead and told Cassidy I wanted to see him about Harlan Beale. I'd said I knew they weren't shooting today and asked if he would have some time to talk. He'd jumped at the chance.

The first words out of his mouth when he opened his front door were, "The police came to my house in the middle of the night. They thought I'd killed Nancy."

"Really?"

"Yes. Can you believe it? Nancy and I had a misunderstanding yesterday that someone must have overheard. But there was nothing to it. Fortunately, I was at The Thirsty Monk when she was killed."

"Roland, may I come in?"

Only then did he realize I was still standing outside with the threshold between us.

"Oh, my, yes." He stepped aside. "Please come in. I've got coffee set in the den."

I entered a black-and-white-tiled foyer and followed Cassidy to a room on the left that was paneled in rich chestnut and furnished like the movies portrayed a British gentlemen's club— overstuffed sofa and chairs, a Persian carpet, fox-hunting prints, and a few deer heads that I figured he bought on eBay. A silver coffee set was centered on a wooden table in front of the sofa.

Cassidy beamed at me. "Here's where the magic happens." He pointed to a rolltop desk in one corner. "I wrote *Love Among the Ridges* right there. Refused to budge until I'd penned my fifteen-hundred-a-day word quota."

"Does the chair double as a toilet?"

Cassidy jerked his head back like I'd thrown a phantom punch. Then he laughed. "No, but that's a good idea. I could probably turn out two thousand words a day." He gestured for me to sit in a wingback chair and then went to the serving tray. "How do you like your coffee?"

I didn't want any, but I saw he'd gone to the trouble to impress me. "Black is fine."

"Good, because I don't have any real cream or unrefined sugar. My last live-in girlfriend was a cashier at Whole Foods and a stickler for organic."

"Last live-in girlfriend?"

Cassidy gave an exaggerated shrug. "We broke up a few weeks ago. Same story. They want to get married, which I find so conventional."

Translation: the dweeb couldn't find someone to marry him, I thought. No girlfriend and now he's sniffing around the lead actress, Nicole Madison.

"Well, no one can call you conventional," I said, looking straight-faced at the writer who evidently sat in his house wearing his tweed jacket that must insulate him from irony.

"So true, sir." He filled a bone china cup and brought it to me. Then he poured one for himself and sat on the sofa. "I take it you have news regarding Harlan?"

"Roland, what I can share must go no farther than this room. Certainly not into your wordsmith creations…at least not until our investigation is finished."

His eyes brightened. "Of course. Even Dr. Watson wouldn't chronicle Sherlock's case prematurely."

The prospect of Cassidy being our witness to the public flipped my stomach.

"Fine," I managed to say. "Nakayla and I believe Harlan had discovered that your uncle and his investors are being cheated."

"Cheated? How?"

"Some of the construction materials that were stolen showed up again in the replacement delivery. We don't know whether the supplier was behind it or if some third party committed the theft and then resold the lumber to the supplier."

"Have you told my uncle?"

"No. What do you think he would do?"

"Blow his stack."

I nodded. "That's why we can't tell him until we have more evidence to present."

"What are the police doing?"

"At this point, they're quietly asking questions and they might discover the culprit behind the scam." I leaned forward. "But, Roland, the sensitive part is that there's a good chance this theft goes to the inside of the film staff. Nancy Pellegatti had an argument with the state accountant, Raymond Braxton, because he wouldn't produce the two invoices for the construction materials. He claimed they'd already gone to Raleigh."

Cassidy frowned. "That doesn't make sense. Braxton reviews qualified expenses but they're not filed with the Film Office and Secretary of Commerce until the project has wrapped and all qualifying invoices are in."

"And Nancy would have known that?"

"Sure. But she was approving expenses that she negotiated and then sent on to Braxton. He should have had them."

"And she had approval power?"

"Yes. My uncle and she would meet every few days to review where they stood. Nancy could shift money around in categories, but he approved overages. The budget was set at ten million."

"Which is why he had to approve the re-order of construction materials that morning we first met you."

"Exactly. Also Uncle Arnold was to be informed if some vendor went from in-state to out-of-state."

"Because of the incentives?"

"Yes. He'd lose the rebate."

I thought for a moment whether the theft and resell could benefit anyone but the supplier. If Nancy approved the invoices and Braxton reviewed them for incentive qualifications and paid them, why would Braxton not want to show Nancy Pellegatti the invoices? Could he have doctored them to get a kickback? The possibility reaffirmed why I was there with Cassidy. I needed to see the accounting records.

"Roland, I have something very serious to ask you."

"What?"

"I understand Braxton locks the accounting office with a key no one else has other than your uncle's master."

"That's not entirely true. My uncle was afraid he might lose his so he had me make a duplicate. He wasn't supposed to, per the lease agreement, but my uncle does what he wants."

"Where is this extra key?"

Cassidy grinned. "On my key ring."

I left after we'd worked up a plan. Unfortunately, Cassidy insisted on writing a role for himself.

• • ● • •

I have found when dealing with a bureaucracy the best approach is often to approach it at the highest level you can. So, after leaving Cassidy, I decided to go up the food chain in the land of the suits.

The FBI Resident Agency was in the Federal Courthouse on Patton Avenue and I had to clear through security before going to the second floor. The FBI office door was locked but a buzzer alerted someone inside that I sought admittance.

The door opened and a black man about my age said, "I'm Special Agent Vance Gilmore. How can we help you?"

I held up my P.I. identification for his inspection. "I'm Sam Blackman. I'd like to see Special Agent Lindsay Boyce."

"Yes, Mr. Blackman. Is she expecting you?"

I gave my most winning smile. "Call me Sam, and not at all. But it's about a case I'm working and I'm making a courtesy call because my investigation is about to cross into the Bureau. I didn't want her blindsided."

I'd worked with Boyce a few times in the past. Although the FBI didn't like private detectives or local law enforcement getting involved in their cases, Boyce and I had never had a confrontation. I learned how to navigate bureaucratic turf when I'd worked for the largest bureaucracy in the country—the U.S. Army. And I'd learned Boyce's uncle was a sheriff in one of the neighboring counties, which made her more open to working outside agency confines.

Gilmore returned in a few minutes with Boyce behind him. She looked as she always looked—pinstripe navy pantsuit, short brown hair that complemented her tanned face and the pale blue eyes that could equally sweep a room or bore into anyone who drew her interest.

She smiled, but those eyes locked on me with piercing intensity.

"Mr. Blackman." She offered her hand. "Good to see you again. Agent Gilmore says you have some information for me."

"It's Sam, please. And, yes, information coupled with some questions."

"Then let's go to my office."

I made a point of shaking Gilmore's hand before following Boyce down a short hall. You can't have too many friends in the FBI.

Her office was sparsely furnished with a desk stacked with folders, a laptop on a side credenza, and a single guest chair. The walls were devoid of diplomas, plaques, and commendations. The only picture was a large framed photograph hanging on the wall across from her desk—a yellow lab splashing in a rock-lined pool at the base of a mountain waterfall. Normally, I'd only glance at such a picture for a second and forget it. But, with Blue in my life, I was noticing dogs everywhere.

I stepped closer to admire it. "Is that your dog or do you just like the photograph?"

Her face lit up. "That's my Jewel. She's eight but still has the energy of a puppy."

I noticed Boyce's left hand was minus a wedding ring. "But you must work long hours. What do you do with her during the day?"

"If I can break away for lunch, I'll run home for a quick walk. Otherwise, I use a walking service."

"You mean you pay someone?"

She laughed. "Yes. It's a growing business in town. There are days I've thought about a career change." Her blue eyes studied me. "You have a dog?"

"Sort of. Right now he's communal property between us and the law firm next door." I told her about Beale's murder and Blue and Nadine with her raccoon Ricky that nixed her as a coonhound heir.

Boyce motioned for me to sit in the guest chair. She stepped behind her desk, sat, and fished out a business card from a drawer. "Here's the service I use. 'Lease A Leash.' They're very reliable, and if Blue likes other dogs, they can arrange a playdate."

"Like a social mixer?"

"Yes. But without the small talk."

Her expression turned serious and I knew the small talk was over.

"What do you have to tell me, Sam?"

"I'm looking into a suspicious death from 1948."

Her eyebrows arched. "Really? And you think the Bureau's involved?"

"Not necessarily. But I'm exploring the context of the times and that involves the Bureau."

Boyce said nothing but waited for an explanation.

"Nice suit," I said.

Her eyes flickered with uncertainty. "What?"

"You're wearing a nice suit. Agent Gilmore has a nice suit. That's what I've learned from people close to the deceased in

1948. The investigation seemed to be crawling with nice suits. Now, nothing against the Buncombe County Sheriff's Department, but they are not known for wearing nice suits. I suspect in 1948 the detectives wore ill-fitting sport coats and lunch-stained ties. Extremely forgettable to the rest of the locals."

Boyce shook her head. "I'm sorry, Sam, I'm not following where this is going."

"Suits, to me, says FBI or some other government agency. And all the records of this man's death, Paul Weaver, have disappeared—police reports, coroner inquest documents, county death certificate, even an M.E. copy that should have gone to Raleigh."

"You think the Bureau's responsible for expunging documents?"

"Well, the documents existed because the death was reported in the local papers. It happened and paperwork should be there."

"How did Weaver die?"

"Fell while hiking was the information released. But I've found no definitive location and his sister says he was raised in these hills and could walk them blindfolded."

"And your interest now?"

"We've been hired by the sister to find some closure to the case. A few days into the investigation, a man helping us was murdered. Harlan Beale. You might have heard about it. His body was discovered in the Black Mountain College Museum."

Boyce nodded. "I did. You're saying it's linked to the Weaver death?"

"I'm saying I don't like coincidences. Harlan Beale was also aiding the production of the movie shooting on the old site of Black Mountain College. The night before last the producer was murdered. The body count is rising. If the FBI knew something back in 1948 that it should have made public, then we might not be talking about a potential embarrassment from the past but rather a culpability for deaths in the present. Neither possibility is particularly attractive, would you say?"

Boyce leaned forward and laced her fingers together atop her desk. "What exactly are you asking me to do?"

I lifted my hands palm up. "Look, I don't want to go through a bunch of petitions and requests like the Freedom of Information Act. You and I have had an honest exchange of information in the past and I have no axe to grind against the Bureau. I want you to find out if the FBI had an interest in the staff and students of Black Mountain College—say from 1946 till 1948 when Paul Weaver attended. Also, two other students, Eleanor Johnson and Leah Rosen. Were any of them informants for the FBI? Were any of them targets or persons of interest? All I'm looking for is an explanation that I can give Weaver's eighty-year-old sister. And if there's a link to these recent crimes, then justice needs to be done."

Boyce pursed her lips and said nothing for a few minutes. Then she came to a decision. "How long do we have?"

"What do you mean?"

"I know how this ends, Sam. You get enough facts to suggest a theory and it winds up in the press. That jumps the interaction above my pay grade and effectively shuts down communication between you and me."

"I understand. But something's either there in the files or it's not. I'm asking straightforward questions that should net straightforward answers."

Boyce opened the desk drawer again and withdrew a notepad and pen. "Give me those names and dates again. And, Sam, if something comes up in the meantime, I'd appreciate a call."

As soon as I was outside the agency door, I checked my phone. One text had come from Nakayla:

> Shirley researched Phillips Building Supplies. Business owned by a holding company. Major shareholder—Arnold Osteen.

Chapter Twenty-two

Roland Cassidy pulled his Lexus sedan onto a side road about a mile from Lake Eden. At eight-thirty, the sun had long set and the cloudy sky meant the world was as dark as we could hope.

He remotely popped open the trunk from the driver's seat. "I spread a couple blankets, so I hope the floor's not too uncomfortable."

I opened the passenger door. "We don't have far to go."

We walked to the rear of the car and I climbed into the trunk.

"I'll try not to wreck." Cassidy closed the lid and plunged me into total darkness.

Our plan was for Cassidy to tell the security guard he was returning to make some script changes that needed to be ready for the next morning. He would be in his office for an hour or so and would be using the copy machine to run-off color-coded rewrites. The trick would be parking so that the angle would mask my emergence from the trunk. Cassidy would lift out an empty cardboard box at the same time I would slide out of the trunk. The box, labeled copy paper, provided a reason for Cassidy to open the trunk.

These elaborate steps would be taken because Nathan Armitage's security team was more efficient than the temps Osteen had passed off as Acme Security. I didn't want to be logged in the guard's records because my presence would raise questions.

The ride was bumpy but not unbearable. When Cassidy stopped, I heard a guard's muffled voice say, "May I help you, sir?"

"I'm Roland Cassidy, the writer of this movie. Here's my driver's license and my name should be on your list."

After about a minute of silence, the guard said, "Very good, sir. Can you tell me what brings you in after hours?"

"Script revisions. The director has last-minute ideas. So, here I am. I hope to be out in an hour or two. Do you mind if I park around the back? I brought special colored paper that I need for new copies and I'll be closer to the machine."

Cassidy was improvising to lessen the chance I'd be observed.

"Do you need help? I could radio my partner to carry something."

Great, I thought. Cassidy's scheme was about to backfire on us.

"Where's your colleague?" Cassidy asked.

"He's on his rounds by the equipment trucks."

"That's not necessary. It's not that heavy. But thanks, anyway."

The car moved forward and I breathed a sigh of relief. When we stopped again, Cassidy released the latch and the trunk lid rose. I stayed curled up with the empty box pushed toward the rear bumper.

Cassidy bent over me. "Looks clear. I'll carry the box just in case." He lifted it up on his shoulder like it weighted twenty or thirty pounds. "The building is between us and the guard."

"And the other guard?"

"I saw the beam of his flashlight by the catering truck. When he makes his rounds here, he'll just check the outside doors. If we're not talking, then there is no reason he should be suspicious."

I rolled out of the trunk and crouched behind the bumper. "Go first and double-check that no one is watching you. Leave the door unlocked and I'll follow in a few minutes."

Five minutes later, Cassidy flipped on the light in the accounting office. He crossed the room and closed the blinds on the windows.

"Since we're on the second floor, the guard can't look directly in," Cassidy said.

"Yes, but we might cast a shadow so let's be careful not to both be standing near the window at the same time."

There were two desks in the office.

"Which one is Raymond Braxton's?" I asked.

"The larger one nearer the window. The other is an assistant who serves more as a bookkeeper and organizes invoices and payments into the proper budget categories."

"Is that person part of Braxton's firm?"

"No. Braxton's from Wilson in the eastern part of the state. Heather's from the local firm that handles my uncle's accounting."

"Then she will have a loyalty to your uncle rather than what Braxton might instruct her to do."

"I guess so," Cassidy said. "You're saying Braxton would make an effort to hide any embezzlement or invoice manipulation?"

"Of course he would. Unless Heather's part of the scam."

Cassidy shook his head. "They never met before. I know Uncle Arnold would have preferred to have people from his own accountants' office, but the state requires outside overview."

"And Braxton has the last word?"

"He signs off on everything reported to the Film Office in the Department of Commerce."

I looked at Raymond Braxton's desk. A computer monitor and keyboard sat on a left-side credenza with the CPU on the floor underneath. His main desk was clear. There was a center drawer and three additional drawers stacked down the right side. The clean desktop told me Braxton must keep all records locked away and his computer was probably password-protected. I was going to be guilty of more than entering an office that had been opened by a key.

"Let's try the computer first." I slipped into the desk chair and pressed the spacebar. A password window appeared. "Damn. I was afraid of that." I'd argued Nakayla out of coming so that we didn't run the risk of both of us being arrested, but now I wished she and her computer skills were here.

"Try O $ T 3 3 N," Cassidy said.

I typed the six-character version of OSTEEN and the password was accepted.

"Braxton gave you his password?" I asked.

"I was with my uncle when he told Braxton to use it. Uncle Arnold was paranoid that Braxton would have a car wreck or a heart attack and then the budget and accounting data would be inaccessible. He'd have to hire some geek to break through the computer's security."

The full desktop screen was devoid of any folders other than the standard trash and various operating system icons.

"Do you know how he might have structured his work?" I asked.

Cassidy leaned over my shoulder. "No. One thing you might try is opening Microsoft Word and Excel. Each has an 'open recent file' option. That could give us what we need or at least show us the file's location in the root directory."

"That's good thinking, Roland."

"Thanks. I was a computer science major."

I pushed the chair back and stood. "Then why the hell am I flying this plane? Have a seat."

Cassidy grinned and grabbed the mouse. He opened Excel, clicked on "File" and then "Open Recent." A side window appeared with five choices. The top was "Current Budget Expenditures_Pellegatti" and the second was "Current Budget Expenditures_Raleigh."

"Open the first one," I said.

A spreadsheet appeared with several summary pages of categories of labor, materials, camera, lighting and grip, catering, and other services. Two columns were on the right of each page: a total-to-date and a total budget. Cassidy scrolled to the last summary page where the total-to-date was $2,567,980 spent on a $10,000,000 budget.

"Does that look right?" I asked Cassidy?

"Yes. We're not a fourth of the way through the picture and there are upfront costs."

"So, nothing seems out of the ordinary?"

Before answering, Cassidy tabbed through detailed breakouts of each category and its line items. He moved the cursor over one line—"on-location screenwriter."

"That's what they pay me, a thousand dollars a week."

"If this budget was for Nancy Pellegatti's review, who will see it now?"

"The new line producer. Word is that Marty wants Camille Brooks to take over. She's already up to speed on the project and Marty works well with her."

"Is that a big step for her?"

Cassidy shrugged. "I guess. A line producer credit coupled with her A.D. credentials upgrades her resume."

My mind stored Camille Brooks' promotion in the compartment reserved for key information in a murder investigation: *Who Benefits?*

"Let's look at the spreadsheet designated for Raleigh," I said.

Cassidy clicked to close the document and got a "Save" option. He clicked "Yes" and then pounded the desk. "Damn it."

"What's wrong?"

"I shouldn't have saved it. Now there's a new time stamp on the file. If Braxton notices, he'll see someone else saved the spreadsheet at a late hour. The guard will tell him I was here."

"Then have a story ready for him. You have a key, you know the password, and you were curious as to how the film's budget was faring with the construction overages. All he can do is complain to your uncle. He might not want to draw attention to the budget."

Cassidy took a deep breath. "You're right. I'll be sure not to save the Raleigh file. If Braxton goes deeper into its history, he might see it was opened, but at least it won't be in front of his face."

An identically formatted spreadsheet filled the monitor's screen.

"This is odd," Cassidy said.

"What?"

He pointed with his finger. "The date of the document is the same, but the figures are different. Look at these summary columns."

"I didn't really look at the others that closely."

Cassidy scrolled through the pages. "Here's the total-to-date, $4,809,890, almost double the first version." He clicked to the detailed page with his screenwriter fee. "And it shows they're paying me two thousand a week. I can tell you that ain't happening."

"Do you think he's trying to hit your uncle up for more money?"

"I don't see how that would work. Uncle Arnold would have gone screaming to Nancy Pellegatti."

"And she's dead," I said. "What about the investors? Would they be on the hook for more?"

"I don't know how those deals were structured." He paused a moment as an idea hit him. "What if Nancy was in on it? Or if she found out and threatened to go to my uncle? Braxton could have killed her."

"Dustin Henry told me that accounting on a movie is the most creative part of film production. Braxton might have some scam going we don't understand."

"What do you want to do?" Cassidy asked.

"Close the file and see if we find anything in the Word documents."

He repeated the process and opened a recent document labeled "Investors." There were about twenty names with Arnold Osteen at the top. I scanned down the list, recognizing a few from Asheville's well-heeled elite. Then one jumped out. Woody Farmer. The man who rented the guesthouse to Nancy Pellegatti. The man who told me and the police that he wasn't an investor.

"Hold that list on the screen." I reached for my phone, switched it to camera mode, and took a photograph. "Let me do the same thing for the two versions of the spreadsheet."

"What are you going to do with them?"

"For now, I'll hold them until I figure out the best approach to take. Don't say anything to your uncle. In fact, however this turns out, it might be safer if no one knows you helped me."

"You think I'm in danger?" Cassidy couldn't mask the quiver in his voice.

"I don't know. Better safe than sorry."

"Better safe than dead." Cassidy re-opened the Excel files, I photographed the spreadsheets, and then he closed down the computer.

If Raymond Braxton was cheating Osteen and the investors, I didn't understand how he could avoid detection when the bank's canceled checks and payment records were examined. Maybe as the state's auditor, he worked under minimal oversight.

I looked at the file cabinets lining the walls. "Are hard copies kept in this office?"

"I've seen Heather go in and out of the file drawers."

I tugged on the handle of the top drawer of Braxton's stacked three. It was locked. "You wouldn't happen to have a key to his desk, would you?"

Cassidy stood up from the chair. "No, but these old metal desks Uncle Arnold rented have a lot of play in them. I lost the key to my desk and use this." He pulled a single-bladed folding knife from his pocket. "You wedge the blade above the lock, then twist to pry open a gap that's bigger than the short bolt protruding from the lock."

I stepped aside to let Cassidy have a go. He inserted the blade a few times until he found the sweet spot where the metal gave and the drawer popped open. He lifted out a ledger-sized checkbook.

"Braxton doesn't print checks by computer?" I asked.

"No. They're hand-issued. The biggest checks go to a payroll company. Braxton writes one very big check and then workers are paid by an individual check that has taxes and Social Security deductions. Technically, the crew's employed by the payroll company. Checks are issued weekly." He pointed to the stub from one check still attached to the ringed binder. "See, Media People Services is a payroll company in Charlotte. This was last week's check for $58,500."

"Does that include your fee?" I asked.

"No, I'm not hourly or a day-player so I don't have to go through a payroll service."

"Can you find a stub from your check?"

The blank checks were laid out three to a sheet. Cassidy flipped back through the stubs of the written ones. "Here's one from two weeks ago. A thousand dollars."

I pointed to a similar checkbook still in the drawer. "And what's this?"

"Extra checks, I guess." He lifted it out and opened the cover to reveal the same check pattern, three to a sheet, with the stubs held by the notebook-sized binding rings.

"He's written checks out of this one as well," I said.

Cassidy peered closely. "And he's written them to the same companies as the other set, but these amounts are different. See, here's the same check number for me but the amount is two thousand. He's jacked up the dollar amount on each of them."

"How would he get identical check numbers?"

"Easy. You can order checks online. Give them the routing and account numbers and the starting number for your sequence, and you have a duplicate set."

"But what would be reflected in the bank statements?" I asked.

"If he's embezzling the difference, then maybe he's doctoring the statements. With Photoshop and other software programs he could scan the real statements and revise."

"So, Nancy Pellegatti and Harlan Beale uncovered only the tip of the iceberg with the construction materials."

Cassidy nodded. "And got themselves killed. We've got to tell Uncle Arnold."

Something gnawed at my gut. Something out of place. "Your uncle has a financial interest in Phillips Building Supplies. Why would his own company be stealing from him?"

"My uncle has interests in a lot of companies in Asheville. He's a big believer in vertical integration."

"Meaning?"

"He says it's smart to have an interest in the companies you do business with."

"Well, I think we need to hold off on telling him till I can check out a few more things. If Braxton gets word we're snooping around, all this goes up in smoke like the construction supplies. Then we have no evidence. We've obtained what we have illegally, and we're outside the jurisdiction of the Asheville Police Department. I'll take photos of these checkbooks and anything else we find in the drawers. Then I want you to sit tight. Can you do that?"

"Yes," Cassidy assured me.

We pried open the rest of the drawers and found blank invoices from Phillips Building Supplies, the payroll company, the temp agency, the rental car company, and the catering service.

"Here's where he could create support for a superficial audit," I said. "It's like printing money for himself."

I finished taking the photographs with my phone and Cassidy used his knife to close the drawers. A few new scratches marked our intrusion, but the desk had enough mars already that I believed these would be unnoticed.

Cassidy returned to the car carrying the dummy box of copy paper. He opened the trunk, scanned the darkness for any sign of the patrolling guard, and waved me to join him. Back in the trunk, I heard the guard log out Cassidy at ten-forty. A mile away, the car turned onto the side road and Cassidy freed me.

As we headed back to Asheville, Cassidy said, "I know I'm on the sidelines while you weigh the best approach to the authorities, but could I ask a favor?"

"What?"

"Can I be with you when you tell my uncle? He doesn't value what I write or what I do. I know he's disappointed in me."

"I would think you're very successful," I said. "He shouldn't define your life."

"I know. My dad died when I was eight, and Uncle Arnold stepped in and told my mother what I should be doing. He pushed me into sports that I didn't like and paid for a college degree in computer science I didn't want. This movie is the first thing we've done together, and I'd like him to see I helped uncover something that was happening under his nose. I guess that sounds silly, but it's important to me."

"No. I understand." I thought about my father and my rebellion to join the Army rather than go to college. I wished he were alive to see the successes I'd had. Not so much to prove him wrong, but to hope for his approval and maybe that he'd feel some pride in his son.

I looked at Cassidy as he stared with determination at the illuminated road, seeing only what the headlights revealed.

Roland Cassidy had hidden wounds, I thought. We all do.

Chapter Twenty-three

The next morning I beat Nakayla into the office. The day promised to be one of multiple encounters as I tried to gather the divergent threads of our investigation into a coherent pattern. One thing I felt certain was that Paul Weaver's death in 1948 hadn't unleashed something in the present. Rather, Beale's killer had seen our case as an opportunity to obscure what was the real motive. And Harlan Beale had conveniently called me, not because he had information about Weaver but because I was a detective and he wanted me to help him with what he discovered in the replacement construction materials.

So, whoever killed him had to know about the research assistance Beale was providing us. But that could have been anyone on the set, including Raymond Braxton. And someone had either met or lured Beale from his home because we found the Black Mountain College book there. Perhaps that was the location where Beale was murdered.

I wrote down the elements at play. Someone had stolen construction materials that reappeared in the replacement delivery. Raymond Braxton was keeping two sets of books and creating discrepancies between actual expenditures and falsified ones. The scam offered the opportunity for embezzlement, although the magnitude seemed too large to hide.

And there was Woody Farmer, who owned the guesthouse where Nancy Pellegatti had been shot. He denied being an investor but his name appeared on Braxton's investor list. Farmer deserved another conversation, one without Newly since I couldn't tell the police detective about breaking into Braxton's desk.

All of these factors had nothing to do with the case we were being paid to investigate. I hoped to hear from Special Agent Lindsay Boyce and I wanted to talk to a doctor at the VA hospital. A theory was beginning to percolate in my brain and the medical information would be crucial.

The office door opened and I heard the click of paws on the hardwood floor. Blue trotted to my desk and put his head in my lap, tail wagging like a maniacal metronome.

"You're the early bird," Nakayla said.

"You know me. Never one to let grass grow."

"Actually, I don't know you. What happened to Sam?"

"Very funny. How'd Blue do last night?"

"Fine. He was a little restless, expecting you to come in."

"It was so late and I knew I'd be restless too." I stood. "There's fresh coffee in the pot. Grab a cup and let me tell you what I've been thinking."

We sat in the conversation area, coffee in hand, coonhound underfoot.

"I've transferred all the photographs from the accounting office onto my hard drive for you to review," I said. "Clearly something fishy is going on."

"Are you going to tell Newly?"

"Yes. But I want to nail down a few more things first."

I told her my plan to talk to Woody Farmer about his investment and ask why he'd lied. And I would contact Lindsay Boyce if I hadn't heard anything from her by early afternoon. I said I planned to talk to someone at the VA hospital about Paul Weaver's condition. Since I volunteered with wounded veterans, I felt I could get access to the information I needed.

"All that sounds good," Nakayla said. "And are we thinking the same thing for the accounting evidence?"

I laughed. "You're ahead of me, aren't you?"

"Aren't I always? I'll call her and see when I can run by. Violet Baker might not know much about the movie business, but as a career accountant, she should have some insights into what's really going on with these checks."

"And no one in Asheville knows her," I said. "There won't be a leak from a local accounting firm about what we're doing."

I decided to try Woody Farmer first. Although I hadn't asked specifically, I suspected he was retired and morning might be the best time to catch him at home. The street was calm and quiet, a far cry from the spectators and flashing police lights of the other night. I parked on the driveway between the main house and guest quarters.

I knocked on the back door, the one we had entered the night of the murder. At first there was no answer. Then I saw Mr. Farmer approach, clearly surprised to see me again.

He opened the door. "Mr. Blackman. Are you like Columbo?" He laughed. "One last question?"

"Yes, I am. Can we talk a moment?"

His smile faded, but he waved me in. "Let's go back to the den. Mickey's run down to Whole Foods. Would you like some coffee?"

"No, thanks. I won't take too much of your time."

I chose the chair I'd sat in before. Farmer took the near end of the sofa.

"Now how can I help you?"

I gave him a hard stare. "Why did you lie to me about being an investor in Osteen's film?"

Color rose in his cheeks, but he didn't seem angry. More embarrassed. "What do you mean?"

"I think it's pretty clear. I asked you point-blank in front of the police whether you were an investor and you answered no. I'm reviewing documents as part of my investigative responsibilities and I see that you are. So, are you or aren't you?"

Farmer sighed. "Yes. But I haven't told Mickey."

"Why not?"

"She's not one for, shall we say, risky investments. Arnold said the secret is to keep the budget in line and make a film with a ready market. Roland's book sold well enough and then the rebate guarantees a twenty-five percent return."

"You mean the state incentive?"

"Yes. Arnold explained all the angles. How if most of the film is made in North Carolina with North Carolina workers and suppliers, then twenty-five percent of the expenses are returned."

"What's the film's budget?"

"Ten million. We might have up to two and a half million returned before ever selling a ticket."

"Has Arnold Osteen said anything to you about cost overruns?"

"No. Not so far. Maybe the producer's death will have an impact, but Arnold hasn't asked for more money. Any overages are supposed to be taken out of the rebate."

"Have you talked to him?"

Farmer shook his head. "Well, I really can't. Not when Mickey's around."

"Sounds like a well-conceived plan, as far as minimizing risk in a risky venture. Did your wife know about the opportunity?"

"Yes. Arnold first mentioned it in front of her." Farmer looked away as if deciding to say something more. He turned back. "Look. Mickey gets these vibes off of people. She said as smart as Arnold might be, she didn't think he'd have our back if everything went south. I reviewed the investment documents before signing, and we're as protected as anyone. I'll tell Mickey when the checks start coming in."

"Mr. Farmer, you know the film's producer was shot on property owned by an investor in the movie that she was responsible for bringing under budget. You are not a disinterested party and you lied about your status. That doesn't look good. In fact, the police might want to make it an obstruction of their investigation."

"I had nothing against that woman. Ask Arnold. He assured me everything was going fine."

I believed him. Now I had to calm him down. "All right. I'm sorry if I seemed to impugn your integrity. But look at it from my perspective, especially since I asked the original question."

"I know, I know."

"So, just to avoid a bigger mess, I won't mention this to anyone and I suggest you do the same. If you tell Osteen, he might feel obligated to report it to the police and that would put both of us in a bad light."

Farmer nodded like his neck was a spring. "I understand. You have my word."

I stood and offered my hand. Farmer rose and shook it firmly.

"I hope your investment returns a bundle," I said.

"Thanks. First check, Mickey and I are taking you out to dinner. Might be a good time to tell her." He laughed. "She won't hit me in public."

• ● ● ● •

If they ever make a movie called *The Onslaught of the Amazon Women*, Sheila Reilly would be cast in the lead. Sheila was the physical therapist who put me through hell during my rehab and pushed, cajoled, challenged, and intimated me into coming out the other side as a man not only able to walk but run. We also developed a friendship that thrived beyond my discharge.

I found her in her office in the physical therapy section of the Charles George VA Medical Center on Tunnel Road filling out paperwork after a morning session.

"Hi, beautiful. Killed anyone yet today?"

Sheila stood up from her desk. I do mean up because she was well over six feet and more physically fit than any drill sergeant in my boot camp.

"Sam, you one-legged wimp. You back for a refresher course?"

"Only before my funeral."

She laughed and came around her desk. I braced myself for a hug that could crush a grizzly.

"Good to see you," she said. "Why have you been a stranger?"

"You know. Work gets in the way of life."

"Why do I have the feeling you brought work with you?"

"Because it's about a vet?"

"Somebody here?"

"No. He died in 1948."

"A little late to the parade, aren't you?"

"His eighty-year-old sister wants to know how he died."

Sheila's mood turned somber. "Oh, then I don't mean to make light of it. I don't know how good the records would be going back that far. Did he die in the hospital?"

"No. He was an outpatient. He was under care for chronic asthma brought on by a fuel explosion, maybe accidental, maybe sabotage, in Germany right after the war."

"That's not my area of expertise."

"I know. But you'd give me a straight answer on who would be the best person to ask."

"Ask what?"

"About how a person could die from asthma."

"That would be Dr. Pete Misenheimer. He's top-notch in respiratory and pulmonary medicine."

"Do you know if he's in today?"

Sheila nodded. "I saw him in the cafeteria this morning after his morning rounds. I'll take you to his office."

We found Dr. Misenheimer at his desk, reviewing some X-rays on his computer monitor. Sheila knocked softly on the open door.

He turned and smiled. "Come in, Sheila." He hadn't noticed my puny body dwarfed behind her.

"Sorry to bother you," Sheila said. "I want you to meet a friend of mine and a former patient, Sam Blackman."

"Mr. Blackman." He stood and stretched his right arm across his desk. I squeezed past Sheila to shake his hand.

"You're the detective, right?"

"Yes."

"Sheila told me about you before, and she doesn't brag on many people."

"I guess that's cause she didn't kill me."

"I told you he was a charmer." Sheila crushed me with another hug. "Sam's got a question for you, so I'll leave you to impress him with your vast knowledge."

She left and Misenheimer pointed to the chair facing his desk. "Have a seat. What can I do for you?"

I gave him what I knew about Paul Weaver's condition and how stress seemed to exacerbate it.

"Asthma can be a killer," he said. "That's for sure. Most cases can be controlled, but in severe cases, death can ensue. Is that what the coroner reported?"

"No. Records have either been destroyed or lost. If you can, I'd appreciate you asking if Paul Weaver's file still exists here. That would be 1946 to 1948."

"Okay. Anything else?"

"Yes. If someone is having a lethal attack would a tracheotomy be a possible lifesaving procedure?"

Misenheimer clicked his tongue on the roof of his mouth as he thought. "That depends. An asthma attack is usually the result of a bronchospasm. That's the tightening of muscles around your air passages. Because this is usually below the incision point of a tracheotomy, such a procedure would be ineffective. Also the lining of the airways swells and becomes inflamed, which would further decrease any benefit of a tracheotomy.

"Now I've read of some cases where an early tracheotomy has been effective when coupled with a mechanical ventilator to force air through. But you said your veteran wasn't in the hospital at the time of his death."

"That's correct."

"Then I doubt if performing a tracheotomy would have saved his life."

"Could an observer tell from a patient's behavior that the blockage was above or below the point of a tracheotomy?"

Misenheimer shook his head. "No. Not unless they were trained to recognize the onslaught of the asthma symptoms. A rapid, lethal attack leaves the patient unable to speak. He's doing all he can just to draw a single breath."

A single breath, I thought. The difference between life and death.

Chapter Twenty-four

On the second day after Nancy Pellegatti's murder, I figured the Asheville Police Department must have a forensics report of some kind. I also knew Detective Curt "Newly" Newland might be hesitant to bring me in since I wasn't tied to the dead producer like I had been with Harlan Beale. The old-timer had placed his last phone call to me.

But I had a sure-fire method for getting Newly to at least talk to me—offer to buy him lunch. So, as I left the VA hospital, I called his cell phone, caught him at the department, and made my pitch.

"I don't think so, Sam. I'm pretty busy."

"I was thinking 12 Bones."

I heard a faint groan of anguish.

"And I was thinking the Sweeten Creek location," I added. "It's less crowded."

The 12 Bones Smokehouse is a renowned barbecue restaurant with two locations in the Asheville area. President Obama had made it a "must stop" whenever he came to town. Not only was the meat done to perfection, but the sides offered the likes of corn pudding, pickled okra, collard greens, and smoked potato salad.

Newly's groan rose to a whine. "I guess I should eat if only to keep my strength up for this caseload."

"Want me to pick you up?"

"Tuck's with me. Why don't we meet you there? Say, thirty minutes?"

"You got it." I'd now be picking up the tab for both their lunches—and no one eats food like a cop when it's free. I'd be lucky to hold them to one entree each.

• • ● • •

"So, how are you getting along with the cold case?" Newly asked the question, and then gnawed the last bite of meat off a barbecued rib.

"I think we might have some answers soon."

"I'm impressed." Tuck Efird mumbled the compliment through a mouthful of pulled pork.

"Yeah," Newly agreed. "What do you think happened?"

I raised my palms. "Sorry. Bad luck to speak prematurely. Fastest way to jinx a case. I will say I'm certain our investigation is linked to the Beale murder only because the killer tried to send you down the wrong trail."

"I agree," Tuck said. "We've talked to the manager of Phillips Building Supplies who's pleading complete ignorance as to how the stolen materials came to be in their inventory."

"Are you looking at other vendors?" I asked.

"What's to look at?" Newly asked. "Nothing else has been taken."

I stuffed my mouth with a spoonful of corn pudding, giving added restraint to admitting I knew the theft went deeper than lumber.

"We matched up the invoices and the itemized deliverables," Efird said. "But all the Phillips' employees have alibis."

"What about Pellegatti?" I asked. "Wasn't there an argument between her and the state accountant over those invoices?"

Efird shook his head. "You mean Raymond Braxton? He said the argument was over timing. He'd boxed them away and told her she'd have to wait. But he had them for us. He was also in the bar of the Aloft Hotel at the time Pellegatti was shot."

"You identify a murder weapon yet?"

"Thirty-eight caliber," Newly said. "Not what I'd expect of a trained assassin. No silencer. Only professional aspects of the murder are dousing the lights before leaving and the absence of prints or DNA."

"Forced entry?"

"No," Newly said. "And where she was found, she had to have let him into the house and then led him back to the middle of the room."

"Someone she knew," I said. "But then no prints. Would the killer have been wearing gloves on such a mild evening?"

Newly and Efird looked at each other.

"We think he had a handkerchief at the ready," Newly said. "He pops her, thrusts the gun into his pocket, grabs a handkerchief, and kills the lights before slipping out into the night. By the time Woody Farmer reacts, the killer is down the block and in his car."

"You sure the killer is a he?" I asked.

Efird mopped up barbecue sauce with a hunk of cornbread and then pointed it at me. "Fair question. We're checking out the woman we've heard will be named to her job."

"Camille Brooks," I said. "I've been told it's a big career step for her."

Efird nodded. "I've heard the movie business is cutthroat so I wouldn't put it past anyone to take extreme measures to get ahead."

"Like murder?" I asked

Efird shifted in his chair. "Well, I'm not saying everyone on the movie is a suspect, only that we're winnowing them down. And we're not even forty-eight hours from the crime."

Efird took a large bite of his cornbread and we all chewed in silence.

So, Braxton had an alibi and was probably staying at the Aloft rather than with the crew in Black Mountain. Useful information and worth the price of two lunches.

● ● ● ● ●

My phone had vibrated a few times during lunch, but I'd waited until I was back in the CR-V before checking to see who had tried to reach me.

No e-mails, no voice messages. But two texts, one from Nakayla and the other from Special Agent Lindsay Boyce.

Nakayla wrote:

> Saw Violet Baker and gave her printouts of
> all the photographed accounting documents.
> She will be in touch. Working with Shirley on
> researching other vendors involved with film.

The second text read:

> Can we meet in my office this afternoon?
> —Boyce

Her message surprised me. There was no hint as to what the meeting was about. More striking, she didn't want to talk over the phone but rather on the sanctity of her turf. That was fine with me. I felt ready to lay out my cards.

I dropped a quick text to Nakayla telling her I was headed to a summons from Boyce and would catch up later. Then I sat in 12 Bones' parking lot organizing my thoughts on paper and thinking how Hewitt Donaldson, master of the courtroom, would present my case.

A few minutes after two, Special Agent Vance Gilmore admitted me to the FBI office.

"Good afternoon, Mr. Blackman."

"Sam, please." We shook hands. "Agent Boyce asked me to stop by."

"Yes, of course. Do you remember the way, or should I escort you?"

"I think I can find her, thank you, especially since she's standing in the hall."

Agent Gilmore turned around and saw Boyce outside her office. He laughed. "She said you were a smart detective."

"I hope she's right."

Boyce greeted me in her doorway and we took our seats from the day before, she behind her desk and I in the chair in front of her. I touched the notepad in my pocket for reassurance.

"How's the case going?" she asked.

"Wrapping up a few loose ends. Then I can write a final report to the client and maybe she'll want to hold a press conference."

Boyce shifted uncomfortably. "What did you find out?"

"Probably something similar to what you did. FBI agents picked up Paul Weaver. My guess is that it was an interception off the campus of Black Mountain College as he was going for what he thought was a rendezvous with Nadine Oates, a meeting in which he planned to tell her to leave him and his friends alone. But, out of spite, Nadine had already reported him as a Communist or Communist sympathizer. He was taken somewhere for interrogation. The interrogation got physical. After all, the Bureau would have known Weaver was a proponent of equal rights for blacks and had even fought local vets over discrimination. Creating racial unrest was a Communist ploy, or so thought J. Edgar Hoover, the omnipotent FBI director at the time. The agents probably thought Weaver guilty by association."

"All speculation," Boyce said.

"Not really. You see, Weaver was being treated for chronic asthma contracted during his military service. One of the agitators of his attacks was stress. Now I submit that being sweated by a team of FBI agents is a stressful situation, one which brought on a major attack. Suddenly, the agents found their suspect unable to breathe. He didn't have an inhaler with him. He might have desperately pointed to his throat. Someone tried a makeshift tracheotomy to try to get air into his lungs. But asthma doesn't work that way. The swelling and muscle constriction happened below the point of where the windpipe was punctured. Paul Weaver died right in front of his interrogators."

Boyce shook her head. "And you know this how?"

"From the coroner's report."

Her eyes widened. "Where did you find that?"

"An interesting question since the report should be readily available in county records or the office of the state medical examiner. Sorry, I failed to mention the report on my first visit."

Boyce's face flushed. She'd made a mistake and she knew I knew it.

I pressed on. "You learned from some buried file that a version of what I said happened. The coroner reported a puncture to the windpipe. There were fragments of bark found in the wound, but that was placed there to make it look like some stick had penetrated the throat. A fall would also explain the bruises, which I believe came from what is now euphemistically called 'enhanced interrogation techniques.' But the real evidence is the lack of evidence. From police reports to medical reports, all documentation has disappeared. Except for one copy of the coroner's report that was probably sent to Paul Weaver's father by a friend in the coroner's office who didn't like what was going on. But Weaver's father did nothing. Instead, he sold the farm for a low price and moved to Pennsylvania, either intimidated or bribed to leave the area."

Boyce stared at me for a moment, her lips drawn into a thin red line. When she finally spoke, her voice dropped to a tight, controlled whisper. "You think we would throw this man's body off a cliff to hide how he died?"

"No. But I think you'd do what was necessary. That wasn't necessary. I don't think Paul Weaver's body ever went over a cliff. The FBI could have said they were following him as a person of interest and they saw him fall. They claimed to have retrieved the body. The local authorities wouldn't challenge them. No one wanted to cross the FBI."

"Apparently you do."

"This is now, that was then. And you invited me here. What are you going to tell me? That you couldn't find anything? I don't think that's true, Lindsay. You work for the Department of Justice, but I know it's really justice you work for. You're going to see that Paul Weaver receives justice, and that his sister receives some answers. That's the kind of person you are behind your badge."

Boyce took a deep breath. "Thanks for the vote of confidence. It wasn't the Bureau's finest hour, and I got some pushback just requesting the information. But, I figured if I didn't find out the truth, you'd bring in *60 Minutes* and learn it before me."

She sat back in her chair. I waited for her story.

"Have you ever heard of the Venona Project, Sam?"

"No. Should I have?"

"Not really. You were only a kid when it was declassified by the NSA."

Her mention of the National Security Agency piqued my interest and I leaned forward.

"The Venona Project was a top-secret and successful effort to break cryptic messages cabled in the 1940s by the KGB and the GRU, the Soviet Union's military intelligence agency. By breaking the code, we were able to learn the identities of Soviet spies and Americans targeted for recruitment. Decoding Soviet cables provided crucial evidence against Americans working for the Communists, particularly those with knowledge of our atomic weapons program. You see, just because Joe McCarthy was paranoid and overzealous didn't mean that there weren't Communists, both U.S. citizens and foreigners, engaged in espionage."

"Paul Weaver was a spy?"

"No. But Black Mountain College was mentioned in a cable as a potentially fertile environment for recruitment, and Paul Weaver was described as a disenchanted veteran who might be vulnerable. So, when Nadine Oates contacted the FBI with her suspicions that her former boyfriend was a Communist, the Bureau took her seriously. As you said, his civil rights actions in an era of the Red Scare meant he was probably considered guilty until proven innocent."

"So, he was innocent," I stated.

"That was the conclusion of the review after the tragedy. Several agents were reprimanded and the senior agent was terminated for the way the Weaver investigation was conducted. But that's only half the story. The Bureau couldn't have its interrogation of Weaver made public because there was no overt reason he should have been singled out. Except for that decoded cable. The fear was that the Soviets would realize we were decrypting their messages. It was like the Nazi Enigma code. Once you break it, you can only use the collected information if the enemy doesn't believe you got it from their own communications. The Venona Project was so secret that even President Harry Truman wasn't told the source of the information."

I nodded that I understood the importance of the Venona Project to national security. "What did the FBI do to Weaver's father that caused him to uproot his family?"

"Gave him fifty thousand dollars. And he was told if he stayed in the area, questions would be raised about his son's patriotism. That Paul was seen in compromising situations with a colored girl and with people who didn't think like Americans. That the FBI couldn't guarantee the safety of Weaver's family, and that he'd already lost two children."

"That's despicable."

"It is. But in less than a year, the Soviets would test an atomic bomb and the Venona Project identified individuals in our country who helped make that possible. That's the context, Sam. I'm not defending what was done. I'm just asking you to understand the pressures of the time. Think present-day Islamic extremists and the fear their acts of terror engender. Now the NSA eavesdrops on everyone."

"I would hope we're not using enhanced interrogation on our own veterans," I snapped.

"I agree," Boyce said firmly.

"Sorry. I know you do. Where do we go from here?"

"That's up to you. You can call a press conference if you think it serves a purpose. But I believe you overrate the public interest. We've already released documents in 2015 admitting we had the college and some of its professors and students under scrutiny. Maybe a press conference will give your client satisfaction, but it could cause her pain. After all, her father took the money and moved the family. I'm not sure how sympathetic the public will be to that."

"She deserves to know," I argued.

"Yes. She does. But how does it serve anyone else?"

"It serves the Department of Justice whenever justice is done. Even if the only result is an apology." I stood. "Thank you for your candor."

Boyce rose and looked me firmly in the eye. "And yours."

Chapter Twenty-five

The solution to a murder often breaks down into a clear-cut case of good and evil. There's an innocent victim whose life was violently ended by someone so vile that personal desires held more value than the life of another human being. The motive might not be money but rather jealousy, pride, or power—motives fueled by narcissism and perceived self-interest.

I didn't think of Paul Weaver's death in those terms, although a prosecutor would call it murder. Paul died as a consequence of aggressive action by men who didn't intend to kill him. His medical condition was triggered by their acts, making them responsible for his death.

I'm certain the FBI agents saw themselves as protecting their country from an enemy as real as Nazi Germany. Special Agent Lindsay Boyce was right. It was a tragedy. But Paul Weaver was just as dead as if he'd faced a firing squad. The man who dreamed of being an architect, of building things in this world, who studied under Buckminster Fuller, was undone by that world. A world of spies and secrets. A world at war in a new way, a cold war where friend and foe were often indiscernible from each other.

The irony wasn't lost on me that Paul Weaver, World War II veteran, holocaust liberator, and crusader for equal justice had been killed by his own government, the government he fought to defend. His wound might not have been as visible as my amputated leg, but walking is secondary to breathing, and his military service had cost him his breath and thereby his life. No,

Paul Weaver wasn't a typical murder victim, and the solution to his case wasn't easily presented to our client. After nearly seventy years, what was to be gained by opening the scars of old wounds from the past? God knows, we were creating enough new ones.

But, Nakayla and I had an obligation to Violet Baker to tell her the truth. That didn't mean I had to like it.

I opened our office door, ready to share the story of my encounter with the FBI and to seek Nakayla's counsel on how to best present our findings to Violet Baker.

Violet was there, sitting on the sofa with papers spread on the coffee table in front of her. For a second, my mind shut down. Had she heard I'd been to the FBI? Was she here expecting a report?

Nakayla rose from one of the leather chairs and turned to face me. Blue scrambled to his feet and hurried to greet me.

"You okay, Sam?" Nakayla asked. "You look like you saw a ghost."

"No ghost. I'm fine. I was just trying to walk and think at the same time. You know that's hard for me."

Violet laughed politely. Nakayla gave a slight nod, her back to our client, and her expression telling me she knew something was wrong, but she wasn't going to inquire.

"You won't believe what Violet uncovered," Nakayla said.

"I took the liberty of coming unannounced," Violet said. "I wanted to show you in person."

"Did I miss the presentation?"

"No," Nakayla said. "Violet's only been here a few minutes. Come, sit down."

I patted Blue on the head and settled in a chair, grateful not to have to talk about Paul Weaver.

Violet waved a hand over the papers. "You can look at the numbers, but I've found a definite pattern to the occurrence of inflated figures between the two budgets."

"What are they?" I asked.

"All of them are North Carolina vendors. Like the Phillips Building Supplies. Those categories from companies out-of-state, like some specialized camera rig that can't be rented locally, are entered at the same amounts."

"So, you think the accountant is inflating these local companies because they're giving him a kickback?"

Violet Baker shook her head. "Not at all. At some point, the movie runs out of money thinking they're on budget when they're not. You're looking at this backwards. The accountant's not stealing from the movie. The movie is stealing from the state of North Carolina."

"Osteen," I said. "Osteen and the accountant are in it together."

Nakayla nodded. "And we should have seen it. Why embezzle money when you can get twenty-five percent back on phantom receipts that never deplete the real budget?"

"I reviewed the state guidelines," Violet said. "The rebate is capped at five million dollars, which means any expenses over twenty million don't qualify. But if the real budget is ten million and Osteen can create phony expenditures adding another ten million, then he's looking at tapping an extra two and a half million based upon falsified checks and invoices."

I shook my head in disbelief. "And there's the stolen construction supplies. I was so taken by Osteen's rant to the crew that I never considered he could have stolen them himself."

"Create a real overage here and there with the money going to a company you're invested in," Nakayla said. "And, as Woody Farmer told you, those cost overruns are charged to the actual investors' rebates. Remember I said I'd investigated a vehicle theft of some of his company trucks? I bet the bastard stole them himself. Now he's stealing from both the state and his investors."

Violet looked a little bewildered at our outburst. "I don't know about all that, but somebody needs to be made aware of the theft."

"I don't know if any theft of state funds has actually happened yet," I said. "He might not submit his qualifying expenses until the movie's finished. An un-submitted audit report isn't a crime, regardless of how erroneous the figures are. They're just numbers on a page."

"You're right," Violet said. "But at some point those numbers do get turned in and the accountant must have had some confidence that they'd be approved. We're talking about two and a half million dollars potentially paid on inflated invoices and doctored bank statements."

"Any ideas?" I asked Violet. "What would you do if you were this accountant?"

"Make sure no one else would cross-check these figures." She pulled a sheet of paper from the coffee table. "Here's the paragraph in the guidelines that caught my eye. She read aloud:

"The general procedures outlined in these Guidelines are intended to be applied consistently to all projects. Significant deviations in procedure should occur only when, in the exercise of discretion and considering the particular and unusual circumstances, the Secretary concludes that the best interest of the State and the purpose of the Program will be advanced. Such deviations should be noted when they occur."

"Who's 'the Secretary'?" I asked.

"The Secretary of Commerce. The rebates are really grants that he or she approves. The Secretary can deviate from the guidelines and the language says deviations *should be* noted, not *must be* noted."

"You're saying the Secretary of Commerce is in on the conspiracy?"

"No," Violet said. "You asked me what would I do if I were the accountant. Well, I would make sure the Secretary of Commerce would have my audit approved without review. Make sure it was rubber-stamped."

"We're moving into powerful political waters," I said.

"But it's a conspiracy that's responsible for two deaths," Nakayla said. "The Secretary is just as culpable as anyone else in the scheme."

"Secretary Lanier Hudson," Violet said. "I looked him up online. And I looked up Arnold Osteen. Did you know they both went to Chapel Hill the same years and were in the same fraternity?"

I looked at Nakayla. "She's making us look bad."

The octogenarian wasn't finished. "You didn't tell me the accountant's name but I read it on one of the documents. Guess how he's tied in?"

I threw up my hands. "Don't tell me he was in the same fraternity."

"No. He's the Secretary's brother-in-law."

"But how do we get to them?" Nakayla asked. "We have no admissible evidence and even what we have isn't incriminating if it hasn't been filed."

"You could wait till the report is submitted and approved," Violet said. "There is a provision for public review of any grant-distribution."

I shook my head. "Two people are dead. I don't want to wait for some paper trail. What if they get cold feet and don't submit? What proof do we have then?"

I stood and started pacing. "Nancy Pellegatti must have had more than just Harlan's photographs of the construction materials to be so brazenly gunned down."

"Like what?" Nakayla asked.

"Like she came across some doctored invoices. Saw the inflated figures and confronted Raymond Braxton. Maybe even Osteen. Remember, he's the one who called Marty Kolsrud into a meeting at his house which left Nancy alone."

"So, if she did have documents, the killer must have taken them," Nakayla said.

I stopped pacing. "Or Newly missed them." I looked at the copies Nakayla had printed from my phone photos. "Violet, can I see the invoices from Phillips Building Supplies, the original and the one made out for twice the amount?"

Violet sorted through the papers. Nakayla eyed me skeptically.

"Here they are," Violet said. "Somebody did a good job doctoring them."

"That's what I want to analyze," I lied. "Sorry, but I've got to run to an appointment."

Nakayla's skepticism turned to a scowl. I think she suspected what I was up to.

"Thanks, Violet," I said. "You're the best detective in the room. Keep Nakayla on her toes."

I went to my office, slid the unfolded invoices into a manila envelope, and headed to see Woody Farmer.

• • ● • •

He came to the back door with a thick biography of Churchill in his hand. The history buff, I recalled. He wasn't happy to see me again. I think he hoped our relationship was history.

"Is your wife here?" I asked.

"Yes. Mickey's on the phone with our daughter in California."

"Good. I need you to let me into the guesthouse."

Farmer stepped back. "I don't know if I should do that."

"Are the police still holding the scene?"

"No. They released it yesterday afternoon, but someone from the movie is supposed to come and get her things."

"Right. And you know I'm helping the police. I think they might have missed something. You're welcome to call Detective Newly if you like, but I'm trying to be discreet here. You know I've found out some things that I'm withholding from the police because they have no bearing on the case and could only embarrass someone."

Farmer understood I was leveraging his investor status to force his cooperation.

"All right," he said gruffly. "Let me get the key."

He opened the guesthouse door and walked inside. "What are you looking for?"

"Something she might have brought from her office. You can go back to your book. I'll let you know when I'm finished." I stepped aside to clear the path to the door.

Farmer looked unhappy but he left.

I pulled the manila envelope from the small of my back where I'd tucked it under my shirt and waistband. I needed to get those doctored invoices into the investigation without revealing we'd broken into Braxton's desk. If they were found with Pellegatti's things, then the police would have cause to question their discrepancy. I knew I was planting evidence, but I only wanted the police to have cause to seek a warrant for a legitimate search of Braxton's office.

I needed to find a hiding place that the police could have overlooked and then call Newly to say I'd found them. But the living room was nicely but sparsely furnished. A multi-colored sofa sat against the long wall. A wooden coffee table was in front of it. A rug was rolled up and tucked against the base of the sofa. I assumed it probably had borne the brunt of the bloodstains.

A writing desk was in the far corner at the end of the sofa. A bookshelf was built into the right half of the short wall that stretched from the desk to a flight of six stairs going up to the next level.

I considered hiding the invoices between larger volumes on the shelf, but the placement wasn't ideal. Would that be the kind of location she'd choose? It sounded like from Roland Cassidy's ten o'clock conversation with Pellegatti, she was going to talk to me the next day. If she had documents, I'd argue she planned to show them to me. Hiding them in some old book seemed extreme. If she thought she was in such danger, why did she let someone in so late at night?"

I went up the stairs to the bath and bedroom. Her makeup case was still on the vanity and a toothbrush stood bristles up in a cup. I turned into the bedroom. It was a good size with a double bed with a high wooden headboard, nightstands on either side, and a small Persian rug on the dark hardwood floor. A dresser with a brass lamp and decorative bowl stood against the wall opposite the foot of the bed.

That was where I saw it. A stack of light green copy paper. Nancy Pellegatti had a shooting script in her bedroom. I could place the invoices within the body of the script and tell Newly I saw a thin line of white in the green. We could assume she stuck them there, either to hide them or simply to mark a place in the script.

I stepped to the dresser and lifted the script, ready to thumb about two-thirds of the way through it before inserting my incriminating documents.

The white pages amid the green were already there. Not just the invoices from Phillips Building Supplies but ones from the temp service and the caterer. Somehow, Nancy Pellegatti had done what Cassidy and I had done, broken into Braxton's files. She had been there before us.

I set the script down on the dresser. What was the best path to follow? Now I didn't need to plant anything. But we needed to link the conspiracy beyond Braxton to Osteen and Secretary of Commerce Lanier Hudson. I'd been around enough Jag prosecutors as a Chief Warrant Officer to know that simply confronting Braxton wouldn't cut it. He'd claim he didn't know how the invoices had been created and he hadn't authorized any payment of the inflated amounts. We needed a confession at least at Osteen's level if we stood any chance of wrapping everyone up.

Osteen wouldn't confess, not with two murder charges involved. We needed a sting operation and we needed someone who could get to Osteen. I looked at the script on the dresser. Pretend parts played by professionals. I knew the cast we needed. Now I needed an audience.

Chapter Twenty-six

"I don't like it." Newly crossed his arms over his chest as a physical exclamation point to his assessment. He looked at his partner Tuck Efird.

"If you think it's such a great idea, why don't you do it yourself?" Efird asked me.

The three of us stood in the bedroom of the guesthouse where I'd called them to see the phony invoices hidden in the script.

"Because I'm not an actor," I said. "Because I didn't have a close friendship with Nancy Pellegatti."

"But we'll be putting him in a dangerous spot," Newly objected. "He'll need to be wired. And I want eyes on him. You know we don't have the quality tech gear of the FBI."

"What if the FBI were part of the operation?"

Efird looked incredulous. "Invite the Feds?"

"Why not? We're talking about a murder conspiracy that may rise to the highest levels of the executive branch of state government. No disrespect, but who has the better chance of bringing these guys down? The Asheville Police Department or the FBI?"

"Why not the SBI?" Newly asked.

"Do you trust the State Bureau of Investigation not to have potential leaks in such a politically charged case? One whiff of our plans and I guarantee you the evidence will disappear."

"But what's the jurisdictional justification for the FBI's involvement?" Newly asked.

"I'm not sure. Maybe RICO charges." I knew that the federal Racketeering Influenced and Corrupt Organizations Act, simply known as RICO, dealt with ongoing criminal organizations. "Maybe RICO can be applied to a department of state government. I'd like to talk to the resident agent, Lindsay Boyce."

"Why you and not us?" Efird asked.

"Let's just say she owes me."

"And have you already approached this actor?" Newly asked.

"No. I called you as soon as I found these invoices. Would you at least be willing to let me talk to Boyce? Then we can proceed from there. We're looking at two cold-blooded homicides and a major corruption scandal. The role of the Asheville Police Department in solving the case won't be minimized."

Newly and Efird exchanged glances. They were only human. Everyone wants a shot at glory.

"All right," Newly said. "We'll take the script and invoices into our chain of custody. Talk to Boyce and we'll go from there."

I followed the detectives back to headquarters where they ran off photocopies of the invoices for me to show Boyce. Then I called her and said I needed to see her about a breaking case. Would she come to our office at six-thirty? She agreed.

When I got to the office, Violet Baker had gone, easing my guilt that I hadn't yet told her about her brother's death.

Nakayla had gathered all the incriminating accounting paperwork into a single pile. "I assume we don't want Boyce to see this," she said.

"Correct. Only what we have from Nancy Pellegatti." I picked up the stack and noticed that the list of investors was on top. Given Woody Farmer's statements, I felt sure the investors were unaware of the rebate scam. They knew a rebate of two and a half million dollars would be credited to the real budget, but had no idea that Osteen, Secretary Hudson, and Raymond Braxton were illegally taking another two and a half million.

One name and address on the list stuck out. Phillip Byrd of Cherokee, North Carolina.

I pointed out the name to Nakayla. "Why does he sound familiar?"

She thought a moment. "I believe he's the tribal chief of the Eastern Band of the Cherokees."

"Really? And in many ways they're a sovereign nation, aren't they?"

"To a certain degree." She smiled. "And he could be a potential victim or a co-conspirator."

"Yes. And what law enforcement agency has broad jurisdiction over the reservation?"

Nakayla's smile broadened. "The FBI."

• • ● • •

Special Agent Lindsay Boyce looked through the accounting documents a third time. She, Nakayla, and I had talked for thirty minutes and I could tell the story intrigued her.

"No other explanations explain the inflated invoices?"

I shook my head. "Not that rise to a motive for murder like two and a half million dollars does."

"And the tribal chief? You're confident he's not involved?"

"Yes. He brings nothing to the scam. But his investment and all of the other investments are making the movie possible and thereby inadvertently financing a criminal enterprise. I hope that's enough jurisdictional crossover to bring you in."

"And Asheville homicide's on board?"

"They agree you have the best resources and bring the most prosecutorial clout if this goes to trial."

Boyce patted the documents. "All right. But first I want to meet this star who we're putting in front of our own cameras."

I stood up from my chair. "Can you stay a little longer? I'll see if I can beam him up here."

"Yes. I'd say speed is of the essence."

I headed for my office.

"Sam," Boyce called. "About that other thing. Have you told her yet?"

"No." I gestured to the papers. "When this broke we decided to wait."

"It's not the kind of thing you rush through," Nakayla added.

"Please let me know when you do. I'll talk to her if she'd like."

"Thank you," I said.

Thirty minutes later, Dustin Henry arrived. I'd told him we had a break in Nancy Pellegatti's murder, but it wasn't for public knowledge. I needed to speak with him and could he come to the office.

The former *Star Fleet* commander came in, excitement radiating from his face. He was surprised to see Boyce and doubly surprised to learn she was an FBI agent. I walked him through what we'd learned from Harlan Beale's photographs as they related to what I'd found in the script in Nancy Pellegatti's bedroom. Dustin Henry's face grew darker with each revelation.

When I finished, he spoke only four words: "How can I help?"

I looked to Boyce. "Tell him your plan."

She turned to Dustin Henry. "Mr. Henry, please feel free to pick it apart. I need to have confidence in it, and, most importantly, I need you to have confidence in it as well."

"Dustin," I said, "this is sketchy at best, but I think you offer the best chance to have Arnold Osteen incriminate himself. The dual accounting figures could be explained away by a slick attorney as innocent errors. The crime doesn't occur until they file and receive their grant. We believe you can pose the best threat to them, a threat that can be negated for a price."

"I'm a blackmailer," Dustin said.

"Yes. And you'll need to convince Osteen of that. Here's the unwritten script for you to improvise. You and Nancy had dinner at Rhubarb, like you described. That can be verified if anyone checks. She told you that she had an argument with Braxton. That will check out. Where you deviate from the facts is that she told you she had taken some documents from Braxton's files that she thinks prove expenses are being fabricated to increase the state's grant. She told you she went back into the accounting office, she didn't say how, but you assumed someone either left the door unlocked or she got a key, maybe Cassidy's since he'd been in her office earlier that day. At Rhubarb, she gave you the invoices she said supported her allegations. We'll give you copies to show Osteen. He'll know they're genuine and worry more that you have them rather than exactly how Nancy acquired them.

"You'll tell Osteen she asked what she should do. You told her you wanted to study the documents, and it would be a mistake to go to the authorities prematurely. Then you learn she's been shot and killed. You could be holding the motive for her murder.

"You spin your tale that you now know someone is falsifying expenses to collect unearned grant money. Since Arnold Osteen is executive producer overseeing the final budget, you've decided it has to be with his knowledge. You offer not to go to the police, but for a price. You know the cap on the grant is five million dollars for a twenty-million dollar production and so half the grant could be illegally obtained. For a cut, you'll keep quiet. Otherwise, you'll go public. You also have given backup copies to your attorney in case something happens to you.

"If Osteen tells you he doesn't know what you're talking about and to go ahead and release them, then it's a good bet we're wrong about our accusations. If he responds otherwise, tell him you'll need some good faith money. He'll probably say the grant won't come through till after the movie's wrapped. Tell him that's his problem. You want two hundred thousand up front. You're not sitting on this when two murders are involved."

"And if he agrees?"

"Tell him to let you know when the funds are coming. He'll probably want a wire transfer rather than cash, but we'll be ready for it." I turned to Boyce. "We will, won't we?"

"Yes. We have an account number we can give you that will send the funds to us. We'll have audio and video of Osteen agreeing to the deal and then proof of the execution. I also hope Osteen opens up during your confrontation with incriminating statements."

"Where's this happening?"

"Where are you staying?" Boyce asked.

I interrupted. "He's at the Aloft. Same hotel as the accountant Raymond Braxton. I don't know if that's a good idea to have your techs wiring his room on the same premises as a prime suspect."

"When is this happening?" Dustin asked.

"I'd like it soon," Boyce said. "If we have a sit-down with the Asheville police tomorrow, I'd like to go Saturday."

"Well, the film's not shooting tomorrow or Saturday because of Nancy's death," Dustin said. "I think only the guards are on location. What about there?"

Boyce shook her head. "No. Not crowded enough. My tech team would stick out, and we have to get in place ahead of time. Osteen could come early, maybe wander through other offices." She turned to me. "I understand your concern, Sam, but having the meeting in the same hotel as the accountant might be a plus. We could get a room either adjacent to Dustin or certainly within wireless signal reach. If we get enough evidence on the spot, the room has only one door and Osteen and Braxton can't get out. Plus we're close to Mission Hospital."

Her last comment raised Dustin Henry's eyebrows.

"Yes. I'm afraid you'll be facing a certain amount of risk," Boyce said. "That's why I need to know you accept these risks, including death, and are volunteering without any pressure from the FBI or Asheville police."

"I understand. I'll sign something if you need me to." Dustin winked at me. "She forgets I've made a career battling terrestrial and extraterrestrial villains. I'm not passing up the chance to do it for real. Let's go get these sons of bitches."

Chapter Twenty-seven

"You're right, Sam. He's a good man for the job." Special Agent Lindsay Boyce gave her verdict after we heard the elevator doors close behind Dustin Henry.

"He's certainly motivated."

Boyce cleared her throat, signally an official pronouncement. She looked at me and then Nakayla. "You know I've got bad news for you."

"Can't you make an exception?" Nakayla asked.

"Look, I know you brought us this case and you brought us Dustin Henry. But I can't have you in the room. In fact, since you found the invoices I'd rather minimize your involvement. The more visible you are, the more likely a slick lawyer will claim you planted those documents to grab a starring role in a trumped-up case against Osteen."

I protested because Boyce would expect me to, but I really couldn't argue. I nearly did plant the invoices and I would have lied under oath if questioned by a defense attorney.

Boyce stood. "I'll let you know how it goes. My advice is stay clear of the movie people until it's over. It might not be safe for Dustin Henry if he's seen talking to you."

As soon as she left, I phoned Newly.

"Be ready for a call from the big leagues," I told him.

"When's it happening?

"Probably Saturday. Boyce will request a meeting with you to review the plan. Dustin Henry will get Osteen and the accountant in his room for the demand. The Bureau will have the room tricked out with all their toys."

"Sounds good."

"Boyce is shutting Nakayla and me out."

The homicide detective was silent for a few seconds. "Not the right pedigree?"

"She wants only official law enforcement involved."

"Even the Feds have to cover their asses," Newly said. "Maybe if you stay off your cell phone, I could check in for a little unpaid consultation. If you're not too busy."

Newly was going to keep me in the information loop. He didn't have to and he risked the wrath of the FBI by doing so. He was a good cop but a better friend.

"Thanks, Newly. I'll always take your call." I disconnected.

Nakayla stood in front of me. "Well?"

"He's going to share what he can."

"Good." She leaned forward and kissed me on the lips. "You've done a great job. Everything's going to be fine."

"I hope. I just can't see Osteen or Braxton pulling a trigger or bludgeoning an old man with a tire iron."

"We've seen Osteen's temper," Nakayla said.

"But he was with Marty Kolsrud when Pellegatti was shot." That fact gave me pause. Marty. I hadn't thought about him. An artistic temperament high in emotional octane to fuel his actors with the passion of his vision. A vision that changed *Love Among the Ridges* to *Battle Scars*. A person Osteen described as hungry. I knew Osteen was probably crooked. How well did I know the man who was his alibi?

"What is it, Sam?" Nakayla studied my face.

I wasn't ready to share a spur-of-the-moment suspicion. "Nothing. I just want to go home with you and Blue."

The coonhound got up at the sound of his name.

"Blue today, Violet tomorrow," Nakayla mused.

"Yes, two colors tied to two cases." I wrapped my arm around Nakayla's waist and pulled her close. "We're a colorful team, you and me."

Nakayla laughed. "Yeah, you can't beat black and white."

• • ● • •

The next morning we were in the office early. Nakayla reached Violet Baker to make arrangements for us to meet her. Violet asked that we join her for lunch, but Nakayla graciously declined. We didn't want to deliver our report and then have Violet have to walk through a dining room full of people. We agreed to be at her cottage at eleven. Blue happily went with Shirley to her office.

Violet ushered us into her living room. Light from a wide bay window filled the air. The walls were a cheery pale yellow with white molding running along the ceiling and floor. Wall-to-wall cream carpet contrasted with a dark wooden coffee table and a deep purple sofa. Two matching floral-print wing-chairs completed the conversation area.

A silver coffee service and tray filled with shortbread sat on the table.

"Please sit down," Violet instructed. "Help yourselves to coffee and some Lorna Doones."

"Thank you," I noticed she had only set two cups on the tray. I poured for Nakayla and me and then sat on the sofa beside her.

Violet Baker nodded her approval. "So, you have news?"

"We do," Nakayla said. "I believe we've taken our investigation as far as we can. We've reached conclusions, some from evidence, some from deductions, and some from off-the-record conversations."

Violet looked at me. "And you're in agreement with these conclusions?"

"Yes. They're consistent with the coroner's report and all we've learned from our research and interviews."

Violet leaned forward. "Then what are these conclusions?"

As Nakayla and I had discussed, she took the lead. "Your brother didn't fall while hiking. In fact, he might not have been near any trail or cliff. Your brother died of a lethal asthma attack."

"Asthma?"

"Yes. We suspect he didn't have his inhaler. That medicine he told you were his breaths. He'd probably left it in his shaving kit." Nakayla went on to describe the context of the Red Scare, the Venona Project, and the FBI's obsession with Black Mountain College as a possible nest of Communists. Violet listened without interruption, but I saw tears form in her eyes when Nakayla described the failed tracheotomy and the cover story given to the press. The sobs came with the news of the payment to her parents and their decision to flee the mountains rather than stand up to the FBI and their threat to spread lies about their son.

Nakayla and I sat silently waiting for Violet to compose herself.

"I'm sorry," she whispered. "I guess Paul's death has really preyed on my mind all these years. I didn't realize how much."

"What would you like to do now?" I asked.

"What do you mean?"

"Although your brother's death was an accident, the circumstances that triggered the attack weren't. Responsibility and accountability can be pursued if you want to go public."

Violet's face registered unfiltered shock. "Why would I do that? Who's still alive? What good would it do?"

I said nothing. She had to come to her own decision.

Violet looked around the room as if seeing it for the first time. "I wondered how my father had been able to send me to the university. He claimed it was from working lots of overtime at the steel mill. Now I suspect he and mother kept some of that money back for my education." She shook her head. "What's done is done. There is no one to prosecute, no one to hold accountable. But at least I know. I thank you for that."

I felt uncomfortable taking satisfaction from closing this case. "Violet, if you'd like, the resident agent in Asheville is willing to talk with you."

"Will she tell me something different from what you told me?"

"I don't think so."

Violet shrugged. "Then why bother?"

My cell phone vibrated. In the quiet of the room, the buzz was audible to all.

"You need to get that?" Violet asked.

I lifted my phone and saw "Newly's Cell" on the screen. "Yes. I'll step outside a moment."

I walked onto the small front porch. "This is Sam."

Newly's voice was scarcely above a whisper. "It's on. Tonight."

"Tonight?"

"Yes. Tuck and I just got out of a meeting with Boyce, her team, and Dustin Henry. Henry said Osteen's going to Raleigh on Saturday."

"Probably to meet Secretary Hudson."

"Boyce says she can have everything ready for tonight. Henry will tell Osteen he's been given information from Nancy Pellegatti and he wants Osteen and Braxton to see it before he takes it to the police. I agree with Boyce that, guilty or not, Osteen will want to see Henry."

"What time?"

"Seven-thirty. Henry's room."

"That's when I usually have a drink at the hotel's WXYZ bar."

"No, Sam. You're not going to be in the hotel. If Osteen sees you, he might be spooked. Are we clear?"

"Of course. I was just yanking your chain."

"About two homicides? I don't think so."

Newly was right. Sitting in the bar at the Aloft was a bad idea and he had waved me off as I'd expected. So, I took that as permission to have free rein outside the hotel.

• • ● • •

Arnold Osteen lived in a large two-story home on Kimberly Avenue, one of the nicest old neighborhoods in Asheville. At six-thirty, I drove slowly by his residence and saw the silver Mercedes parked in front of a three-car garage. Unless he had taken another vehicle, the real estate developer/would-be movie mogul was at home.

Nakayla hadn't been enthusiastic about my plan to follow Osteen to and from the meeting. I wanted to see what he did after Dustin Henry gave him the ultimatum. That meant I needed to know where he parked his car. Nakayla considered my action to be a stake-out that should have backup. She wanted to be with me or at least be in her own car as part of the tail. A two-car surveillance was more effective than a lone operative, but Asheville isn't that big, and at night we could look like a caravan. Besides, Newly might pass me information that she could respond to through the resources at the office.

We compromised when I agreed to keep my phone connected to her while I was in motion.

I circled around and drove down Kimberly in the direction most likely to be the one Osteen would take to the Aloft. The avenue was wide enough to allow parking, so I stopped in front of a stucco home with a tile roof that had a for sale sign in the yard. Osteen's house was about five behind and I could clearly see his driveway in the rearview mirror. I reported my location to Nakayla and then disconnected, promising to phone as soon as Osteen headed for the hotel.

A few minutes before seven, I saw a flash of the setting sun reflect off the silver hood of Osteen's car as he swung onto Kimberly. I ducked down across the seat and speed-dialed Nakayla.

"He's moving."

"All right. Stay connected."

Evening traffic was light and I had no trouble catching up with Osteen. Fortunately, another car had slipped in between us or I'd have been on his rear bumper at the first stoplight. I tailed him till he turned off Biltmore Avenue onto Aston, the side street by the Aloft that ran to South Lexington, and the rear entrance to the underground deck for hotel parking. Following the Mercedes left me at the mercy of available spaces that could put us on separate levels. The odds were Osteen would exit the way he entered so I drove past and pulled into the parking lot of Lexington Glass Works a half block away. The business had closed at six so I could position the CR-V with a clear view of the Aloft's garage exit. It was seven-fifteen. I gave Nakayla my location.

"And you're staying put," she said.

"Yes. I'll call you when Osteen reappears."

"No. Leave the line open. Use your charger if you have to, but I want to stay in contact."

"All right."

A heavy-duty gray pickup, the kind with a four-door cab, parked at an angle right behind me. The vehicle was so close, it pinned me in.

"Hold up. I've got company. Don't talk." I laid the phone back on the seat, facedown so the glowing screen wouldn't be visible.

The driver got out but in the dim light of dusk I didn't recognize him till he stepped up to my window. Mick Ritchie.

I rolled down the glass.

"Hey, Sam, watcha doin' out here by yourself?"

It was a good question and I wished I'd thought to invent a good answer ahead of time.

"You know how it is, Mick. The parking lots cost an arm and a leg and I don't have that many legs."

Ritchie didn't laugh. "So, are you meeting someone in the hotel and parking for free?"

"Yeah. That's what I'm doing."

He nodded, weighing my answer. "You meeting Mr. Osteen?"

That question came out of left field and he must have read the surprise on my face.

"No. Is he here?"

"Yeah. But you should know that since you followed him from his house. You see, one of my jobs is to watch Mr. Osteen's back."

My stomach knotted. Mick Ritchie. Electrician. My mind flashed to the disabled power box at the Black Mountain College Museum. Then to the movie location where Ritchie had access as a crew member. He easily could have been the person calling to Harlan Beale as the old mountaineer left me his voice message. Maybe Beale had told him what he suspected about the construction materials. Ritchie had called Osteen for instructions, and then gone to Beale's house.

"We need to have a little talk, Sam." He drew a thirty-eight-caliber pistol from underneath his denim jacket but kept it low enough that no passing car would notice.

I reached for my phone.

"Leave it," he growled.

"Where are we going?"

He smiled. "Somewhere where nobody's home." He stepped back and ordered me to open the door.

Part of me wanted to resist. To see if he was bluffing and wouldn't dare shoot me on a city street. But this was the man who murdered Nancy Pellegatti within earshot of Woody and Mickey Farmer. He could pull the trigger, be in his truck and gone in less than ten seconds. If I broke and ran, my prosthetic leg would make it easy for him to overtake me, or worse, shoot me in the back.

I tried to stall, hoping that Nakayla heard enough to alert the police. "Mick, there's no need for this. I don't know what you think is going on."

"That's what we're going to find out. Now move it!" He jabbed the gun forward for emphasis.

I did as he said. He instructed me to get in the front passenger's seat of his truck and buckle the shoulder strap. Then, never taking his eyes off me, he crossed in front of the hood and climbed behind the wheel. He pulled his cell phone from his belt and speed-dialed. He said three words: "I have him."

I could only assume he was talking to Osteen, and that Osteen had been aware I'd been following him. I shuddered to think how I'd screwed up. Would Osteen even meet with Dustin Henry? Would he try to silence both of us?

Two people had already been murdered. What were two more?

Chapter Twenty-eight

Mick Ritchie and I rode in silence. I made no accusations against him, figuring the less he thought I knew, the better my chances.

His phone rang once. He listened without speaking a word.

As dusk turned to darkness, I had an idea where we were headed. My suspicion was confirmed when we turned into Harlan Beale's long driveway. Ritchie was the reason nobody was home.

We parked close to the shed with the old tractor.

"Get out and walk ahead of me to the front door." Ritchie brandished the gun openly.

I did as I was told, navigating my steps through the yard by the faint light of a crescent moon.

"Open the door," he ordered.

I tried the knob, but it was locked.

"Step aside." Ritchie struck the pane above the lock, shattering the glass. He reached through and opened the door from the inside. "Now go in nice and slow. The light switch is on the left."

No question that he'd been in the house before. The two-bulb overhead threw a yellow glow across the room.

"Sit down." He pointed the pistol at the bentwood rocker and then sat in an upholstered chair facing me and the front door.

"What now?" I asked.

"We wait. Believe me, you don't want to be in a hurry."

For another fifteen minutes, we sat without speaking. Ritchie kept the pistol resting on his thigh but pointed at me. Then we heard the approaching crunch of tires on gravel. Headlights swept through the front window and across the wall. Ritchie stood and arced toward the door, never taking his eyes off me.

I glared at him, hoping to look angry rather than display the genuine fear I felt in my gut.

The first person through the door was Dustin Henry. He walked as if he didn't have a care in the world. "Good evening, Mick," he said. "Nice work apprehending Inspector Clouseau here."

My mouth went dry. I couldn't speak. Had Dustin been part of the conspiracy from the beginning? Had he fooled me into making a colossal misjudgment? Dustin was followed by Osteen and the accountant Raymond Braxton. Osteen wore a tailored navy suit, white shirt, and red tie. He must have planned on attending some Friday night function after meeting with Dustin. Braxton's pudgy face looked as pale as skim milk. Beads of sweat glistened on his forehead.

"So, has he confirmed my story, Mick?" Dustin Henry asked.

"What story? I ain't talked to him. Just like Mr. Osteen told me."

"Yes," Osteen agreed. "I'd rather hear it from Sam."

"Okay." Dustin Henry raised his right hand to his heart and gave a solicitous bow to Osteen. "Whatever you say."

I saw it, and only I saw it. Dustin kept his hand over his heart a few extra seconds, long enough to spread his fingers in the splayed salute of his character, Captain Jefferson. Dustin's calm demeanor was a façade. He was improvising and it was up to me to play along without blowing the scene.

"All right, Sam," Osteen said. "The time for games is over. We can all walk away without anyone getting hurt. Just tell me what's going on."

I nodded. "Okay. The police were investigating Nancy Pellegatti's murder. They brought me in because of Harlan Beale's death in the museum. They thought that was tied to the research he was doing for me and perhaps there was some connection between the two deaths. They searched the guesthouse but found nothing. I make my living accomplishing what the police can't.

I went back through the guesthouse and found some invoices buried in a copy of the script. They appeared to be doctored. I didn't have any proof that they represented any crime, but I was suspicious. I'd found some pictures on Beale's phone of construction supplies." I looked at Mick Ritchie. "I showed them to Mick. I was curious as to what they meant. I started following you, Arnold, to see if there was more to it. I apologize."

Osteen's lips were thin as wire. His eyes stared without blinking. He said, "How does Dustin fit into the picture?"

Dustin Henry's eyes narrowed and I knew I was heading into a critical part of the story. Would they have frisked him for a microphone? Certainly for a gun, which would have revealed the microphone. How would he have explained it?

"I approached him," I said. "I knew he'd been around the movie business for years. I asked him if the invoices could be evidence of trying to get grant money based on phony expenses. He said that it might, but that I shouldn't go making accusations without proof. I did some research and found Braxton," I nodded to the trembling accountant, "is the brother-in-law of the Secretary of Commerce, who has final say on the awarding of grant funds. I saw an opportunity."

"What opportunity?" Osteen asked.

"See if I could record something incriminating. I borrowed the equipment from Nathan Armitage and convinced Dustin to wear a wire. Nathan's security firm has all the latest gadgets, as you know."

"And then what?" Osteen asked.

"Well, Dustin was supposed to shake you down and we'd split the take. Otherwise, I'd go to the cops and make headlines as a brilliant detective. I win either way."

Dustin Henry smiled. I must have been close enough to what he'd told them.

"How much?" Osteen asked me.

"How much what?"

"How much was the blackmail? Surely you discussed it. You were splitting some figure."

Stick to the story we'd concocted, I told myself. "It was a quarter of what we thought you might make from the fraud. We couldn't be sure but our first demand was for a fourth of two and a half million dollars."

"First demand?" Osteen asked.

"Well, we didn't know for sure. I gave Dustin latitude to get what he could. If our numbers don't match, it's because he made a judgment call."

"And the police?" Osteen asked.

"What police? I told you they don't know anything about your scam. If I was working with the police, why would I have asked Dustin to be part of it? I'd have worn the wire myself. Look, we tried, we failed, and we've got no proof. If you haven't processed any of the false expenses, then even the invoices aren't evidence of a crime."

Raymond Braxton spoke for the first time. "But we have processed invoices." He stepped back toward the door, distancing himself from what was to come.

I felt a cold chill sweep through me. I'd spoken one sentence too many and rubbed their noses in our incriminating evidence.

"So, destroy the invoices I gave you," Dustin said to Osteen. "Nobody else knows anything."

"No," Osteen said. "We're in it now. If you're lying and you've told the police, they've got the evidence. If you told the truth, then tough. You're both loose ends." He nodded to Ritchie.

Dustin Henry jerked his elbow back with a vicious swing that caught Ritchie across the nose. The man stumbled backwards. I jumped from the rocker to go for his gun but Dustin was ahead of me. He wasn't quite fast enough. Ritchie brought the revolver down across Dustin's temple with a blow that sent the actor crashing to the floor. Staggering to stay on his feet, Ritchie pointed the gun at the injured man, but I smashed into him and the shot went wide into the wood floorplanks. I pinned Ritchie's arms to his side. He fired a second shot and I felt my prosthesis vibrate from the bullet's impact. Ritchie spun around, trying to shake me off and we both tripped over

Dustin. As we fell together, I twisted Ritchie's wrist. Whether he fired on purpose or my fingers pressed against his, I'll never know. I felt the sting of the muzzle flash and hot blood on the side of my face—Ritchie's blood as the bullet ripped through his carotid artery.

He went limp and I yanked the pistol free.

"Drop it, Sam."

I looked up to see Osteen standing over me, a small caliber Beretta held rock-solid in his hand.

It would have been suicide to try to swing the pistol around and fire. It would have been suicide not to. But in that split-second of weighing horrible choices, Raymond Braxton stumbled forward as if someone had shoved him.

"What the hell's goin' on?"

Osteen kept the gun on me, but looked over his shoulder.

In the doorway stood Nadine Oates, her shotgun at the ready and a rotund raccoon in a rhinestone collar by her side.

"This man attacked me," Osteen said. "He's crazy."

I let the gun fall to the floor. "It's the men in suits, Naydee. Now they've come for you too."

Nadine Oates' eyes widened as she took in Osteen's wardrobe. Osteen saw the change come over her. He couldn't have understood what was happening, but he knew it wasn't good. He spun around.

She fired the shotgun point-blank at his face.

The gun smoke still burned in my nostrils and the sonic blast still rang in my ears when the cavalry arrived.

Fifteen minutes later, I sat on the edge of Harlan Beale's porch. Nakayla was wiping my face with a damp cloth. My shirt was soaked in Mick Ritchie's blood. Nadine Oates sat in Newly's unmarked police car. Tuck Efird was minding her. Ricky the Raccoon was in the old lady's arms and her shotgun was in the trunk tagged as evidence.

EMTs were in the living room tending to Dustin Henry. Braxton was with Newly and Special Agent Boyce at the other end of the porch. Braxton was retching with dry heaves. Ritchie and Osteen were destined for the morgue. Osteen's funeral would be closed casket.

"What took you so long?" I asked Nakayla.

"You didn't give me a lot of clues. I heard you say you had company and then you spoke Mick's name. The last I heard he was taking you where nobody was home. Then you were gone. I called Newly. He was rattled because Dustin had just disappeared. Evidently, Braxton said he wasn't feeling well and if Dustin wanted to meet, he'd have to come to Braxton's room. Newly figures they nabbed Dustin in the corridor on Braxton's floor. Mick Ritchie must have tipped them off you were following Osteen, and Osteen smelled a rat."

"Dustin came up with a good story," I said. "With me listening rather than the FBI. He hoped we could talk our way out of it."

"I told Newly where you'd parked and I hurried there on foot," Nakayla explained. "Dustin had been quickly removed beyond the range of his transmitter. Efird put out a BOLO on Osteen's Mercedes and Boyce was searching databases for descriptions of Ritchie's truck. Newly was pacing, cursing you one minute and praying the next. I kept turning over the phrase I heard about 'nobody home,' and I thought it sounded like a boastful jab at you. Nobody was at the Farmer's guesthouse, but that was too visible. That left Harlan Beale's, so we threw all our eggs in that basket and arrived in time to see that a ninety-year-old crazy woman had done the job for us."

Footsteps sounded on the warped floorboards. I looked up to see Newly towering above us.

"How you doing?" he asked.

"I've had better Friday nights. Sorry to screw up your big chance to work with the FBI."

"Yeah, there goes my career. On the bright side, I've got two dead criminals that I won't have to see at trial, and I've got a whining blob of Jell-o singing like a choirboy to Agent Boyce. Braxton's selling out the Secretary of Commerce like yesterday's bread. Take my advice. Never trust a brother-in-law."

I looked over the yard to Newly's car. "You know there's a raccoon in your backseat."

"So far he's neater than most people I've put back there. You ought to be grateful to him. The Oates woman said they come at night to set out food and water for the chickens. The raccoon likes the eggs. She says you took care of the coonhound but forgot all about the hens."

"She's right. They're hard to keep in an apartment. What's the word on Dustin?"

"He's conscious. Probably has a concussion. He was asking for you. They'll bring him out in a few minutes. Then Boyce is bringing in forensics and we pay for the body bags."

"You need a statement from me?"

"Not tonight. I'll let Nakayla take you home. We'll talk in the morning. That is after I chew your ass out for your boneheaded solo operation."

"Love you, too."

Newly disappeared back into the house. A few minutes later I heard gurney wheels squeaking as EMTs rolled Dustin Henry out the front door. Nakayla helped me stand. I caught his eye and he told the responders to stop.

"Sorry to have dropped out on you," he rasped.

"If you hadn't thrown that elbow, neither of us would be here."

"Is it true we were saved by a ninety-year-old woman?"

"And her raccoon. In rhinestones."

He grinned and then grimaced as the bruised facial muscles pained him. "And we gave our story a good try."

"Yeah, until I went one sentence too long."

He reached up from the gurney and grabbed my arm. The grip was strong. "They were going to kill us anyway, Sam. But an actor never gives up on a good scene. As for talking too long, sometimes an actor's best lines are the ones never spoken."

Nakayla and I watched as they loaded Dustin into the rear of an ambulance. We didn't speak until the siren's echo faded from the hills.

"Let's go to the office," Nakayla said.

"The office?"

"Yes. I left Blue in charge and we don't have money to pay our dog overtime."

"*Our* dog?"

"Yes. Either that or I find a new boyfriend."

"A good woman, a good dog. What else do I need?"

She stepped back and looked at me. "A bath would be a start."

Chapter Twenty-nine

Roland Cassidy insisted that Nakayla and I ride with him and
Dustin Henry in his rented stretch limousine. Although Asheville's downtown Fine Arts movie theater was only half a block
from our office, Cassidy said there was no one else he'd rather
arrive with than the three of us.

The Friday night world premiere was a sellout with all pro-
ceeds going to a local charity that worked with disabled veterans.
I couldn't say no.

As the chauffeur drove us up Biltmore Avenue, where shops
and restaurants were adorned with Christmas decorations, I
thought back over what had transpired in the eight months
since that bloody Friday night. Raymond Braxton had pled
guilty to a lesser charge in exchange for his testimony. Osteen
had promised him a hundred grand for his role in falsifying
checks and invoices. Osteen and the Secretary of Commerce
would have split two-point-four million dollars in rebates, plus
Osteen created real overages paid to companies he controlled,
overages like those caused by the building supplies theft. A full
audit showed him on track to clear more than three million
dollars by the time the movie wrapped.

Secretary of Commerce Lanier Hudson had been found guilty
of being a co-conspirator in two capital murders and was await-
ing sentencing. The North Carolina Legislature had rewritten its
film incentive program to be more transparent and competitive
with other states' rebate plans.

The investigation after the shootout revealed that Mick Ritchie had been the electrician who had installed the alarm system in the Black Mountain College Museum. He'd set up the security code. Braxton had testified that Ritchie learned Beale was going to tell me what he suspected about the lumber theft. Ritchie warned Osteen who told him to take care of Beale. Ritchie had come up with the museum idea on his own, murdered Beale in his front yard, and staged the museum scene to look like Beale had broken in. He'd driven Beale's truck and body to the museum and then phoned Osteen to pick him up a few blocks away and drive him back to his truck. Osteen was angry with Ritchie for what he saw as an unnecessary and foolish action, but now the die was cast and he had to play it out.

But instead of throwing the police off the trail, it brought Nakayla and me in. That was why Osteen offered to hire us—so that he could monitor our investigation.

The movie had been set up as a limited liability corporation that allowed the funds for filming to flow unimpeded. As Osteen's only heir, Roland Cassidy became executive producer. He and newly promoted Camille Brooks both rose to the occasion and, under Marty Kolsrud's direction, the film was completed on time and on budget. Colvertson Filmworks, a major producer and distributor of independent films, snatched up the rights, and the Hollywood buzz mentioned potential Oscar nominations for Grayson Beckner and Nicole Madison. The money that Osteen and Hudson killed for was likely to pale in comparison to the profits the film would generate.

As for Cassidy, he was finishing up the first draft of a book based on the case, including the connection to Paul Weaver's death so many years ago. Lindsay Boyce had been given permission from the FBI powers-that-be to speak on the record and Violet Baker had not objected.

The limo slowed as we neared the theater. A crowd had gathered on the sidewalk where a red carpet had been spread. It wasn't exactly Hollywood, but for Asheville, it was damned impressive. Nakayla wore a stunning azure dress, and Cassidy,

Dustin, and I were three mismatched penguins in tuxedos. Mine had to be returned to the rental shop by ten the next morning.

A doorman opened the passenger door and Nakayla stepped out onto the carpet and into the flashes of phone cameras. Grayson and Nicole looked up from where they stood signing autographs and waved. I followed and took Nakayla by the arm. The prospect of arriving by limo that had seemed so ridiculously over the top was suddenly the coolest thing in the world. I walked proudly beside my beautiful partner, walked proudly on my new prosthesis since Mick Ritchie's bullet had ruined my old one. A bullet that ballistics proved came from the same gun that killed Nancy Pellegatti.

"Hold up, Sam." Roland Cassidy caught me by the arm.

I turned to find him giddy with excitement.

"I have a little surprise." He pointed to a limousine pulling into the space vacated by our own.

I looked at Dustin Henry who only shrugged. He was as clueless as I was.

"We know there was more behind the stories Harlan told me than I realized," Cassidy said. "I think it only fitting that all my characters be here."

The limo stopped, the doorman went into action, and Leah Rosen and Eleanor Johnson exited arm in arm. Behind them came Ellie's granddaughter, Mercy.

I felt a lump in my throat and regretted that I hadn't suggested it. But they weren't alone. Violet Baker emerged with a spry old gentleman in his ancient Army dress uniform.

Captain was making his move.

We stepped aside, letting the real stars enter the theater first. Then, before Nakayla and I followed, I looked up at the marquee. Chaser lights circled the words "World Premiere" written above the film's title. A title that had journeyed from *Love Among the Ridges* to *Battle Scars* to a new title suggested by Cassidy. A title that reflected what often can't be seen, yet is carried by combat veterans of all wars, by all refugees, by all who've lived in the camps and confines of executioners from Hitler to ISIS. Those who bear the wounds we cannot see but who need healing all the same. The film bore witness to their stories, and so Cassidy's title had struck a chord with me.

"So we beat on, boats against the current, borne back ceaselessly into the past." I left some of my own anxiety from the past on that red carpet and walked forward with Nakayla to see *Hidden Scars*.

Author's Note

Although this book is a work of fiction, many of its elements are based on historical facts. Black Mountain College was an innovative school founded by revolutionary educators and its fine arts-centered approach to learning attracted students and faculty whose names represent some of the leading luminaries of the twentieth century. A trip to the Black Mountain College Museum in Asheville will provide a fuller appreciation of the school's impact.

The Venona Project was a closely guarded secret that allowed the United States to decode Soviet cables and led to the discovery of numerous spies working within the country. I have no evidence that any of those cables mentioned Black Mountain College or specific students or faculty members, however, declassified FBI documents as recently as 2015 prove that the school was on the FBI's watchlist for Communist sympathizers, and students were often approached by FBI agents. The closing of the school in 1957 has been attributed in part to the efforts of the government to disqualify the college's students from receiving tuition funds through the G.I. Bill. I find it encouraging that a renewed interest in the "Black Mountain Experiment" is growing at a time when education budgets are being slashed, arts programs face elimination, and liberal arts degrees promoting imagination are discouraged as "not marketable job skills."

References to the North Carolina Film Incentives are taken directly from their guidelines. The "improvements" in the program claimed by the state legislature have succeeded in drying up film production and sent millions of dollars and hundreds of jobs to Georgia.

Acknowledgments

Special thanks to my friends Woody and Mickey Farmer who not only let me house one of my characters with them, but also were good sports to play a role in the story.

I'm grateful to Poisoned Pen Press, Robert Rosenwald, Barbara Peters, and the staff for making this adventure of Sam and Nakayla possible. Also to my family members Linda, Melissa, Pete, Lindsay, Jordan, and Charlie for being in my life.

In the age of *The Art of the Deal,* the art of being—being loved, being compassionate, being welcoming—is an art I hope all the heroes of my stories personify, and an art we can practice and defend with the assurance that we, readers and writers alike, are on the right side of history.

To see more Poisoned Pen Press titles: